Cast a Long Shadow

Mary E. Pearce

Cast a Long Shadow

ST. MARTIN'S PRESS
NEW YORK

For information, address St. Martin's Press, 175 Fifth Avenue,
New York, N.Y. 10010.

Library of Congress Cataloging in Publication Data

Pearce, Mary Emily.
Cast a long shadow.

I. Title.
PR6066.E165C3 1983 823'.914 83-2953
ISBN 0-312-12353-1

First published in Great Britain by Macdonald and Jane's
Publishers Limited.

First U.S. Edition

10 9 8 7 6 5 4 3 2 1

Also by Mary E. Pearce

APPLE TREE LEAN DOWN
THE LAND ENDURES
SEEDTIME AND HARVEST

Chapter One

When Ellen Wainwright was married to Richard Lancy in July, 1873, the day was so hot that the church doors were left wide open, and towards the end of the ceremony, a stray dog ran in and stood howling in the central aisle.

The incident caused some amusement among the small congregation but the vicar, Mr Eustead, was seriously displeased and waited, tight-lipped, while Dyson the verger drove the dog out. He then turned back to the bride and groom and angrily pronounced them man and wife.

'It warnt hardly our fault the dog got in,' Richard said to Ellen later, 'but the way Mr Eustead bellowed the blessing at us, you'd think it was.'

'Never mind,' Ellen said. 'We *are* married, that's the main thing. – I thought he was going to leave it half done!'

Nothing could mar her contentment that day: neither the terrible sultry heat; nor the disturbance caused by the dog; nor the vicar's burst of temper. She and Richard were now one. The day was theirs and nothing could spoil it.

The dog itself was something of a mystery. It had never been seen in Dingham before, nor was it ever seen again, and the only explanation was that it must have strayed off a barge passing through the lock on the river. The matter was talked of for some days. A few people thought it rather a joke. Others thought it a minor scandal and the vicar was censured for having allowed the church doors to remain open. But it was only a good deal later, when Ellen and Richard had been married five years and things were not quite the same between them, that people remembered the dog in church and spoke of it as some sort of omen.

'The moment I saw it,' Mrs Dancox used to say, 'I felt a shiver go down my spine, and I warnt the only one, I don't suppose.' And Mrs Dyson always said: 'A dog in church is bad enough but a dog at a wedding – anything could happen after that! And nobody never did know how it got there, neither, did they?'

'It came off a barge,' Dyson said. 'Nothing very strange in that.'

'We don't know for sure, though, do we?'

'If you had such premonitions, woman, how come you never said so at the time?'

'On the wedding day?' Mrs Dyson said. 'And cast such a blight on everything? That's not my way, Bob, and never was. Such a fine handsome couple they made that day! And everything seemingly set so fair! It warnt for me to cast a shadow. There's some dark things we must keep to ourselves.'

Dyson gave a little grunt. He had never known his wife to keep anything to herself, dark or otherwise, in twenty-six years of marriage. He had only taken the post of verger to secure some measure of peace and quiet.

One good thing at least had come of the business of the dog in the church, for the Stavertons of Dinnis Hall, on hearing about it, had given a pair of wire-gauze doors, and now the church could be kept aired without the incursion of stray animals and nesting birds. The summers were hot in the mid 1870s.

* * *

Ellen was twenty when she married, and Richard was almost twenty-five. Their courtship had been a happy one, and as they were well-suited to each other, their marriage got off to a good start. Everyone in Dingham agreed that they deserved their good luck, for Ellen's life hitherto, with a jealous-natured mother and invalid uncle, had brought little joy; and Richard, too, left alone at eighteen, with a half-ruined mill on his hands, and his father's creditors at the door, had had a hard struggle to make his way.

Within a month of his father's death, Richard had repaired the old machinery, re-dressed the millstones, and cleared the weeds out of the millstream. Soon the old mill was working again: noisily, perhaps, with many a screech that set Richard's teeth on edge and sent him hurrying round with the oilcan; but working, certainly, and coming slowly to life again after two years of idleness. And when the first grinding of barley-meal came squeezing down the narrow chute, into the open sack below, a few Dingham folk were there to see it, ready to try it between their fingers and offer advice on its quality.

'You'll come to it, young fella,' said George Danks, whose barley it was that was being ground. 'It takes years to make a good miller – ten or twelve at least I'd say – but you'll come to it surely in the end.'

'I shall come to it sooner than that!' Richard said, rather sharply, and his listeners believed him.

True to his word, Richard was master of his trade by the time he was twenty, and Pex Mill had a good name. But the business itself, having been allowed to run down, was not won back again all at once: often there was only work enough for three days' milling in the week; and Richard made money on the side by dealing in various second-hand goods. He travelled about with two donkeys, collecting anything he could find that lay rusting or rotting in farmyards or workshop sheds. Sometimes he paid a copper or two, but mostly he was 'doing a favour', clearing away unwanted rubbish.

'It's a funny thing!' Michael Bullock said once: 'It's a funny thing that if I buy a hen-coop offa you it's a valuable article worth five shillun, but if you take a seed-drill offa me it's only old junk needing clearing away!'

Richard was certainly sharp in his dealings, but most

people admired him for that. He was a man who meant to get on and, the way he worked, he well deserved to.

'You want a cage for your canary?' people would say. 'Or maybe a medal to stick on your chest? Go to Dick Lancy. He'll have one for sure. And if he hasn't, well, you can bet your life he'll know where to find one!'

Although he dealt in all manner of things, there was never any rubbish left lying about the mill, to mar its tidiness and neatness. Everything Richard brought home was carefully mended and made good, given a coat of paint, perhaps, and placed in the shed behind the millhouse. No one was ever taken inside. If a man came asking for elm planking or an old barrel for a water-butt Richard would say: 'I dunno – I shall have to see.' And in a day or two the required item would be delivered. But only Richard himself ever entered the shed.

When Ellen Wainwright came into his life, he worked all the harder. His father's debts had been squared by then and he was beginning to pay his way. Gradually, he made improvements. The walls of the mill and the millhouse were re-pointed, the roofs were re-tiled, and the worm-eaten weather-boarding over the luccomb was replaced by new. The old mill was itself again and, reflected in the millpond, where the water now ran pure and clear, looked just as it did in the old picture, painted by Richard's great-grandfather, that hung above the mantelpiece in the kitchen.

Downriver from the mill, the banks in summer were crowded with tansy and comfrey and flags and the tall spires of purple loosestrife, and it was among these bright flowers that he first saw Ellen Wainwright. She was sixteen then and had come to Dingham with her widowed mother to live with her uncle, a retired seaman, at Victory Cottage, in Water Lane. Old Captain Wainwright was almost a cripple. He suffered much pain and was dying of cancer. He cared little for this sister-in-law of his who had condescended to keep house for him, but he and Ellen became great friends. She was at the river that day looking for the nest of a coot, so that she could report to him on the progress of the young brood. Richard went down to speak to her.

'If the keeper'd known that nest was there, I reckon he'd have smashed the eggs.'

'Why would he?' Ellen cried.

'Because of the fish, I suppose,' he said.

'Surely there are enough for everybody?'

'I shan't say nothing, anyway. I like to see the coot here, larking about.'

And, crouching beside her, he showed her how cleverly the nest was loose-tied to two or three upright reeds so that, when the river rose, the nest rose with it and escaped flooding.

'You tell your uncle there's six in the brood, all of em swimming and doing well. He'll be glad to hear that. It'll cheer him up. He was always down here, before he got sick, watching them birds and making notes. You tell him the kingfisher's here as well. I seen it a day or two, like a streak.'

'Yes, I'll tell him,' Ellen said.

* * *

She was often at the river after that, and Richard soon got into the way of looking out for her. Both were lonely and both were older than their years. There was soon an understanding between them. Once Ellen was caught in a storm and took shelter with him in the mill, and while they leant together over the hatch-door, looking out at the white rain, he talked of marriage.

'I can't afford a wife just yet. I'm only just getting on my feet. There's a lot to do before I can think of such a step. I daresay it might be two or three years.'

'I couldn't leave Uncle John, either. I promised I'd stay with him till the end. I hope that won't be for ages yet, though he's in such terrible pain sometimes – '

'You must certainly stop with him, no doubt of that. It'd break his heart if you left him alone with that mother of yours. She'd have him in the grave in no time at all.'

'Hush!' Ellen said. 'You mustn't say such things. She's not

that bad.'

'Ent she indeed! She's bad enough! And if it warnt for your poor old uncle, I'd up and marry you tomorrow morning, just to get you away from her. But as it is, we must just be patient, and make our plans accordingly.'

'Yes,' she said, 'we must be patient.'

They had known each other for five weeks, but it was taken for granted between them, quietly, without surprise, that their lives were linked and always would be.

Ellen's mother did not approve of Richard Lancy. Meeting him, she was barely civil, and behind his back she was often contemptuous.

'A miller!' she said. 'Why not throw yourself away on a road-mender and be done with it? I will certainly not receive him here!'

But Ellen's uncle took Richard's part.

'This is my house, remember, Adelaide, and Dick Lancy will always be welcome in it, at least so long as I am alive.'

He and Richard got on well together. The old man trusted the younger one and towards the end, when he grew more frail, it was Richard who carried him to bed at night and who came every morning to put him into his chair by the window.

'You've been like a son to me, my boy, and Ellen has been like a darling daughter. Take care of her, after I'm gone, and don't let Adelaide bully her.'

Uncle John died in June, 1873, and Ellen married Richard in July. Mrs Wainwright was disgusted. There should have been a year's mourning at least, but to have the wedding within a month – ! She washed her hands of the whole affair. Victory Cottage was now hers and no wedding-breakfast should take place *there.* Nor would she be present in church.

So the wedding-breakfast took place at Pex Mill and the little parlour was so crowded with well-wishers that they overflowed into the garden, and young Simon Shaw, playing the fool out on the footbridge, fell with a splash into the millrace and had to be rescued by Will Gale, the smith, no less tipsy than himself.

'Drink up by all means,' Richard said. 'There'll be little drinking done in this house after today, cos Ellen and me is both teetotal.'

Indeed, it was noticed that he himself touched not a drop, and his wedding-guests could guess the reason. It was drink that had hastened his father's ruin.

'You can't be teetotal and live in Dingham,' said George Danks of Cockhanger Farm. 'Not when it's got two inns to support.'

'Teetotal or not, I wish you good health and prosperity,' said Bob Dyson, raising his glass, 'and may your waterwheel never stop turning.'

'He'll prosper all right,' said Michael Bullock. 'Did you ever know of a *poor* miller?'

'I knew a poor miller's daughter once . . .'

'Any man will prosper,' said Joe Dancox, 'so long as he has a good wife behind him.'

'Wedlock's a padlock,' said Simon Shaw. 'It's a brave man that turns the key.'

Just after sunset, when a pink moon hung in the sky, the noisy revellers at last went home. The mill and the millhouse became silent, and Ellen, at the kitchen window, stood listening to the quiet sounds of the river: the plopping of fish in the millpond; the fluttering of water-fowl among the reeds; and, in the distance, the rush of the weir. These sounds were now her life. They would fill all her wandering thoughts by day and her dreams by night, heard and yet not heard, like her own heartbeats or the drumming of blood between her ears.

'Quiet, ent it, now they're gone?' Richard said, coming into the room.

'Yes, quiet,' Ellen said. 'I can hear the Abbey clock striking.'

'Can you? Golly? That's all of three miles. Did it strike the quarter? Then our clock is slow.'

He went to the tall grandfather clock and put it right. Then he turned and stood watching her as she leant at the window, a dark outline against the violet-coloured sky.

'I reckon there's going to be a storm. The wind is as hot as a drunkard's breath and I'm d— near melting in this suit.'

'Perhaps a storm will clear the air.'

Ellen came away from the window and they looked at each other in the fading light.

'Shall I light a candle?' Richard said.

'No need for candles,' Ellen said, 'it isn't really dark yet.'

The moon, now whitening, lit them to bed.

* * *

Soon after the wedding, Ellen's mother sold Victory Cottage and bought a house in Lyme Regis, as far away from Worcestershire as she could well manage. The day she left Dingham, she called at the mill in a hired carriage, and handed down a bundle of clothes. Ellen never saw or heard of her again.

Old Captain Wainwright had left Ellen sixty pounds and as soon as the money was in her hands she went to Sutton Crabtree on a secret errand. Three weeks later, as arranged, a brand new waggon drew up at the mill, with a strong grey horse between the shafts, driven by Gleddow, the Sutton wheelwright. Ellen went to the mill-door and called Richard.

'I can't come now – I'm busy!' he said, shouting above the noise of the mill.

'You *must* come!' Ellen said. 'You'll be sorry if you don't!'

Richard followed her out to the road, wiping his hands on his apron. His scowl deepened when he saw the waggon, – he thought it was somebody asking the way – but as he drew close and saw its newness, he began to perceive what was afoot. The waggon was painted dark green, its chamfered panels picked out in yellow, the rims of its wheels fine-lined with black. And along its shafts, dark green on yellow, Richard read his own name: Richard Lancy; Miller and General Dealer: Pex Mill, Dingham, nr. Rainborough, Worcs. .

'Would you believe it!' he kept saying, walking round the horse and waggon. 'Would you ever in the Lord's name . . . Oh,

I shall be somebody, driving this!' And, after Gleddow had gone, he said: 'Seems I was onto a good thing, Nell, when I married you!'

'It's only right that a miller should have a horse and waggon. How can you carry on your trade with only a couple of old donkeys?'

'I'm not just a miller,' Richard said. 'I'm a miller *and* a General Dealer. That's what you got them to put on them shafts, and very well it looks, too.'

His pride in the horse and waggon was boundless. He kept them always in perfect condition. And the fact that Ellen should have spent her legacy in such a way moved him deeply. But there was one matter arising out of the gift that was less pleasing. She made him give the two donkeys away.

'You don't need them now. You'll never have to use them again. So why not give them to someone in need?'

'D——t, woman, I can always sell them! The money would pay for that new hursting. I ent so rich that I can afford to give things away.'

'Just this once you can,' she said. 'Just this once, to please me.'

So the two donkeys were given away: one to old Trussler, the fishmonger, whose pony had only recently died; the other to Mr and Mrs Grey, to pull their little home-made cart, so that they could take their invalid daughter for drives.

'Don't thank *me!*' Richard said, parting with the donkeys. 'It was my wife's idea, not mine.'

The matter rankled for a long time, though he managed to turn it into a joke.

'I seen one of my neddies in Sturton this morning. He don't look too happy, delivering fish. I hardly knew how to meet his eye. I reckon he liked it a lot better when he worked for a miller and general dealer!'

* * *

In September, 1874, their son was born, and they called him John after Ellen's uncle. Richard was a proud and boastful father. There was nobody like this baby son. No one so forward, so clever, so strong. And his customers often felt the urge to take him down a peg or two.

'Is he talking yet, Dick, that boy of yours?'

'Talking? D—t! He ent hardly more'n eight weeks old!'

'Oh, he's only an ordinary baby after all, then. From what you'd said, I thought he'd be keeping your books for you by now!'

In November that year, something unusual happened to Richard. He spent an evening in The Old Tap and got very drunk. The landlord, Archie Shaw, had wanted an old cattle-trough for his stable-yard, and Richard as always had known where to find one. The night he delivered it, the weather was cold and wet, and when the trough had been unloaded, Shaw invited him inside and together they shared a bottle of brandy.

Richard, unused to strong drink, was soon helpless, and Will Gale, the blacksmith, a regular customer at The Old Tap, volunteered to take him home. Ellen, waiting anxiously, heard the horse and waggon coming, and the two men's voices upraised in song. She also heard the commotion they made as they bedded down the horse in his stall. Then Richard stumbled into the kitchen, looked at her with rolling eyes, and fell insensible at her feet. Will Gale stood grinning in the open doorway.

'One handsome husband delivered safe and sound to his wife,' he said. 'There's nothing to pay, though I wouldn't say no to a little nightcap.'

'Safe and sound?' Ellen said, stooping to loosen Richard's collar. 'Do you call this safe and sound?'

'He's all in one piece, surely? No broken bones? Nothing wrong that a night's sleep won't cure?'

'What *use* is he? You tell me that!'

'It all depends what you had in mind.'

'If there's one thing I detest,' Ellen said, 'it's the sight of a man in a drunken stupor.'

'Me too,' Will said. 'I'll help you to get him up to bed.'

'Thank you, no! Just leave him be.'

'Maybe you're right. He's better lying as he is. He won't be much company for you tonight, though he'll need your sympathy in the morning.'

'He won't get it!' Ellen said. 'And I'll say goodnight to you now, Mr Gale, while I've still got patience enough to be polite.'

'Don't I get no nightcap, then?'

'No,' she said, 'you've had enough.'

She moved to the door and pushed it against him. Will fell back a few paces, still with a foolish grin on his face, and, finding himself shut out in the rain, hammered three or four times on the door.

'Mrs Lancy, ma'am, you're a darned shrew! Thank God I'm a single bachelor chap and can come and go as I darn well please! I never knowed a woman yet that hadn't got rennet in her veins!'

Will went off singing and his heavy footsteps pounded the bridge. Ellen lit a storm-lantern and went out to see that all was well with the horse in his stall. She returned to the kitchen, where Richard, except that he snored loudly, lay on his back as though dead. She covered him over with a blanket and went up to bed. Baby John lay asleep in his cot.

In the morning, Richard was surly and sick-faced. He went to his work without any breakfast. At twelve o'clock, when he came in to dinner, he fidgeted with his knife and fork and eyed Ellen, who ate in silence.

'Well, woman?' he said at last. 'Has the cat got your tongue?'

'What is it you want me to say?'

'It's the first time it's ever happened!'

'I hope it's the last,' Ellen said. 'I hadn't bargained for a drunken husband.'

'You can be sure it's the last,' he said. 'There's no pleasure in drinking for me. My head is boiling like a kettle.' A sudden thought came to him and he thumped the table. 'Archie

Shaw is a fly devil! He never paid me for that trough. I shall have to see him about that.'

But although he went to The Old Tap again, to collect his money, he could not be persuaded to take a drink.

Chapter Two

Their second child was stillborn, a sad disappointment to both of them, and to little John, too, who had hoped for a brother. But at least this one son was strong and healthy and full of spirit, growing straight and tall and clever; able to count at the age of three; able to read before he was four; always eager to ride with his father in the waggon and especially when he went to the market in Runston or Sturton or Rainborough.

'One of these days,' Richard said, 'you'll be a miller the same as me and then that name on the shafts there will have to be changed to something else.'

'Why will it?'

'It'll have to be changed to 'Richard Lancy and Son' instead, cos you and me will be partners together, both of us millers and general dealers.'

'When will we?'

'Why, when you're a man like me, of course. And the way you're growing, that won't be all that long, neither.'

One day, when they were delivering meal at Brooks, the farmer, Mr Rissington, seeing this little boy, not yet four, sitting erect with the reins in his hands, came right up to the side of the waggon.

'Lord almighty! What have we here?'

'Richard Lancy and Son,' said John, 'delivering beanmeal from Pex Mill.'

And the old man was so amused that he asked John into the dairy and gave him a cup of buttermilk, a rare honour, Richard said, for the Rissingtons were very close.

When John, soon after his fourth birthday, began going to the village school, Richard insisted that he should have the best of everything. Best boots, best clothes, and a smart leather satchel with his name on it. But Ellen set her face against this. She refused to obey Richard's orders.

'Do you want our son to be disliked? They are ordinary folk in this village, with ordinary children, mostly poor. If we set John above the rest, how is he ever to make friends?'

'I hadn't thought of it like that. Seems I'd better leave it to you. But I want my son to be tidy, mind! No great patches on his seat. No knots in his laces nor nothing like that. He ent going scruffy, as I had to do when I was a boy.'

Richard, if he could have had his way, would have seen wife and son clad always in the finest clothes, and once, when Ellen was turning up the hem of a dress, he snatched it from her and threatened to throw it into the fire.

'There's no need for you to do all that mending. I ent so poor as all that!'

'Don't be ridiculous,' Ellen said. 'Everybody renews frayed hems. This dress is my favourite. I've only had it six months.' And she took it, crumpled, from his hands. 'We've had so many new things lately. China. Curtains. That new Indian rug. Folk will be taking advantage of you if they think you're growing so well off.'

'They'll have to get up pretty early in the morning, Nell, before they can take advantage of *me.*'

But although he wanted everything to be of the best for his wife and son, in other matters he was cautious to a degree, and would never buy anything if instead he could make it or mend it or persuade someone else to lend it to him.

'Always look after the pennies,' he said, 'and the pounds will surely look after theirselves.'

Once he travelled all the way up to Derbyshire because he had heard of an old millstone quarry having closed there and he hoped for a bargain. He was gone four days and returned in high triumph with two good stones.

'Were they a bargain?' Ellen asked.

'A bargain, yes. I got them for nothing. And if it hadn't been for considering the horse, I'd have brought another couple more, cos they was just lying there, scattered about.'

'You mean you just took them?' Ellen said.

'That's right. I helped myself.'

'But surely the stones belong to someone? Didn't you try to find out?'

'No, not me. I was there at night.'

'Then many people would call it stealing.'

'Stealing? Rubbish! I ent having that! The quarry is closed and out of business, and the stones is just lying there, going to waste. They're no use to no one, except men like me.'

Ellen was silent and Richard, meeting her steady gaze, became annoyed. He did not care to be called a thief.

'D——t, woman, they're only rough-hewn! Think of the work I've got to do, dressing them and setting them up. They was just lying there, out in the weather, so much rubbish throwed aside. I'm d—nd if I'll let you call me a thief!'

'How did you load them onto the waggon?'

'I managed all right. No trouble there. There's nothing much a man can't do, given a horse and the right tackle.'

'You shouldn't have done it all alone – you might have killed yourself,' Ellen said.

'I've got too much nous for that,' he said. 'It'd take a mighty clever stone to catch me napping, be sure of that.' He became very busy, making notes in a little book, and then he said, without looking up, 'You'd have minded about it a bit, then, if your thieving husband had got hisself killed?'

'Don't be silly,' Ellen said.

*　　　*　　　*

The mill was half a mile from the end of Dingham, and because of this Ellen lived a life apart, meeting other women only when she went to the shops.

'I reckon that's lonely for you,' Richard said, 'with no neighbours nearby to pop in and out like they do in the village.'

'No, I'm not lonely,' Ellen said. 'I like it down here beside the river. I see enough people to satisfy me, what with the barges when they pass, and the coming and going at the mill.'

'But that's all menfolk,' Richard said, 'and business at that.'

'I enjoy the business,' Ellen said, and she always knew who had been to the mill that day, what grain they had brought for Richard to grind, or how much flour they had taken away. 'I wouldn't change places with anyone.'

But for little John, an only child, it was a very different matter, and that was why she sent him to school as soon as Miss Robinson would agree to take him. From that moment she had no more fears. John made friends easily and every Saturday and Sunday there would be a group of children playing all day on the river bank or fishing from the footbridge over the stream.

Once, when Richard was going on an errand to Runston and had promised that John should go for the ride, he found a group of seven boys sitting waiting in the waggon.

'What the deuce is all this?'

'These are my friends. They're coming with us into Runston.'

'Oh no they're not!' Richard said, and made them all get out at once. 'Either you come along by yourself or else you stop at home with your friends. You can't have it both ways. You've got to choose.'

On that occasion, out of loyalty to his friends, John decided to stay behind. His father went to Runston alone and afterwards, when he returned, he spoke to John in a serious manner.

'Them boys is all very well, but I don't want everyone knowing my business, and that's what'd happen if they came along. So just mind your p's and q's and don't be so free with your invitations.'

On every other occasion, of course, John chose to go with his father, for this was the greatest excitement of all. To visit so many outlying farms; to drive down the narrow streets of towns; to see the barges tied up at the wharves in Rainborough, and to watch their cargoes unloaded into the warehouses there: the sacks of grain or wool or hops hoisted so high on the chain and pulley: John would not miss it for the world. The whole of Worcestershire, it seemed to him, was full of the most exciting things, and over the border, not far away, was the unknown county of Herefordshire.

Not far from the mill, in Water Lane, which ran with the river for a mile or so, an old rough grey stone stood out of the grass at the side of the road and marked the boundary for all to see. On one side there was an H; on the other a W; and the children of Dingham liked to straddle this stone, for then they stood in two counties at the same time. But they always took care to stand so that Worcestershire was 'on the right' and Herefordshire was 'in the wrong'. It was said that the people living over the boundary were all left-handed and had four thumbs, and John sometimes wondered if this was true.

'Why don't we never go driving into Herefordshire?' he asked his father in the mill one day.

'I dunno. I just don't happen to have no business there, that's all. Not that I try for it. No, not me. Why, if you go into Herefordshire, you're very nearly in Wales!'

'Do they speak English in Herefordshire?'

'Not as good as you and me. But they manage to make theirselves understood.'

'Are they left-handed and got four thumbs?'

'I shouldn't be surprised,' Richard said. 'They're funny folk, sure enough. And then of course Old Rag-Face is said to ride over there.'

'Who's Old Rag-Face?' John asked.

'Old Rag-Face on his flying horse. He swoops down on

travellers out of the dark and carries them off to his lair in the hills.'

'What does he do to them?'

'I dunno. Nobody knows. The travellers is never seen again. But they say there's a cave under Willer's Knob that's full of human skulls and bones.'

Richard turned to look at the boy and saw that his face was very white.

'It's only an old tale,' he said. 'You've got no call to look like that. Here, come and help me tie this sack, and let me see how you manage a knot. You ent scared of an old tale? A big boy like you, past his fourth birthday? Surely not? I don't believe it!'

John shook his head. He would never admit to being afraid. Not to his father, anyway.

But he had bad dreams for several nights after that, and once when Ellen went in to him he flung his arms around her neck, crying and sobbing against her breast. It took a long time to comfort him and get him to go to sleep again and Ellen, returning to her own room, shook Richard roughly and woke him up.

'Frightening the child with such horrible talk! I should have thought you'd have more sense! Old Rag-Face indeed! Skulls and bones in a cave! He was in such a sweat, the poor mite, that I had to give him a clean nightshirt.'

In the morning, at breakfast-time, Richard looked at his small son across the table.

'You got me into trouble, you know, crying out in the night like that. Your mother says it's all my fault on account of my talking about Old Rag-Face, but I told you it was only a tale, didn't I? I said there warnt really nothing in it.'

John hung his head, unable to meet his father's eye.

'Laws!' Richard said. 'You ent scared of Goldilocks or Jack the Giant Killer or Simple Simon, are you, boy? And that Old Rag-Face is just such another. Nothing more than an old tale.'

'Don't he live over the border, then, and carry folk off on

his flying horse?'

'No. He don't. Cos there's no such man. Herefordshire is pretty much the same as Worcestershire. I'll take you one day and you'll see for yourself. So promise you won't have no more bad dreams?'

'Yes, I promise,' John said.

'Good! That's the spirit. You're a sensible lad.'

And Richard sought his wife's eye, as much as to say, There! You see? That's soon settled that! A lot of fuss about nothing at all.

* * *

Not long afterwards, on a wet windy day in the new year, Richard announced that he was going into Herefordshire, to the old watermill at Cutlowell Park. The mill had recently had a fire and there was to be a sale of tackle. It was a Saturday afternoon and Richard suggested that John should go along for the ride.

'I promised I'd take you there one day so's you could see what it was like. You ent too scared to go, I suppose? You ent still thinking about them bad dreams?'

'No,' John said, 'I ent scared.'

But his face was very white indeed as they set out in the waggon that day, and he sat very close at his father's side, looking about him with wide-stretched eyes. The day was cheerless, for big black clouds moved low in the sky, and rain blew down on the northwest wind. Still, the lanes they travelled along were commonplace enough; the fields on either side were peaceful; and the three villages they had to pass through were not much different from Dingham itself. The people, if anything, were more friendly. Some of them even nodded and waved. Richard spoke of it to John.

'Does it seem the folk is all left-handed?'

'No, I don't think so,' John said.

'Seen anyone with four thumbs?'

'No.'

'There! You see! The people here ent no different from us.

Nor we ent seen no sign of Old Rag-Face neither.'

'You said he mostly rode out at night.'

'Well, he don't!' Richard said, impatiently. 'I told you before, it's a fairy-tale, so let's not hear no more about it. Just look around you and see what you see.'

'That old woman was smoking a pipe.'

'Ah. I saw her. She'd got a black nose.'

'We're getting near the river again. The cattle is going down to drink. I can see two men fishing. I wonder if there's salmon here?'

The boy's fears were soon forgotten. Herefordshire, as his father said, was not so different after all. He saw nothing frightening. Nothing strange. Nothing to bring back those horrible dreams. But the places were new and therefore exciting, and when they arrived at Cutlowell Park, he was the first down from the waggon, eager to join the knot of men gathered at the door of the burnt-out mill.

The fire had occurred eight days before, and the mill was in ruins. The roof and both floors had gone; even part of one gable wall; and the other walls, where the bricks themselves had been on fire, had cracks in them more than three inches wide. Above the doorway was a notice saying: DANGER: BEWARE OF FALLING MASONRY.

Most of the mill machinery had been rendered useless, but some smaller tackle, though badly damaged, was being offered for sale as spare parts, and this was laid out on the stone-flagged floor, in a space cleared among the rubble. Everywhere, all around, the floors were covered with burnt corn and blackened brick-dust and timbers reduced to bits of charcoal, and in a far corner stood a few sacks of flour that had kept their shape, though charred and blackened all the way through. And all this, soaked by the rain, gave off a strong sharp choking smell that burnt the lungs and turned the stomach.

The mill belonged to Sir Godfrey Sayer, and his agent was there to conduct the sale. Sir Godfrey would not be rebuilding the mill, and the hired miller had been dismissed, for it was his carelessness that had caused the fire.

'Take a good look, boy,' Richard said to his little son who stared, appalled, at the burnt-out shell, 'and let it be a lesson to you that a miller must always be on his guard against getting up heat between stone and stone.'

There were four other men there beside Richard, all millers like himself, looking out for a bargain. The sale had been set for three o'clock but already, when Richard arrived, the best bits and pieces had been knocked down and the men were loading them into their carts. The agent, Mr Jones, was unashamed. He did not seem to think he was in the wrong.

'What was you wanting, Mr Lancy? Anything in particular?'

'I wanted some four-pound weights,' Richard said. 'And some pitwheel parts if they was still sound.'

'Too late, I'm afraid. These gentlemen here have cleared the decks. There's only a few odds and bobs still left, but you're welcome to look around, of course.'

'Three o'clock was the time of the sale. I was here at quarter to. How come I'm late when I was early?'

'Mr Hilliard was keen to begin. He's got another appointment elsewhere. We didn't expect no one else to come.'

'You mean Mr Hilliard greased your palm? Is that how you always do business in these parts? If it is, I'll be sure to remember.'

'Now look here, young man!' the agent said. 'The sooner you take a quick look round, the sooner I can call it a day. It's not the weather for standing about in.'

'Dirty weather for dirty work,' Richard said, as he passed the millers loading their carts. But they were silent, avoiding his glance.

* * *

Inside the mill, he kicked at the worthless items of junk laid out in rows among the ashes, turning them over with the toe of his boot. Three bundles of sacks, badly burnt, and a coil of belting, about the same. A wallower wheel, badly buckled. Two hoppers; two bins; a rigger chain: all these things were beyond repair and he walked among them in growing anger. Little John followed behind, coughing because of the acrid fumes.

'Well?' said the agent, from the door. 'Do you see anything there you want?'

'I ent finished looking yet,' Richard said.

'Then how much longer are you going to be?'

'If you're in such a tarnal hurry, man, you get off by all means and leave me to look round in peace.'

'So that you can help yourself? I'm not such a fool! My men are waiting to clear this stuff up. They're taking it down to the smith at Lodding.'

'Your men can wait,' Richard said. 'I ent leaving till I've looked my fill.'

The agent, swearing, turned and went out. Richard, in an obstinate mood, went through the mill and into the house, inspecting the shoddy items for sale as though he had all the time in the world. John trailed after him, gazing at the cracked walls, bulging out high overhead as though they would topple at any moment.

'I don't like this place,' he said. 'I don't like the *smell.'*

'We shan't be long,' Richard said. 'Just mind you don't touch nothing, that's all, or you'll get yourself as black as pitch.'

He was in the millhouse kitchen now: a sad place, all blackened with soot, empty save for the mess of ashes covering the floor. All the furniture had been burnt and lay, mere sticks, among the rubble. The glass had burst from the casement window and a ragged fringe, like burnt cobwebs, hung from the curtain-rod above.

Richard was about to leave when he kicked something heavy in the ashes. He knelt down and uncovered a bag full of millwrighting tools, all in good order, unharmed by the fire. A proof-staff in its wooden case. A couple of dozen mill-bills of the finest steel, with three beechwood hafts. Two millpecks, a brush, and a pair of gloves. How they came to be in the house and how they could have escaped the fire was altogether rather strange, but the only thing that mattered to Richard was that he had found something worth buying, and he laughed very softly to himself, because his persistence had brought some reward.

Outside the mill, the agent was shouting to him again, demanding to know how long he would be. Richard stood up with the bag in his hands and carried it with him to the door. But then, suddenly, irritated by the agent's shouts, he hesitated and looked around.

In the middle of the kitchen floor, amongst the big square flagstones, he saw that there was a wood trapdoor with an iron ring in it. He went to it quickly and kicked away the ash and rubble. He raised the trap about eighteen inches, dropped the bag of tools into the cellar, and let the trap down again, carefully, without a sound. Then he kicked the ashes over it, wiped his hands on the seat of his trousers, and turned away feeling pleased.

John, who had come to look for him, stood in the doorway, watching intently, but Richard put a finger to his lips, and the little boy remained silent. They walked out together, hand in hand.

'Well?' said the agent. 'Did you find anything you wanted?'

'No, nothing,' Richard said. 'He done a pretty thorough job, burning the place down, that miller of yours. There's nothing left worth having here, so I'll bid you good day.'

He passed between the agent's men and lifted John onto the waggon. He climbed up beside him and took the reins, and as they drove slowly past the agent, he spoke a last word over his shoulder.

'You should take care how you waste a man's time, holding a sale that's no sale at all, cos time is money to a man like me and I can't afford to throw it away on fools' errands like today.'

He pulled a little on the nearside ribbon and turned the waggon towards home. It was raining coldly, steadily now, and John sat huddled close beside him.

'Now you know what it's like in Herefordshire. Folk are

the same wherever you go. No more honest than they are at home.'

That evening, as she gave him his supper, Ellen asked how he had got on.

'There warnt nothing there worth having,' he said. 'The crows had been down and picked the place clean. All I done was waste my time.'

He glanced at John, who sat in a chair beside the fire, intending to warn him against mentioning the tools, but John, half dozing as he sipped his milk, had not even heard what his father was saying. And in the morning, after a long night's sleep, the matter had faded from his mind.

* * *

Richard allowed three weeks to pass and then, after dark on a Friday evening, he set out again for Cutlowell Park.

'Don't wait up,' he said to Ellen, 'cos the chances are that I shall be late.'

'Why, where are you going?' Ellen asked.

'Nowhere much,' he said, shrugging. 'Just a bit of business to attend to, that's all.'

He went to Cutlowell Park on foot, following the course of the river, keeping to the towpaths all the way. The night was a rough one, with a gale blowing from the northwest, threatening a heavy downpour of rain. The trees along the river bank were loud with the noise of the wild wind, and the river itself was very high, sloshing over in many places, whipped up choppily in white-edged waves.

The whole of the month so far had been wet, and the waning moon, showing now and then through the tattered clouds, had its worst quarter still to go through. When the wind dropped and the rain fell, coming together with the spring-tide, there would be floods along this valley, as there had been in many a winter past. And as he approached Cutlowell, a few drops were already falling, cold and stinging in his face.

The burnt-out mill was a skeleton, black and jagged against

the sky, its gable walls broken off in rough steps. Some of the brickwork had crumbled and fallen in the three weeks since he had last been there, and he had to clear away a heap of rubble before he could find the trap in the floor. He swung it up, both hands in the ring, and propped it open on a stout stick of wood.

When he lowered himself into the cellar, there was water lying at the bottom, and he hung for a moment, wondering about the probable depth. Then he let himself go, dropping down with a mighty splash, and when the water had stopped surging, it reached about half way up his thighs.

Very slowly he waded about in it, feeling with his feet for the bag of tools, but although he moved in widening circles, until in the end he had covered every inch of the floor, he encountered nothing but a small empty cask. Plainly, the agent's men had searched the cellar, and the bag of tools had been discovered. Richard, once again, had wasted a journey, but this time, as he told himself, he had nobody but himself to blame. He waded back to the open trapdoor and reached up to haul himself out.

The opening, when he raised his arms, was almost a yard away from his hands. He had to jump to get a grip. But his hands were wet and coated with slime, and when he tried to haul himself up, his fingers slithered on the ledge and he fell back clumsily into the cellar, knocking away the piece of wood that was keeping the trapdoor propped open. As the water surged about his body and he staggered, trying to keep his feet, the trapdoor fell shut with a heavy thud, and the shock that ran through the ruined millhouse brought one of the gables crumpling down, so that timbers and masonry fell with a terrible rumbling crash, covering the trapdoor above his head.

He groped his way about the cellar until he found the empty cask. He climbed on it to reach the trapdoor. His strength had always been a source of pride. Often when loading his waggon at a farm he had run to and fro perhaps twenty times, with a hundredweight bag of grain under each arm, and scarcely even sweated at it. But in this moment, when he needed it most, his strength was nothing. Although he pushed with all his might, the trapdoor never budged an inch, for three tons of rubble were weighting it down.

Standing quite still in the utter darkness, he told himself he would have to die. He was five miles away from his own home and nobody in the world would know where to find him. Cutlowell Mill was a lonely place, a mile and a half from the nearest village, half a mile from the nearest road, and, it being nothing but a ruin, no one now had reason to come there. No barges plied this stretch of the Ail, for the canal did not join it until Sutton Crabtree, and no pleasure craft would be out in winter.

The cellar was small. It was twelve or thirteen feet high and perhaps about fifteen by fifteen across, with only a slight amount of air finding its way through cracks in the walls. But worst of all was the river water surrounding him, for if the gale brought heavy rain to coincide with the month's spring-tide, the river might easily fill the cellar and he would be drowned like a rat in a trap.

He took his watch from his waistcoat pocket and wound it carefully to the end. He could see nothing of its face, but its ticking brought him a measure of comfort, and he put it into his breast pocket, so that it should be safe from the wet. He got down from the little cask and began feeling his way round the cellar. The floodwater washed about his thighs.

Chapter Three

In the days following Richard's disappearance, Ellen became more closely acquainted with the people of Dingham than she had ever been in all the nine years she had lived there, and she learnt that, in times of trouble at least, they were good neighbours. Many were ready to set aside their own affairs and go searching the countryside around. Others came to the millhouse with words of comfort and stayed talking by the hour, feeling that she should not be left alone to brood. Among these was the vicar, Mr Eustead, and on the next Sunday, at each of the day's services, he offered up prayers for Richard Lancy, asking that his wife should not be left long in such terrible doubt as to the fate that had befallen him.

But although they were kind and sympathetic, Ellen was far from comforted, for nobody offered her any hope. Will Gale and Archie Shaw, with all the helpers they could muster, were dragging the river below the mill. Bob Dyson and his son had searched the railway line from Runston to Milby, a distance of nearly eleven miles. And the constable from Sutton Crabtree, calling on Ellen at the millhouse, seemed to think that Richard could have been attacked and robbed by a man from Sturton, already wanted for several crimes.

'Everyone's looking for a dead body!' Ellen burst out to Jerry Trussler, when he and some others returned from searching Skyte Quarry. 'Why does no one believe he's alive?'

'As to that, we all hope so, of course. But if he's alive, then where's he got to? Why's he missing all this long time?'

'Perhaps he's been taken ill,' Ellen said, 'or hurt himself and can't move.'

'Then we shall find him, never fear. Though in this bad weather we been having – '

'You sure he never said where he was going, Mrs Lancy?' asked Bob Dyson. 'No hint nor nothing of what he was doing nor who he was going to see that night?'

'No, nothing,' Ellen said. She had been through the matter a hundred times. There was nothing new she could tell the men. 'He said he was going out on business. No why or where or what about. But he did say he'd be late coming home.'

'It's a blooming mystery, that's what it is!' said George Danks of Cockhanger Farm. 'I don't know what to make of it nohow.'

'You don't think it's some sort of joke on his part, do you, George?' asked Joe Dancox.

'No, no. Not him. Richard liked a laugh well enough but he warnt what you'd call a *joking* man. And what sort of joke would it be, anyway, doing a thing like that to his wife? No, it's no joke, be sure of that. Something's befell him. You mark my words. And what with the floods and the bad weather – '

George broke off and looked at Ellen, who stood erect, staring before her. The five men were silent, sitting awkwardly, hands on their knees, wishing themselves elsewhere yet unwilling to leave her all alone. But at last Joe Dancox rose to his feet.

'Mrs Lancy, ma'am, you shouldn't ought to be by yourself. Just say the word and I'll get my missus to come along and sleep in the house till it's all over.'

'No, Mr Dancox,' Ellen said. 'It's kind of you but it won't do. If I'm to be left without a husband, I must get used to it as best I can. Thank you all for your kind help, and thank you for coming to tell me the news.'

'We shan't give up!' said Jerry Trussler, and the others,

following him out of the kitchen, echoed his words: 'No lections of that! Oh dear me no! We shan't give up till we've tarnal well found him and brung him home!'

Ellen closed the door on them and stood for a moment listening to their footsteps thudding across the wooden bridge. Then she went upstairs to the back bedroom, where little John lay fast asleep. So far, although he knew of his father's absence, he took it for granted that all would be well, and she had done everything to encourage him in this belief. But soon the holidays would be over and he would be going back to school, and there he would hear the worst rumours. In the morning, therefore, she would have to tell him the truth of the matter: that his father was lost and might be dead; for by now it was the seventh day.

* * *

Now that the mill was no longer working, the little millhouse seemed dreadfully quiet. The gales had blown themselves out at last; the rain was no longer sluicing down; and sometimes, in the course of the day, the silence was so encompassing, it seemed to her that the whole world outside had gone dead. She had to go to the door and open it, so that she should be reassured by the sound of the weir pouring into the stream, and the sight of the sparrows squabbling for crumbs on the garden path.

Sometimes, alone in the kitchen, she would sit and concentrate her mind, thinking of all the places where Richard might be, and of all the possible accidents that could have befallen him. Surely, surely, so close as they were, her mind should be able to reach out to his? She had to *concentrate* with her whole being. And at these times, her small son, coming in from school, would find her sitting in a trance. He would come to her and touch her hand.

'He ent gone for good, has he, mother? He ent gone and left us all by ourselves?'

'I hope not, John. I hope not indeed.'

'I wish he'd come back this very minute. I wish he'd come

walking in at the door. I don't like it without my dad. I'm scared Old Rag-Face will come and get us and carry us off on his flying horse.'

'You mustn't be scared,' Ellen said. 'Nothing will happen to you while I'm here. I won't let it. And you mustn't start thinking about Old Rag-Face or you'll have bad dreams like you did before.'

'Maybe my dad has gone on a journey to Derbyshire. Maybe he'll bring back another stone.'

'I'm sure he hasn't gone on a journey. He would have told us all about it. He would have taken the horse and waggon.' Ellen got up and began moving about the room. She struck one hand against the other. 'We ought to be able to *think*!' She said. 'We ought to be able to work it out!'

The boy looked up with wrinkled forehead. He watched her walking to and fro. The fire in the stove had burnt low, the lamp was unlit, and the kitchen was growing very dark. He thought of his father out at night, stumbling into the swollen river.

'Don't let him be dead!' he said, trembling. 'Don't let him be dead, mother! – Not my dad!'

Ellen turned to him with a little cry. She knelt and took him into her arms.

'Of course he's not dead, John! He can't be! He *can't*! I won't believe it and neither must you. We must both be brave and strong about it and keep on praying for his return.'

But there were times when even the worst news would almost have been welcome, if only to end the uncertainty. She pictured someone coming to tell her that Richard's body had been taken from the river or the railway line, and the feeling that came over her was one of relief, like the melting away of a heavy burden. For at least such a thing could be understood: death was straightforward, however dreadful: it struck at people in broad daylight and those who were left did at least know what had happened and why; whereas, with her, there was only blankness; a tormenting bewilderment that left her a prey to every fancy and superstition. So that once or twice, in her innermost mind, she almost wished she could see Richard's body brought to the door. But immediately she would feel ashamed; would feel herself guilty of betrayal; and then it seemed to her, somehow, that Richard's safety depended on the strength of her faith.

'We *must* go on searching!' she said every day to Jerry Trussler. 'We must! We must!'

But, as Jerry said to Joe Dancox, there were not many places left to be searched, even outside the parish boundary, and he for one was losing hope. Twelve days had now gone by and Richard Lancy's disappearance looked like remaining a mystery for ever more.

'I'll tell you what, Mrs Lancy, ma'am. I reckon you ought to see Grannie Franklin. You never know. It might be worth trying, as a last chance, and it can't do no harm one way or the other. Of course, some people say it's a lot of nonsense, and maybe you're against such things – '

'What would Grannie Franklin do?'

'Well, she'd need something belonging to Richard, and she'd need a map of the district too. That's easy enough, it seems to me, so why not try it and see what happens?'

'I'll try anything,' Ellen said.

So, that afternoon, in the tiny cottage next to the churchyard, old Mrs Franklin took the penknife Ellen had brought her and, dangling it on the end of a string, allowed it to swing slowly to and fro, above the map laid out on the table. Ellen watched, willing to believe in any magic, and Jerry Trussler held his breath, following every move of the penknife as it swung like a pendulum back and forth.

'D'you get any feelings, Grannie?' he asked.

'No, not much,' the old woman said. 'A slight pull northwards, that's all, and you generally nearly always get that.'

'Then what use is it?' Ellen asked.

'Sometimes it shows a will of its own. I feel it twirling in a certain direction.'

'But you get no such feeling now?'

'No, not a thing, I'm sorry to say. You sure this knife

belonged to your husband?'

'He was using it the night he disappeared.'

'Then I reckon I'll give it another chance.'

The old woman closed her eyes. The penknife swung slowly to and fro, northward to southward, above the map.

'No, nothing,' she said again. 'Just the slight pull northwards and that's nothing.' She opened her eyes suddenly and looked at Ellen. 'But one thing I feel and the feeling is throbbing right up my arm. – Richard Lancy is still alive!'

Ellen's heart moved painfully. She found it impossible to speak. Jerry Trussler spoke for her.

'Is he hurted, Grannie? Can you say?'

'Hurted? Maybe. I dunno for sure. But he's alive, I'm sure of that. I can feel the throbbing of his blood. Now it's up to you to find him.'

'Can't you say *nothing* of where he is? Not even the *sort* of place to look?'

'No, no more,' Grannie said, and began folding Jerry's map. 'I've told you all there is to tell. I'm not a magician, you know, nor a witch neither. It's a special power in my hands and the power ent so good today.'

Ellen gave the old woman a florin and left the cottage with Jerry Trussler.

'The trouble is,' he said to her, ' she says what she knows folk want to hear, and we ent much the wiser for that, I'm afraid.'

'We *must* go on looking all the same.'

'Ah, but where?' Jerry said.

* * *

Ellen herself was out every day with the horse and waggon, driving to every neighbouring village. She travelled a great many weary miles, calling at the remotest farms, questioning everyone she met on the road, but no one could help her to find her husband. The people of Dingham, seeing her driving through the village, treated her with a solemn respect, because of the nature of her errand.

'There she goes again, poor woman, wearing herself to a tarnal shravel. She don't never give up, does she, poor soul, but what good can she ever do, toiling about like that, day in, day out? Better if she was to face the facts.'

Some felt ashamed at seeing her pass, because they themselves had abandoned the search, and her perseverance was like a reproach. And now that so much time had passed without Richard's body being found, the gossip began to blossom out. There was speculation on all sides.

'You don't think,' said Jem Williams in The Feathers one evening, 'that Dick Lancy's gone off with another woman?'

'And left a good business behind like that? Not him, by golly! He's a sight too smart. Besides, he ent never favoured no other woman, apart from his missus. He ent that sort.'

'All things is possible, however, I reckon. Nobody knows another man's mind.'

'Oh, anything's possible!' Jerry Trussler said with scorn. 'He could've gone off and jumped in the sea or took a ship to foreign parts. Or maybe his missus upped and killed him and fed him to the little fishes. Or maybe he got catched up in the moon for grinding corn on a Sunday! Anything's possible in this world – so long as there's big enough fools to believe it!'

'All right, all right!' said Jem, nettled. 'And what do *you* think has happened to him?'

'I dunno,' Jerry said. 'We've just about turned over every stick and stone between Sturton and Runston. That's a rajus of eighteen miles, southwards and eastwards and mostly downriver. Dick didn't hardly ever go upriver. He always said it was like foreign parts.'

'He was upriver, though, not long ago. He went to that sale at Cutlowell Park.'

'Ah, I know. And some pretty hard things he had to say about it too. He never thought much of folk in them parts and I'm inclined to feel the same. Herefordshire is a queer country.'

Jerry drank the last of his beer and watched the froth

sliding back in his tankard.

'It's his missus I feel so sorry for. It's enough to turn a woman's mind. And them such a well-suited couple together! It's a blooming mystery, that's what it is, and I'd give a fortune to fathom it out.'

'How long is it since he went missing?'

'A fortnight tomorrow,' Jerry said. 'Too long, I reckon, for any hope of his being alive.'

* * *

Richard was trapped in the cellar for sixteen days and during that time, at the height of the gales, the floodwater rose to such a level that even when he stood on the cask, it reached to his waist. Then, after a day and a night, it fell again slowly, little by little, till only ten or twelve inches remained, a thick sludge on the cellar floor.

On the seventeenth day, in the early morning, two young gipsies, picking over the ruins of the burnt-out mill, heard a knocking from below and a faint voice calling. They set to work to remove the rubble and discovered the trapdoor with its ring. They opened it and Richard was free.

The day was a dull one, the sky close-packed with low grey cloud, yet its light to Richard was a blinding glare, and he pulled his cap down over his eyes, cowering a while with his head in his arms before allowing them to haul him out. The gipsies took him to their camp nearby and he sat at their fire with a horse-blanket round him. The womenfolk gave him hot soup and bread and afterwards, when he had eaten, an old man proffered a bottle of brandy. Richard took it and drank many times, gulping the brandy with a kind of lust and making little grunting sounds as it ran hotly down his throat. The old gipsy leant across and took the bottle away again. He had to use force to loosen Richard's tight-clasped fingers. By then, only a cupful of brandy was left, and he emptied it into Richard's boots.

'Did somebody put you into that hole?'

'No,' Richard said, in a hoarse whisper. 'Accident. Nothing

more.'

'How long was you there?'

'I dunno,' Richard said, and sat quite still, looking into the fire. His strength was almost at an end. His eyes kept rolling in their sockets. 'A long time,' he said, and his voice broke in utter weakness.

They put him up into one of their waggons and drove him to Dingham, wrapped as he was in the horse-blanket, and wearing his cap down over his eyes. They were seen as soon as they entered the village, and as they drove down the long main street, people gathered to watch them pass. Richard saw them, but only dimly, like faces and figures seen in a dream. And they in turn stared in silence, for his face showed how close he had come to death.

'Leave him be,' the old gipsy said, as one or two people moved forward. 'Leave him be. He wants his home.'

When they set him down at the millhouse door and took the blanket from his shoulders, he stood for a moment as though puzzled, as though asking, What is this place you've brought me to? – What am I supposed to do? And he half looked round, with a little gesture of appeal, as the gipsy waggon began moving off, leaving him standing all alone.

Ellen, hearing the sound of wheels, went to the window to see who was there. The gipsies were already driving away. She saw Richard with his hand on the door and she hurried to open it, reaching out to him, saying his name, and weeping to see him so changed, so gaunt. Supporting him, she led him indoors, and there he stood like a hollow man, looking at her with burning eyes, unable to speak a word to her, unable even to move his lips. Ellen put her arms around him, giving him her warmth and strength, and he clung to her as the giver of life.

* * *

Nursed by Ellen, and with Dr Reed in attendance on him, he soon recovered. He had always been a strong healthy man, and possessed an iron will besides. His strength and his will had saved his life.

In less than two weeks he was up and about again, eager to get the mill working, determined to make up for lost time. But his ordeal in the cellar had left its mark: his brown hair was streaked with grey, and his face was deep-lined, the nerves pulsing visibly under the skin of jaw and temple; and sometimes, when something upset him, the sweat would come out on his upper lip, and his eyes would take on a blind-staring blankness.

'My dad's gone old,' John said once, alone with his mother.

'No, he's not old,' Ellen said. 'He's still sick, that's all, but he's getting better all the time.'

'He never laughs nor nothing now. He wears a long face like old Mr Groom.'

'He'll soon be better, you'll see. It's up to us to try and be helpful and not make his head ache with too much noise.'

Ellen watched over Richard anxiously and always, if he left the house, tried to find out where he was going.

'Don't worry!' he said. 'I shan't get into a scrape like that again. I ent going nowhere near Cutlowell Park.'

When Ellen asked what had taken him to the ruined mill, he was inclined to be evasive, but the story came out eventually.

'I was looking for something, that's all.'

'Something that wasn't really yours?'

'A bag of millwrighting tools, that's all. They owed me something, them upriver folk, for wasting my time at the sale that day. But the tools had gone when I went back, and now you'll say it served me right.'

Ellen, however, said nothing. She was too thankful to have him back. But the villagers, calling at the mill, anxious to welcome him back to life, eager to hear the whole story, might have been less indulgent towards him, and for them he had a different answer.

'I thought I'd lost my watch and chain there. I went back to look for it and got buried alive.'

'And did you find it, your watch and chain?'

'Yes, I found it,' Richard said, producing it and showing it round, 'and I reckon it just about saved my life.'

'How do'you make that out?' asked Fred Byers.

'I dunno. It was just an idea I got into my head. I felt, somehow, that so long as my old watch kept going, well, I could d— well keep going too!'

'Then I reckon you took good care to wind it?'

'I did,' Richard said, 'and I took good care not to let it get wet.'

'It was company, like, I suppose?'

'It was all the company I had!'

'I dunno how you could've stood it, being shut up so long like that, in the cold and the dark, with not a bite of nothing to eat, and only that dirty water to drink. I'd say it's a marvel you're alive.'

'Was there rats in that cellar?' asked Joe Dancox.

'Rats and all sorts!' Richard said. 'Dead uns, mostly, drowned in the floods, and they floated around on the top of the water. But here! Lumme! Look at the time! I got work to do today. I can't stand gossiping hours on end – not like some folk I could mention.'

He talked very little of his sixteen days trapped in the cellar. It irked him if they pressed him too hard. He would say just so much and no more, and afterwards would turn to his work, being brisk and busy and preoccupied until his questioners went away. But one day, suddenly, alone with George Danks in the mealroom, he said: 'I had to eat *slugs*, George, to keep alive! Slugs and snails and dead worms. I had to *eat* them to keep alive.' And then, avoiding George's pitying gaze, he said: 'Don't tell no one else about that. It's something I generally try to forget.'

* * *

Every day now, after school, John hurried home and went straight to the mill, hauling himself up on the half-door until he could see over the top and call to his father, busy inside. He followed Richard everywhere, watching everything he did, wanting to help at every turn.

'Glory, boy!' Richard said at teatime one day. 'You look at me as though you could eat me. Don't you believe it's really me?'

'He missed you dreadfully,' Ellen said. 'He used to pray for you every night.'

'If he used his headpiece,' Richard said, 'he'd maybe have known where I could be found.'

'How on earth could he?' Ellen exclaimed. 'When nobody knew where you had gone?'

'Seems to me he didn't think. If he had done, he'd have figured it out.' Richard was eating a piece of cake. He removed a cherry and gave it to John. 'Well, boy, where was your wits? You remember going to the sale at the mill?'

John nodded, eating the cherry.

'Of course you do,' Richard said. 'And what happened when we got there?'

'It warnt no good,' John said. 'There warnt nothing left worth buying.'

'And what about that bag of tools? You saw me put it in the cellar? You was watching me, warnt you, when I closed the trap?'

'Yes.'

'Then if you'd used your headpiece,' Richard said, 'you'd have known I meant to go back and get it.'

John sat quite still and said nothing. He looked at his father with dark frowning eyes. Ellen was indignant on his behalf. She rounded on Richard and spoke sharply.

'You seem to forget he's only a child. He's four years old, not a grown man. How could he know what you meant to do? Did you ever say you were going back?'

'I would've thought it was plain enough.'

'Were you so clever when you were his age?'

'Ah, that's going back a bit, ent it, Nell?'

'You expect too much of him,' Ellen said. 'You even expect him to read your thoughts.'

'Maybe you're right,' Richard said, and leant across to

ruffle John's hair. 'You're only a tiddler, ent you, boy? You're only tailings and a bit of bran? We've got to wait a good long while before you're grown up and using your brains. Still, I hope you won't be too slow a-learning, boy, cos you don't get anywhere in this world unless you got a bit of nous.'

Richard's recovery of his physical strength was something of a miracle to Ellen, and she never ceased to marvel at it. Within a month of rising from his bed, according to his own boast, his weight was back to normal again, and when Ellen doubted his word, he took her into the mill and weighed himself in her presence.

Within two months, he was working harder than ever, on the go at all hours, for he still travelled about the district, dealing in all manner of things, as well as running the water-mill and grinding, most days, for a good seven or eight hours. And in the mealroom, as of old, he would demonstrate his strength by raising a full sack of flour from the ground until he held it above his head. Sometimes he did this special trick with John sitting astride the sack, and the little boy, having no fear of heights, would hang his cap on a nail in the beam, shouting with laughter all the while.

'My dad,' he would say to the customers, 'is the strongest man in the whole world.'

* * *

But Richard's recovery in other respects was much slower. He showed signs of strain and weakness. One wet Saturday afternoon, when he was in the woodshed, splitting logs, John crept up to the door and shut it, twisting the hasp and locking him in. It was a favourite trick of John's; it had happened often in the past; and the joke had been for Richard to bargain with his son, offering a penny or a shoulder-ride in exchange for his release. But this time, as soon as the door slammed shut and the place became dark and close about him, Richard felt himself trapped again. There was not enough air for him to breathe. The roof was pressing lower and lower, and unseen water swirled about him, waiting for him to topple and fall. And suddenly, with a loud cry, he sprang at the door in a kind of frenzy and hacked it open with his axe.

Outside, in the yard, John stood and stared in fascination as the axe came splintering through the door. His grin of expectancy faded away, yielding to the chill whiteness of fear as his father burst out and lunged towards him. Too late, he tried to run. Richard caught him and swung him round.

'D'you think it's funny to shut me up in there like that? Would you like it yourself if I done it to you? Maybe you don't think I had enough of being shut up the way I was, day and night for sixteen days? Maybe you'd like me gone for good?'

Richard was holding the boy by the arms and was shaking him savagely to and fro. With every word another shake, and his fingers pressed harder all the time. John was crying, hurt and frightened, when Ellen ran out from the back kitchen.

'Richard! Please! Whatever are you doing? Control yourself! The boy is choking.'

'Ent it likely I've had enough, without his shutting me in that shed? I've a mind to do the same to him – shut him up in the dark with the rats and see if he thinks it's funny then! What d'you say, boy? Will you go in?'

'Control yourself, Richard, for pity's sake! It's only a little childish prank. He's done it often enough before.'

'I'll d— well make sure he don't do it again after today! By the time I've finished with him—'

Ellen thrust herself between them and tried to unfasten Richard's fingers, pressing hard into John's arms. Richard's rage was slow to die down, but gradually he loosened his hold, and the little boy turned to his mother, hiding himself against her skirts.

'Poor boy! Poor boy!' she said, holding him close. 'It's all over now. There's no need to cry. Your daddy didn't mean to hurt you. It's just that he doesn't know his own strength.'

And, over his head as he sobbed against her, she challenged

Richard with anxious gaze. His face was wet with perspiration. Anger was still a film on his eyes. But gradually, little by little, his breathing became steady again, and his voice when he spoke was more like his own.

He shouldn't ought to've shut that door. He knows what I've been through. If he don't, he ought.'

'He's only a child. He can't imagine your sufferings. He's just glad to have you back.'

'He ent got enough to do on Saturdays and Sundays, seems to me. Where are them kids he plays with sometimes? Why don't he go off with them?'

'He was hoping you'd take him to Rainborough today, when you go to Henden's with that flour.'

'Oh, he's always ready to go gadding about! He's bright enough when it comes to that. But I ent going to Rainborough today. I've put it off till Monday or Tuesday. I've got too much to do at home.'

Richard went back to his work in the woodshed. Ellen took the boy indoors. And at bedtime that night, after he had said his prayers, she tried to explain his father's bad temper.

'He's not really well yet. He gets upset. We've got to be careful not to annoy him, and if he flies out at us now and then, well, we must try not to take it to heart.'

'Does he fly out at *you*, mother?'

'He's very touchy with me sometimes. He gets bad headaches that makes him cross. He was very ill, you see, after being in that cellar. You remember how ill he was, lying in bed? You remember the doctor coming in? Well, he's not really strong yet, and we've got to help him to get better.'

'He *is* strong,' the little boy said, and showed her his arms, which were badly bruised from the elbows upwards.

'I know, I know. But he didn't mean to hurt you, John. You must try and forgive him and be very good. He'll soon get well if we don't vex him. Promise me you'll do your best?'

John's face was still stubborn. He looked at her with rebellious eyes.

'Won't you promise,' she said again, 'even if only to please me?'

This time he gave her the briefest of nods, and, knowing it was the most she could hope for, Ellen kissed him and said goodnight.

All through Sunday and during the week, John kept out of his father's way. He no longer went to the mill after school but marched straight past, into the house, and stayed with his mother in the kitchen. At mealtimes he sat like a little image, speaking only when spoken to, and when Saturday came round again, he took himself off to play by the river.

'Is he sulking, that boy?' Richard asked, coming into the house from the mealroom. 'Is he paying me out cos I went for him?'

'I don't think he means to sulk,' Ellen said. 'I told him he must be good and quiet, and it seems to me he's doing his best.'

'That don't mean he's got to be dumb, however, and sit like a malkin on a stick. Why, he looks at me with such eyes sometimes, you'd think I was some kind of wild fierce bear.'

'You frightened him badly in the yard that day. You hurt him, too, inside himself. You made him feel you didn't love him.'

'That's rubbish, that is. I've no time for that. He's supposed to be a boy, not a whey-faced Mary Ellen. There's no call for him to be so soft.'

Richard walked about the kitchen, fidgeting with the backs of the chairs. He went to the window and looked out and could see John, on the riverbank, poking with a stick into the deep holes where the martins had nested in the summer.

'He ent got enough to do, that boy. I reckon I'd better take him fishing. Would he like that, Nell? D'you think he'd come?'

'You've only got to ask him,' Ellen said. 'Just open that window a few inches and see what happens when you put your question.'

And, a quarter of an hour later, watching the two of them setting off, the one a small counterpart of the other, she saw that the sun was shining again, after several days of darkness.

Chapter Four

Richard had quite a few new customers at the mill that spring, some of them strangers from as far away as Aston Charmer, for the story of his amazing survival after sixteen days underground had gone round the county, and many people were curious to see him.

'I know why they come,' he said to Ellen. 'It's to see the man that rose from the dead. You'd think I was something out of a raree show, the way they go on, but it's all right by me! – It's good for trade! I ent been so busy in all my born days. I shall make the most of it while it lasts.'

The mill was certainly doing well, and Ellen was glad to see him happy. But often she worried about him, too, for he still did everything himself and sometimes worked throughout the night, re-dressing the stones by candlelight, so that no precious milling time should be lost next day. She wished he would take on a millboy to help, or employ one of the travelling millwrights who called occasionally, asking for work. But Richard scoffed at the idea. He would not pay outsiders for doing what he could do himself.

'I ent made of money, Nell. Besides, I can't trust them to do a good job.'

'You'll wear yourself out,' Ellen said. 'The doctor warned

you against too much strain.'

'Work never hurt us. It's *lack* of work that wears a man down. A man with business coming in is thankful for it and finds the strength of two or three.'

True, he never seemed tired, physically, but there was strain of a kind, all the same: a certain excitement of the mind as though, having defied death, he felt he had nothing more to fear and could drive himself as hard as he pleased. His energy was unnatural. It overflowed the normal bounds.

One night in April, Ellen awoke in the small hours to find that Richard had gone from her side. His clothes, too, had gone from the chair. She pulled a shawl over her shoulders and went downstairs, drawn by noises in the mealroom. And there, by the moonlight entering the south window, she found him moving sacks of meal.

For a little while she stood and watched him, half in amusement, half in worried exasperation, with some teasing remark beginning to form, ready on the tip of her tongue. But as he crossed the white path of moonlight, dragging a heavy sack by its 'ears', she became aware of some strangeness in him and sensed that he was still asleep.

Her teasing remark almost hung in the air, so near had it come to being uttered, and the quietness thrummed like a drawn string. At the back of her neck, a coldness crept upwards into her scalp, sending a tremor through her nerves, and she stood undecided, half inclined not to interfere. But Richard, sleepwalking in the mill, could easily do himself an injury, so she went and put a hand on his arm.

'Come along, Richard,' she said in an ordinary, quiet voice. 'This way. We're going to bed.'

A touch was enough. He turned towards her silently, eyes wide open, seeing nothing, and meekly allowed her to lead him away. She kept her hand upon his arm, and they went together like two grey ghosts, through the kitchen, into the passage, and up the narrow wooden stairs. His feet found their way without hesitation, and the lightness and quietness of his walk, although he wore his heavy boots, made him an

unreal presence beside her, not a living man at all. Yet his arm was warm and solid enough, under her own icy fingers.

Once in the bedroom, he undressed and lay down without prompting, and drew the bedclothes up to his shoulders. He was soon breathing heavily, and did not stir again that night, but Ellen lay on her back beside him and watched the moonlight on the ceiling giving way to the light of dawn. The night, for her, was an anxious vigil.

When she mentioned the matter the next day, Richard threw back his head and laughed.

'Sleepwalking? Me? You're having me on. I never walked in my sleep in my life.'

'You did last night. I had to bring you back to bed.'

'Without my knowing naught about it? Get away! I ent having that!'

'I'm sure it's because you've been working too hard instead of trying to take it easy. It's got on your mind. It's a worry to you. Your health is not so good as it was before you were trapped in that cellar.'

'That's rubbish, that is. I'm as fit as a flea. Sleepwalking? Get away! You must've dreamt it and thought it was real.'

'Have you been in the mealroom yet? Is everything there as it was yesterday?'

'I've had enough of this!' Richard said. 'I don't want to hear no more about it. I've got enough to occupy me, without you adding your woman's fancies.'

A week later, it happened again. Ellen followed him downstairs and all the way through into the mill. She saw him remove three bricks from the wall and take something from the space behind. It was a bottle of some sort, and she saw him put it to his lips. Afterwards, he hid it again, putting the three bricks back in their place. Then he walked into the mealroom, passing quite close to where she stood. Deliberately, she moved forward, almost directly into his path, and waved a hand in a circular movement in front of those seemingly wide-awake eyes. He passed, however, without a sign, merely stepping aside to avoid her, and there was the

same strangeness about him, the same remoteness as before. He was walking in his sleep. Now, if she woke him, he would have to believe it. But such a course was said to be dangerous, and she hesitated to take the risk.

But the thing that disturbed her most of all was the smell of brandy he left behind him. She thought of the bottle in the wall and wondered how many were stowed elsewhere. Was it possible for a man to be a drinker in his sleep and not know it? No. It was not. For he had known what he was doing when buying the brandy, and had gone to a good deal of trouble to keep the matter to himself. The secrecy of it cut her off. He seemed a stranger, suddenly. The distance between them was cold and dark.

Shivering, she pulled her shawl close about her, and followed him into the mealroom. He was moving among the sacks, apparently counting them, touching each one. She went to him and took his arm and led him back upstairs to bed.

* * *

Now that she knew of his secret drinking, the signs of it were plain enough. The slight slurring of his speech sometimes and the uncertainty of his gaze; the bursts of temper arising out of nothing at all; the habit he had of chewing a mouthful of wheat-meal several times in the course of the day. These things spoke for themselves and she wondered that she had not noticed before.

It was easy to understand how the habit had come to him. Working so late into the night, alone in the mill, doing tedious, exhausting work such as dressing the stones or making new cogs for the spur-wheel, surely he could comfort himself in whatever way he chose? But much of his work could be dangerous if his judgment were ever impaired by drink, and Ellen, being afraid for him, decided that she must speak her mind.

'Don't you think it's unwise to drink so much, when you're working all alone in the mill? If the stone were to slip when you're turning it up, or if you should knock the candle over – '

'What're you on about?' he said, and his eyes slid away, as they so often did nowadays, till he seemed to be looking, not at her, but at something shadowy moving behind her. 'What're you on about, drinking indeed? How many times have I been to the inn? Once! That's all. Just once! No more.'

'I'm talking about what you do in the mill. You've always said how easy it is to start a fire in such a dry, dusty place and if you were to have an accident – '

'What do you take me for? A fool?'

'Drink can make any man foolish, even you.'

'Drink is nothing to do with me. I dunno what the h— you mean.'

'Oh, Richard!' she said reproachfully. 'I've seen you, myself, with my own eyes. I've seen where you hide the brandy bottle. I've even seen you drinking from it, so why deny it all the time – '

'Seen it?' he said, with a quick glance, and began moving about the kitchen, fidgeting with the chairs at the table. 'What've you seen, I'd like to know? You take me and show me what you've seen! Let's go this minute into the mill and get it settled once and for all!'

'No, I don't want to. Where's the point? I know what I mean and so do you. You've got a hiding-place in the wall.'

'All I know is, you've been snooping around. That's the truth of it, right enough, and I don't like it, I'll tell you straight. When a man's wife starts spying on him – '

'I never meant to spy on you. I followed you down when you walked in your sleep.'

'Here we go! Them fancies of yours! Are you saying it's happened again?'

'Yes, it happened on Monday night. You went down to the mill and I followed you. I had to bring you back to bed.'

'Get away!' he exclaimed. 'I shan't swallow that!'

'How else would I know?' Ellen asked, watching him as he flung about. 'How else would I know of your hiding-place if

I hadn't seen you go to it? You haven't been out of the mill since Monday. You were there all day yesterday and today and I never came in for a single moment.'

'That's nothing. You could've been in there before.'

'And what would I have seen then, any different from what I've said?'

Ellen stepped in front of him and tried to make him meet her eye, but he merely flung away from her and went towards the mealroom door.

'You won't have seen nothing! Not a stitch! Cos there's nothing there for you to see! As for my walking in my sleep, if I hear that old tale again – '

'Richard! Please! If only we could talk this out!'

Richard, however, would not stay and talk. He went back to the mill and worked on into the night, and when he came in, after midnight, he went to bed without a word.

But, strangely enough, although he denied it had ever happened, the sleepwalking stopped after that, and Ellen's nights, in part at least, were free of anxiety on his behalf. She noticed, too, on going into the mill one day to ask for a new bag of flour, that the three loose bricks in the far wall had been cemented into place.

* * *

The drinking went on as before. Ellen was beginning to know the signs. And although Richard took such care in his attempts to keep it secret, it was soon suspected in the village. Ellen was at Whitty's shop one morning, buying the week's groceries, and one of the items on her list was a bottle of sarsparilla. Mr Whitty fetched it for her and put it into her shopping-basket.

'So long as it's nothing stronger, eh?' he said with a laugh, and Ellen, taking money from her purse, pretended that she was busy counting.

That same morning, returning home, she heard voices inside the mill, raised so loud that they could be heard above the noise of machinery. An old cart stood in the roadway, loaded with sacks of meal and bran. It belonged to George Danks of Cockhanger Farm. And after a moment, as she stood, George came stumping out of the mill, red in the face and scowling fiercly, slamming the half-door shut behind him. He went to his horse and removed its nosebag with trembling fingers. He threw it into the back of the cart.

'George! What is it?' Ellen said. 'Whatever's the matter?'

'Ask *him*!' said George, jerking his head towards the mill. 'That husband of yours! The miller hisself! Ask him what's wrong with his weights and measures!'

'Do you mean he's made some mistake?'

'Twelve years I've been coming to this mill. I was one of the first, when Dick was a lad, and I did my bit in starting him off. But I shan't be coming after today. I shall trade with Holt in Runston in future, where I can get an honest deal.'

'Whatever it is that's happened today surely it can be put right?'

'Nobody likes to be cheated, ma'am, and I've had more'n I can take. That husband of yours is too sharp by half.'

'Isn't there anything I can do?'

'No, no, there's nothing to do. It's past mending and I'm away off.' George climbed onto the box and took the ribbons from the cleat. He looked at Ellen, standing below. 'There's only one way to help your Dick — keep him away from the blasted bottle!'

Ellen watched him drive away. She put down her shopping and went into the mill. Richard had a sack on the hand-barrow and was wheeling it towards the hoist. His handsome face was dark with anger. A pulse was beating in his cheek.

'What happened?' she asked, above the rumble of the mill. 'How come you've quarrelled with George Danks?'

But although he heard her and glanced round, he made no attempt to answer her, and she saw by the tightening of his mouth that to question him now would make matters worse.

At midday, when he came in for dinner, he was chewing a mouthful of wheat-meal. The dust of it was on his lips. He washed himself in the back kitchen and splashed cold water over his head. He came to the table with wet hair.

'Well?' Ellen said, bringing his dinner. 'Are you going to tell me what happened?'

'If you mean George Danks, and I daresay you do, I d— well threw him out of my mill.'

'That's no answer. I want to know what it's all about.'

He accused me of giving him short measure. Now you know as much as me. Lord! But the fool has got a nerve! He's lucky I didn't break his neck. Him and his tuppenny tinpot farm! Accusing *me* of giving short measure!'

'And did you?' she asked, quietly.

'Lord!' Richard said, striking the table. 'That's your loyalty, I suppose? That's your idea of being a wife! Supposing you think of the day we got married, how you promised to honour and obey! Is this how you keep that sacred promise, accusing me the same as Danks?'

'I notice you don't really answer my question.'

'No, nor shan't, if you ask for ever! It's not a wife's place to ask questions. Not *them* sort of questions, anyway, concerning a man and his private business.'

'Since you don't deny it,' Ellen said, 'I suppose that's an answer in itself.'

'Is it? Is it?' he exclaimed. 'And what in h—'s name do you mean by that?'

Hands flat on the table, he leant towards her, jaw outthrust, the blood rising in his face and burning darkly in his cheeks. His anger leapt out at her like heat, causing a prickling in her skin, but before either could speak again, John came running in from school with a wren's nest he had found in the lane, and while Ellen inspected the nest, Richard took up his knife and fork and began eating.

Throughout the meal, as they ate together, Richard scarcely spoke at all, but stared at his wife across the table and followed every move she made. John's bright prattle gradually ceased. He saw that his father was in a mood. He looked at his mother questioningly and she gave him a reassuring smile. She asked him about his school lessons. Then suddenly, in a pause, Richard put down his knife and fork and pushed his empty plate aside.

'I might've known you'd side with Danks! It's not the first time you've called me a thief! You done it that time when I fetched the stones. Don't think I've forgotten cos I ent!'

'I'm not taking sides,' Ellen said. 'But why quarrel with George Danks, who's been so good to you all these years, helping to set you on your feet?'

'Why does he up and quarrel with *me*?'

'You've lost his custom. I suppose you know that. He's going to Runston in future, he said, and he's a man who means what he says.'

'Let him go, by all means! What loss will it be if he gets his pigfood ground elsewhere?'

'I don't understand you,' Ellen said. 'George has always been your friend. When you were missing all that time, he was out with the other men, searching everywhere day after day.'

'Don't tell me he lost any sleep!'

'Does it mean nothing at all to you that so many people were worried about you, doing their best to find where you'd gone?'

'People?' he said contemptuously. 'Danks and Bullock and Rissington? I doubt if they was concerned for *me*. They just wondered who'd grind their corn!'

Ellen was silent, looking at him, and under her unwavering gaze his own fell away, uneasily, trying to focus elsewhere. He gave a shrug and tried to laugh, as though it was nothing but a joke and she was at fault for taking it all so seriously.

'Anyway! What use was it? They never looked in the right place, did they? I could be there still, just bones in a cellar, for all the good they done searching around.'

'How could they know where to look for you? How could anyone know, even me, your own wife, when you chose to be so mysterious, poking about where you'd no right to be and telling no one what you were doing? How *could* we have known where you had gone?'

In the silence that followed Ellen took herself to task, ashamed of her outburst in front of her child. John sat quite still, his shoulders drooping, making himself very small in his chair. His dinner, half eaten, lay before him, the food growing cold upon the plate. And in his hands, hidden down in his lap, he held the tiny wren's nest, made of sheepswool and moss and bits of dried grass. Looking at it, he shut himself off. Harsh words between his mother and father were becoming common nowadays. He crouched beneath them and made himself small.

Richard got up and rattled his chair in under the table. He looked at Ellen and at his son.

'You should have asked the boy where I was. He could've told you, Cutlowell Park. He could've told you about that cellar.'

'That's ridiculous!' Ellen said. 'We've been through all this once before. John couldn't know you were going back.'

Richard took his cap from the peg and opened the door. He stood for a moment with his hand on the latch, looking back over his shoulder.

'*He* knew,' he muttered, half to himself, and went out, shutting the door.

Soon the waterwheel was turning again, swish and clack, swish and clack, and the house became filled with the muffled rumbling of the mill. John slid from his chair and came to lean in Ellen's lap, still holding the wren's nest in his hands.

'What's the matter with my dad?'

'I think he's not feeling so well today.'

'Is it his elbow?' John asked.

'Elbow?' she said. 'What do you mean?'

'Jacky Williams said he reckoned my dad had been tipping his elbow. Did he hit it in the mill?'

Briskly, Ellen rose to her feet. She began clearing away the dishes.

'Just look at the time!' she said, laughing. 'You'll soon be running back to school, and you haven't finished telling me how you came to find that nest.'

*   *   *

One Saturday afternoon in June, Richard loaded the waggon with flour, and drove towards Sutton Crabtree. He always locked the mill door these days and he alone kept the key. No one was ever allowed in except when he himself was there.

John was on the footbridge, fishing in the stream with two other boys, Ernie Horn and Lukey Strudwick. They watched Richard driving away.

'I've never been in the mill,' Lukey said. 'Is it spooky like they say?'

'No! It's not!' John said. 'Who says it's spooky, I'd like to know?'

'Can we go in and look around?'

'How can we?' said Ern. 'You saw his father lock it up.'

'Can't we get in through the house instead?'

'No,' John said, 'that door's locked too.'

'Glory be!' Lukey said. 'Ent you allowed in your own dad's mill?'

John withdrew his line from the stream and examined the cube of cheese on the hook. It was sodden and beginning to crumble. He squeezed it into a lump again and dropped it back into the water.

'*I* can always get in,' he said, 'if you really want to see the mill.'

'Ent you afraid?' Lukey asked.

'No,' John said, 'I ent afraid.'

A little while later he led the way to the side of the mill, to the small slatted doors that covered the cog-hole. He opened them and crept inside, and the others followed his example, clambering over the pit-wheel and sidling along the greasy axle. John led them through the wooden shutters, and they were in the mill itself, with the sun coming in through the three windows, making three separate shafts of light, each one showing the dust in the air.

'Lumme!' said Lukey. 'Ent it big?'

'I don't like it in here,' said Ern. 'It feels the same as it does in church.'

'Is that why you're whispering?' Lukey asked. He was

older than John and Ern. He was almost ten and a half. 'Are you going to say your prayers?'

A sudden sound startled them, and the mill cat leapt down from a rafter above. Lukey's face was as shocked as Ern's. He gave a little nervous laugh.

'What's up that ladder?' he asked John.

'The stones is up there,' John said.

'Come along, then, let's have a look.'

From the stone-floor they climbed yet another ladder and mounted to the top floor of all and from there, peeping through the cracks of the luccomb door, they looked down on the open yard, thirty or forty feet below.

'Makes me feel giddy,' Lukey said. 'I shouldn't like to go down on that chain.'

They returned again to the stone-floor and looked at the tools laid out on the bench. Lukey picked them up in turn and asked John what they were for. He picked up the little haresfoot brush and tickled Ernie under the chin.

While they were playing like this together, John heard the sound of the horse and waggon. He whispered urgently to the others and they all lay on their stomachs on the floor, peering down between the cracks into the sunlit millroom below.

Richard walked in carrying a sack over his shoulder. He set it carefully down on the kist, untied the string about its neck, and took out a roll of paper money. The boys could see him counting the notes. They even heard the crisp rustle. And Lukey, lying next to John, gave him a sharp nudge in the ribs.

Richard walked across the mill, unscrewed a tie-plate in the wall, and hid the roll of money behind it. He screwed the plate back very hard. He returned to the sack, took out three big round black bottles, and put them into the wooden kist. He covered them over with a bundle of sacks and let down the lid.

When he had gone, driving away in the waggon again, the three boys hurried down the ladder and crept through the cog-hole, out of the mill.

'Whew! That was close!' Lukey said. 'If your dad had come and found us up there – '

'He wouldn't have done nothing,' John said.

'I dunno so much. I dunno. I reckon he'd have skinned us alive.'

They returned to the upper bank of the stream and took their fishing-rods from under the bushes. John sat down to re-tie the hook on the end of the string.

'Your dad's a miser,' Ernie said, 'hiding his money away like that.'

'Oh no he ent!' John exclaimed. 'Miser your own-self! You mind your tongue!'

'He *is* a miser,' Lukey said. 'Ask any one. Ask my dad. *And* he's a tippler, on the quiet. Anyone'll tell you that.'

'What's a tippler when it's at home?'

'You saw them bottles, didn't you?'

'Bottles is nothing,' John said. 'It's none of your business, anyway!'

'Seems to me you're green as grass.'

'My dad's not a tippler!' John said. 'Nor he ent a miser neither!' And, wriggling forward a little way, he kicked hard at Lukey's foot.

'What is he, then? You tell us that!'

'He's nothing,' John said, twisting the ravelled ends of the string and tying them to the tiny hook. 'He's my dad, that's all.'

'Are you coming to fish at the weir?'

'No! I'm not. I'm stopping here.'

'Suit yourself,' Lukey said. 'Suit yourself – miser's boy!'

They left him sitting on the bank.

* * *

Richard came home at four o'clock but left the horse and waggon outside because he had business elsewhere at five. He ate a very hurried tea and rose immediately from the table. He was on his way out when John came in, and as the boy walked past, Richard took hold of him and dragged him back. He had seen a red smudge on the boy's jacket.

'How come you got ruddle on yourself? You been getting into the mill? Answer me, boy, and be quick about it! I ent got time to waste on lies. You been larking about in there the moment my back was turned today?'

'No!' John said, white-faced. 'Not larking, no!'

'What, then? You was in there for sure. That smudge of ruddle tells the tale. So what was you up to while I was out?'

'Nothing, honest. Just looking round.'

'Touching things and interfering? Poking your nose into my affairs?'

'We was just looking at things, that's all. We never touched nothing. Cross my heart!'

'We? Who's we? What others was there?'

'Lukey Strudwick and Ernie Horn. Lukey wanted to see the mill.'

'You been playing about with my tools? Taking the edge off? Doing them in? How many times have I told you – '

'Richard!' said Ellen, stepping forward. 'Is it such a terrible matter? The boy always *used* to go into the mill. Why should it be so different now?'

'You keep out of this, Nell. It's a matter between the boy and me.'

'He's my son as well as yours.'

'Then you should learn him he's got to obey!'

'Leave go of him and let him sit down. He'll answer you if you give him a chance. He's not a dog, to be shaken so!'

'Get out of my way!' Richard said. 'The mill is my business, not yours, and I'll deal with things as I think fit.' With his fist twisted in John's collar, pressing hard against his neck, he shook him and lifted him off his feet. 'The mill is my business!' he said again. 'And what I want to know is, how the hell did you get in?'

'Through the cog-hole!' John said, gasping.

'You and two others? Kids like yourself? Poking about everywhere, letting them know about my affairs, getting it spread about the place! If you've interfered with anything – '

'I haven't! I haven't!' John cried. 'Leave me alone! You're hurting me! What do I care about the mill? I hate it! I hate it! I hope it falls down!'

Squirming, he managed to wrestle free, and when his father lunged towards him, Ellen quickly stepped in the way. The boy escaped and ran headlong from the house. Ellen clutched at Richard's arm.

'My Lord!' he said, and his face, close to hers, was ugly with temper. 'You dare to take his part against me? You let him defy me and treat me as though I was nothing at all? No wonder he thinks he can do as he likes!'

'So much anger?' Ellen said. 'And all for such a little thing! Is it the drink that makes you like this?'

'I can't stop to argue with you! I've got to go to Whitestone Farm. But I shall be home in due course and young Master John had better watch out!'

He left the house and drove away, and Ellen went out to look for John, walking along the bank of the stream to where it flowed into the river. The boy, as she guessed, was up in his place in the old pollard willow, sitting in the crutch of it, hidden among the grey-green leaves.

'You can come out now. Your father's gone.'

Reluctantly, he climbed down. She helped him and lowered him to the ground. His face was cold and white and stiff, his gaze fixed, defying the tears. The feeling she had, of wanting to take him into her arms, had to be set firmly aside, for, young as he was, he had his pride, and softness from her would have meant his undoing. They walked together hand in hand.

'I don't like my dad,' he said. 'I wish he'd never come back that time. I wish he'd stopped away for good.'

'You mustn't say that. It's very wrong. You shouldn't have taken your friends into the mill. You saw the lock was on the door. You knew that meant you were not to go in.'

'What'll he do to me when he gets home? Will he whip me?'

'No, of course not,' Ellen said. 'He won't do anything.

I won't let him.'

She put him to bed early that night and sat up late waiting for Richard. She steeled herself for the sound of wheels. But when at last he returned home he was steady-eyed, quiet-voiced, in great good humour with himself, having spent the evening with the new tenant at Whitestone Farm.

'Mr Temple farms six hundred acres. He's promised he'll let me grind his corn. That more'n makes up for George Danks and his paltry bits of peas and beans. I reckon I've done a fair evening's work.'

'Yes, that's good,' Ellen said. 'Very good. It is indeed.'

'I reckon I must've kept you up. You're about dropping with sleep, I can see. Still, at least it's Sunday tomorrow, eh?'

Of the trouble with John he said not a word. Nor did he mention it the next morning. The whole of Sunday passed in peace. Ellen was relieved but also puzzled. Richard was not a forgetful man yet the matter it seemed had been forgotten, and even John's white, fearful face did not remind him.

The next time she went into the mill, however, she saw that the shutters over the cog-hole were now fastened with a padlock and chain. No one would enter that way in future. The mill was as safe as a fortress these days, and Richard's pocket was full of keys.

'What are you afraid of,' she asked, 'that you always keep the place locked up?'

'I don't want people snooping around. They got light fingers, some of them, and I can't afford to lose my stock. I reckon they done pretty well for theirselves when I was missing all that time but they'll never get the chance again.'

'That's not true!' Ellen said. 'How can you say such a wicked thing?'

'You don't know. You wasn't here all the time. You was out looking for me. Or so you told me, anyway.'

'Don't you even believe that?'

'Of course I believe it. People saw you driving out. I've heard them say so often enough. And that's what made it easy for them to help theirselves out of my mill.'

Chapter Five

It was a wet summer that year, and harvests everywhere were spoilt. Richard knew this as well as anyone. He had seen the corn laid low in the fields, the soaked grain sprouting in the ear. Yet when autumn came, and farmers like Bullock and Rissington had only a few bushels of grey peas to grind, Richard accused them of holding back. He had already lost three customers, and he blamed George Danks.

'It's him that's turning folk against me, you know. Him and his lies about short measure. I reckon he means to ruin me. He'd like to see me go down the drain.'

'No one's against you,' Ellen said. 'You know the crops have been bad this year. It's the same for everyone, everywhere. But you *will* turn them against you, certainly, if you keep accusing honest men.'

'Oh, I knew it'd all be my own fault! I expect no sympathy at home. My wife is as bad as all the rest.'

All through that summer, the change in him had grown more marked. He was not the Richard she had married. His attitude to everyone, friends and strangers alike, was hard and suspicious. He trusted no one. And often some petty hinderment would put him into a sweat of rage.

The millstream had always attracted children, especially boys, and whenever they had a holiday they would come very early in the morning, bringing a satchel full of food, and play along the banks all day. It had always been so, years without number, and sometimes if rain had fallen hard they had taken shelter in the mill. But now, if a boy so much as set foot on the footbridge, Richard would lean out over the hatch and shout to him to be off at once.

'Ent there enough river for you, without you got to come just there? How'd it be if I chopped that bridge down? I reckon you'd look pretty silly then!'

But the boys still came to the bridge just the same, and the more he shouted to them to be off, the more inclined they were to stay, drumming on the boards with their hobnailed boots and doing their best to provoke him further.

'Mr Lancy! Yoo-hoo! We're on your bridge! Aren't you coming to chop it down?'

Sometimes they went even further than that and closed the upper sluice-gate, so that the waterflow was reduced and the waterwheel gradually slowed to a halt. Then Richard would rush out and pursue them as much as half a mile, trying to trip them up with his broom as they ran along the narrow towpath.

'Why don't you leave them alone?' Ellen asked. 'Boys have always come to the bridge. You used to be friendly and make them welcome.'

'And see where it's got me!' Richard said. 'Great big boys of eleven and twelve, they ought to be going out to work. And what're they *doing* on my bridge? Not fishing! Oh, no! They're looking for ways to get me riled. Well, they'll go too far one of these days and then they'll be sorry, you mark my words!' And, turning to John, he would say: 'Friends of yours? Is that what you said? Then tell them to keep away from my mill or they'll regret it sure as fate!'

Sure enough, the next time the boys interfered with the sluices, Richard was ready with his shotgun and fired both barrels over their heads. Ellen was in the back garden. She and John were picking peas. When she ran round to the mill door, Richard was leaning over the hatch, the twinbarrel smoking dirtily, and a small powder-burn on the side of his face. Three or four boys, with frightened faces, were running like hares towards the village.

'For heaven's sake, Richard, what are you doing? Surely you didn't use real shot?'

'A full charge! Both barrels! And I reckon they must've felt the draught!'

'But they're only children!' Ellen said. 'You might so easily have done them harm!'

'I ent a fool. It's not the first time I've used this gun. It was only to scare them, that's all, and learn them a lesson to keep away.'

'You've got no right to do such a thing! That old gun is dangerous. You've got no right to take such risks.'

'Ent I, though! We'll see about that! I've got a right to protect my mill!'

He was perfectly matter-of-fact. Nothing she said affected him. He went to see to the sluice-gate and returned to his unfinished work in the mill, and that afternoon, in the kitchen, he sat down with powder-flask and bag of shot and carefully reloaded the gun. He put it into the long-case clock and locked the door.

'If they come meddling with the water again, I'm ready for them and so's my gun!'

John, sitting quietly whittling a stick, looked up and sought his mother's gaze. Ellen, sighing, turned away.

But that was not the end of the matter, for later that day, Dave Jukes and Alfred Meadows came knocking at the mill-house door, threatening Richard with the law if he ever shot at their boys again.

'I suppose you'd been drinking,' Meadows said. 'It's the nearest thing to an excuse I can find for you. But if you ever harm them boys of ours, that'll go hard with you, miller, so don't say you was never warned!'

Richard said nothing in answer to this. He merely shrugged and spread his hands as though it was nothing but a joke. Still, their threat seemed to carry weight with him, and he was more circumspect after that. And the boys, too, less bold than before, kept away from the sluice-gates and contented themselves with hurling stones into the millstream. Richard by now had a bad reputation with the people of Dingham, and although there were some who felt sorry for him, knowing what had caused the change, many gave him a wide berth. He became known as the Mad Miller.

People felt even more sorry for Richard's wife and little son, shut away with a man of such uncertain temper, down at the millhouse beside the river, without the solace of near neighbours. And it was at this time that people remembered the stray dog that had run through the church on the day of the wedding. Plainly, it must have been an omen, they said, and the marriage that had seemed so promising had in fact been ill-fated from the start.

Ellen, whenever she shopped in the village, was aware of receiving pitying glances. She tried to ignore them. She tried to preserve a cheerful manner. But it was not easy and sometimes, when the pity overstepped certain bounds, it became irksome.

'Good morning, Mrs Lancy, and how are you, my dear, today? How's *Mister* Lancy, the poor man? It's your little boy I think of most, and the three of you down at the mill like that, cut off from the rest of us, all by yourselves. Why, if that was me – '

'We're perfectly well, Mrs Whitty, thank you. Now if you will kindly look at my list . . . I *am* in rather a hurry this morning.'

Ellen's rebuffs were not well received. She soon had an enemy here and there. The habit she formed, of walking quickly through the village, gaze fixed upon the ground, soon called forth a few spiteful remarks.

'She's like her mother, after all, and what with never speaking nor nothing, I'd say her and Lancy is all too well matched. The two of them is best left alone.'

* * *

Custom was falling off at the mill because of Richard's

strange behaviour, and although he scoffed at the loss of trade, he took such good care of his few remaining customers that they often called him Smarmy Dick. He was always offering to do them favours, and gave them presents of fish he had caught in the river.

Yet he trusted no one. He thought the villagers spied on him, and he put a gate across the footbridge, with an odd assortment of cowbells and sheepbells tied, trailing, along the bottom, so that no villager could approach that way without a loud warning clangour. The Dingham children delighted in this. They would open and close the little gate and, having set the bells jangling, would retreat to the shelter of the blackthorn bushes, where they watched for Richard's suspicious face to appear at the hatch. And often they teased little John about it.

'Why've you got bells on your gate, John? Does your father like the tune? Your dad's a bit touched, ent he, John? He ent quite right in the upper storey?'

'Touched your own-self!' John would say. 'Shut your rattle and get off my tail!'

Throughout that wet and dismal summer he played less and less with the other children, for he could not bear the way they talked about his father and it led to quarrels. He therefore withdrew and when the long holidays came he took to wandering off alone to be rid of them; to find his own refuge in some secret place where he could lie among the reeds and watch the fish in the quiet water.

He was turning in on himself, growing more silent day by day, and Ellen, seeing the change in him, seeing how rarely he smiled or laughed, would leave her housework and follow him, to keep him company on his walks. One day in September, she took a basket and a stick, and they went together to Sanditch Common to pick blackberries.

The day was dull and rather cold. The blackberries were poor withered things for lack of sun to ripen them. But John went from one bramble clump to another, peering into every thicket, hoping to see a stonechat's nest or a whitethroat's, perhaps, and collecting every fallen feather until he had a little bunch to stick in the band of Ellen's hat. And she, seeing some light come into his eyes, gladly gave herself up to him, allowing the day to spin itself out, until he was prattling as of old. Until, for a little while at least, he was a child like any other, fully enjoying childish things.

Then the coming home again, with Richard sitting, tight-lipped, drumming with his fingers on the table, waiting for her to give him his tea.

'Where've you been to all this time?'

'We've been to Sanditch, blackberrying. We know how you like a blackberry pie.'

'I've been waiting nearly an hour but that don't mean nothing, I don't suppose, when you and your lambkin go off together?'

'You could at least have laid the table. You knew I'd be back by and by.'

'It's women's work, getting a man his tea,' he said, 'and I don't care to be kept waiting.'

'I'm sorry, Richard, but I never know when you'll finish work.'

Ellen put her basket aside and began laying the table for tea. She motioned John to help her with it and obediently he went to and fro, setting out bread and cheese and pickles, honey and jam and black treacle.

'Seems to me these holidays of yours don't never finish nowadays,' Richard said, taking the tin of treacle from him and planking it down on the table. 'You spend more time at home than you do at school.'

'They had an extension because of the late harvest,' Ellen said, 'but he'll be going back next week.'

'Can't he answer for hisself?'

'I don't think he realized you were asking him a question.'

'He ent very bright, then, that's for sure! Though he's bright enough when it d— well suits him!'

'Richard, please! Not again today! Can't we have just one mealtime in peace, without you swearing and picking a quarrel? Must you spoil a pleasant day?'

'*You* may have had a pleasant day but *I've* been working for twelve hours, breathing mill-dust all day long and slaving my guts out for small thanks!'

Ellen was silent, tilting the kettle on the hob, filling the teapot with scalding water.

'Didn't you hear me?' Richard asked.

'Yes, I heard you, Richard,' she said. 'I'm sorry you've had a bad day.'

She often made herself humble before him. Only thus could she keep the peace. His mood that day was sneering and sullen. The meal was eaten in total silence.

* * *

But sullenness was the least of evils. Worse, much worse, were the quick and ungovernable rages that nothing, even her utter humility, could avert or appease. For Richard, worried by poor trade, seemed to find relief only when his feelings had overflowed in some act of violence in the home.

One day at dinner, John left a piece of fat bacon on his plate, and Richard ordered him to eat it up.

That's good food. I won't have waste in my house. Eat it up or there'll be trouble.'

'It's nasty gristle,' John said. 'I don't like it.'

'Like it or not, you don't leave this table to go to school until I've seen you eat that bacon, so you might as well get on with it.'

'No. I shan't. I don't like it.'

'Good Lord! I've stood enough! I'll teach you to sniff at good clean food that's cost me money I can't afford! You're getting a lesson you won't forget!'

Richard got up and hurried out into the garden and Ellen, watching from the window, saw him stooping among the plants. He returned with three big yellow slugs and flipped them onto John's plate where they uncurled, wet and pudgy, showing their wrinkled underbodies. John recoiled, looking sick. His lips were tightly pressed together. Ellen went forward in disgust and tried to take the plate away but Richard pushed her roughly aside.

'Well?' he said, nudging John. 'How would you like to eat *them*?'

John looked away, his face a sickly greenish-white. He leant back, shrinking, in his chair.

'Well?' Richard said, with another nudge. 'I asked you how you'd like to eat *them*!'

'I *wouldn't* like it!' John exclaimed. 'Nobody would! I shan't neither!'

'Well, *I* had to eat em!' Richard said. 'All that time I was in that cellar, *I* had to eat them to stay alive!'

'For pity's sake!' Ellen said. 'Will you stop this or are you completely out of your mind?' She pulled at his arm with all her strength, but again he merely thrust her aside.

'Keep out of this. No son of mine is turning his nose up at good wholesome food. After today, he'll know better!'

He put his hand on the boy's neck and pushed him forward against the table. The three slugs were moving on the plate, leaving glistening trails of slime.

'Are you going to eat what I've brought you, boy?'

'No! I'm not!' John cried shrilly. 'Nor you can't make me, neither, so there!'

And he pressed his lips together again, stubbornly enduring pain as his father's fingers, squeezing his neck, forced him forward towards the plate.

'Can't make you? We'll see about that! We'll see who's strongest, you or me!'

Richard was enclosed in his own anger. It gave him a look of blind dogged calm. He picked up a slug between his fingers and held it against the boy's mouth.

Ellen went quickly round the table and leant across from the other side. She struck sharply at Richard's hand and the slug fell onto the plate. She snatched it up before he could stop her and took it to the open stove. She brushed the slugs off into the fire.

'Richard, you've gone too far today! Do you really expect

me to stand by and see my child subjected to this? Take your hands off him at once and try to behave like a normal father!'

'*Your* child, did you say? Is he any more yours than he is mine? Yes, come to think of it, maybe he is, seeing you set him against me so much!'

But he loosened his hold on the little boy and watched as he went to stand by his mother, hiding his face against her body and pulling the folds of her skirts about him.

'Ah, that's right! That's touching, that is! Put your arms around him, Nell! Whisper to him how clever he is, defying his father and answering back! Kiss him and make it up to him and tell him he can do as he likes!'

'Do you want him to hate you?' she asked. 'You're going the right way about it if you do.'

'I want him to have a bit of respect and do as he's told once in a while. He's got no right to leave good food.'

'It's no good demanding his respect when your drinking makes you behave like this.'

'Oh, you'll turn it round in the end, I know, and make out that I'm the one to blame! But what about him and the way he provokes me? What about all I went through that time? Have you any idea what it was like?'

'I know how terrible it was. I can see what it's done to you clearly enough. But must you take it out on us?'

'Sixteen days I was in that cellar and every day I said to myself, "My boy John will know where I am. – *He'll* soon tell them where to look." That was the thing that kept me going. I thought of it over and over again. I even used to call to him – '

'Richard, if only you'd see the doctor!' she said. 'He could help you and give you advice.'

'Yes, it suits you to try and make out I'm sick, instead of listening to what I say. But I'm paying no doctor to fuss over me. No doctor can take away the truth and the truth is what I had to live with all the time I was trapped underground.'

'What truth?' Ellen asked.

'That nobody cared if I lived or died!'

'You are indeed sick,' Ellen said. 'The sickness is in your mind, Richard, and it gives you bad thoughts.'

'What'll the doctor do for that? Will a bottle of medicine cure bad thoughts?'

'No, perhaps not, but the brandy bottle only makes them worse.'

'I ent listening to you no more, twisting everything I say. I've got to go out and look for business. I've got to make a living somehow to pay for the food *he* throws away!'

When Richard had gone Ellen spoke to the little boy and unclasped his fingers from her skirts. She knelt before him and dried his tears; straightened his tie and his torn collar; and tried not to notice the marks on his neck. He looked at her and his lip trembled.

'I hate my dad! He's horrible! I wish he was dead!'

'Hush, now. You mustn't say that. It's a very wicked thing to say.'

'It's him that's wicked, not me! When I'm bigger I'll run away!'

'And leave me behind?' Ellen said.

'No,' he said in a small voice, and his face puckered uncertainly.

'I should hope not indeed!' she said briskly. 'What should I do without my son? Who'd stone the raisins for me when I bake a cake?'

'You could come too. We'd go together. We could go to the lock and get on a barge. We could live on the barge like the bargemen do and nobody wouldn't know where we was.'

The little boy reached out to her and put his hands against her breast.

'Shall we, mother? Shall we go? Shall we run away on a barge?'

Ellen, with an effort, managed to laugh. She touched his face with her fingertips.

'We'll have to see!' she said lightly. 'But now it's time you went to school, otherwise you'll get a bad mark. What are the lessons this afternoon? Reading? Counting? Doing sums?

Miss Robinson says you're good at sums. Are you learning tables yet? Well, you will be soon, I daresay. Come along, then, and I'll walk with you as far as the gate.'

Alone in the millhouse that afternoon she made herself busy, bottling the last of the apple jelly and drying the last of the garden herbs. Outside, a cold grey mist rose from the river and pressed up close against the windows, squirming as though to gain admittance. Ellen felt herself confined. The mist was a presence, shutting out the light of day. She lit the lamp and turned the living flame up high. She stood arrested, stilled by thought.

A wife's duty was to her husband, for better or for worse, according to her vows, and Richard had need of her, now more than ever. But what of her duty to her son whose bright little spirit, day by day, was being dimmed while she looked on? He was only five years old. He had no defence, no strength but hers. What was her duty to her child?

She asked the question in her prayers, but received no guidance.

Chapter Six

Richard would never admit that he had been drinking, even when the smell of it was strong on his breath. Even when he stumbled, crossing the threshold. Even when it made him sick.

'I don't feel so good today. It's a touch of something on my stomach. I reckon maybe I've got a chill.'

'You know what it is that makes you like this.'

'Do I? Do I?' he exclaimed.

'Yes,' she said, 'we both know.'

He never bought his drink in the village. He dealt with a man in a back street in Runston, and he could say with perfect truth that he never set foot in a public house. Yet although he took care in smuggling his bottles so secretly into the mill, once they were empty he made no further attempt to hide them, but let them accumulate in corners here and there, till Ellen quietly took them away.

Sometimes he stayed in the mill quite late, 'doing the accounts' as he always said, and Ellen, as she lay in bed, listening to the slamming of the mealroom door and his clumsy footsteps on the stairs, could tell at once how bad he was and what his behaviour was likely to be. She would lie very still, her face averted, and try to pretend that she was asleep.

'Funny the way you're always asleep! Always lapped up tight like that, set on keeping yourself to yourself. But you needn't worry! It's no odds to me! I don't want where I know I ent wanted!'

But at other times he would strip the blankets away from her and force her round until she faced him.

'You ent much of a wife lately. Not like you ought to be, loving and kind. D'you think I'm going to beg for you? Why should I beg when you're my wife?'

His strong hands punished her flesh. There was no tenderness in him as there had been in the early days. He used his strength and humbled her. She prayed she would not have another child.

Often, during that autumn and winter, he drove about the countryside, buying and selling all manner of goods. He bought eggs and butter at different farms and sold them in the market at Runston. He bought a few bullocks and fattened them up in the mill yard, feeding them on cheap 'misky' corn which he ground, black and smutty though it was, and mixed with molasses to hide the bad taste. As always, he worked hard. Bad times or not, he would make his way. And as Michael Bullock said to his son, 'Dick Lancy may tip the elbow but he's never so far gone in drink that he can't sniff out a fourpenny piece and soon turn it into five-pence!'

But one good thing was said of him: he paid every tradesman on the nail. He always grumbled, certainly, and wanted something knocked off 'for cash', but that was business and why not?

'You may not be doing well these days,' Rissington said, selling him butter, 'but at least you never ask for credit and that makes you one all on your own.'

'Who says I ent doing well?'

'I meant the mill,' Rissington said. 'How much do you grind? One day a month? Maybe two? It surely ent more, from what I hear.'

'You shouldn't believe the tales folk tell. A good miller has always got trade. I'm miller first and general dealer afterwards, and don't you make any mistake about it!'

That the mill should so often be standing idle was a thing that hurt Richard through and through, and Henry Rissington's remark weighed heavily on his mind.

'I know what they're likely saying, Nell. They're saying it's gone back to what it was, that I've done no better than my dad who muddled all his business away and let the mill go down and down. But it ent true, you know. I ent like my dad. It's just their spite.'

'It's been a bad year,' Ellen said. 'Things will improve, given time.'

They were together in the mill. She was helping to mend torn sacks. They sat on two big bags of bran where the light was best, at the south window, each of them busy with bodkin and twine. Richard for once was talking to her in the old way, quietly, in a friendly tone, and his sadness as he looked round the mill, swept and garnered but oh! so bare, brought them together in sympathy for the first time in almost a year.

'Just look at it!' he said. 'I built up such trade in this here mill. Now it's all gone down again. But it ent my fault, is it, Nell? It ent my fault it's all gone down?'

'No, Richard, it's not your fault. And next summer, God willing, the harvest will be a better one and you'll be as busy as you were before.'

She leant across and took his hand, and he looked at her for a long while, with something of the old warmth and with a gleam of cheerfulness too.

'You're right,' he said. 'I ent finished yet and they needn't think it. Rissington shall eat his words. Just cos *he's* got no corn for me to grind he seems to think I'm out of business. But I'll soon make him change his tune, and all the other gossips too!'

Early next morning, the waterwheel began to turn, swish and clack, swish and clack, splashing water in an arc. Ellen, astonished, went into the mill. No corn had come as far as she knew. She asked Richard what he was doing.

'Never you mind!' he said gruffly. 'You attend to your own work and leave me to attend to mine.'

He had put the two pairs of stones out of gear and was letting the waterwheel run by itself. He would not have it said that he was a miller without any trade, and anybody passing by would soon know better and spread the word.

Two or three times a week after that he opened the sluices and worked the wheel, and if anyone passed the open hatch he would make sure that he was seen, wheeling the sack-barrow, fully laden, or working the chain-hoist to the loft.

'You seem pretty busy this morning, Dick?'

'Busy enough!' Richard would say.

And if somebody, putting his head inside, listened for the rumbling of the stones and remarked on its absence, Richard had his answer ready.

'I'm just about finished for today. I'm on my way out to see to the sluices.'

It was not believed for long. Soon it became a village joke. 'The miller's milling air again. He'll soon have enough to fill a sack!'

* * *

Early in November John was ill with whooping cough and Ellen wanted to fetch Dr Reed. Richard said she was making a fuss. She had only to keep the boy in bed and let the fever take its course.

'All children get whooping cough. It's one of them things that go through the school. It's up to you to nurse him through it.'

But Ellen was worried. The boy's face and body burnt with a terrible throbbing heat, and yet he complained of feeling cold. His throat was so sore he could hardly speak. The soreness brought the tears to his eyes, and sometimes he whimpered wearily, mouth open, in distress. Ellen kept him as warm as she could with plenty of blankets and a stone hot water bottle wrapped in flannel. She fed him on gruel and chicken broth. On the third day, seeing that he was just the same, she fetched the doctor.

The old man examined John and even managed to make him smile by the way he twitched his bushy eyebrows when listening with his stethoscope. He left a bottle of medicine to bring down the fever and some 'drops' that would help the boy to sleep.

'Go on nursing him as before and give him warm milk with honey in it. Try to get him to eat if you can. Custards, you know, and things of that sort. I'll call again in a couple of days.'

Richard was out when the doctor came, but returned in time to see him drive off.

'So you went against me as usual? You called him in behind my back!'

'Yes,' Ellen said, 'and any mother would do the same.'

'You'll be sorry for doing that.'

'No, I don't think so, Richard,' she said.

'Yes, you'll be sorry,' he said again. 'You mark my words.'

His behaviour daily grew more strange. He never went up

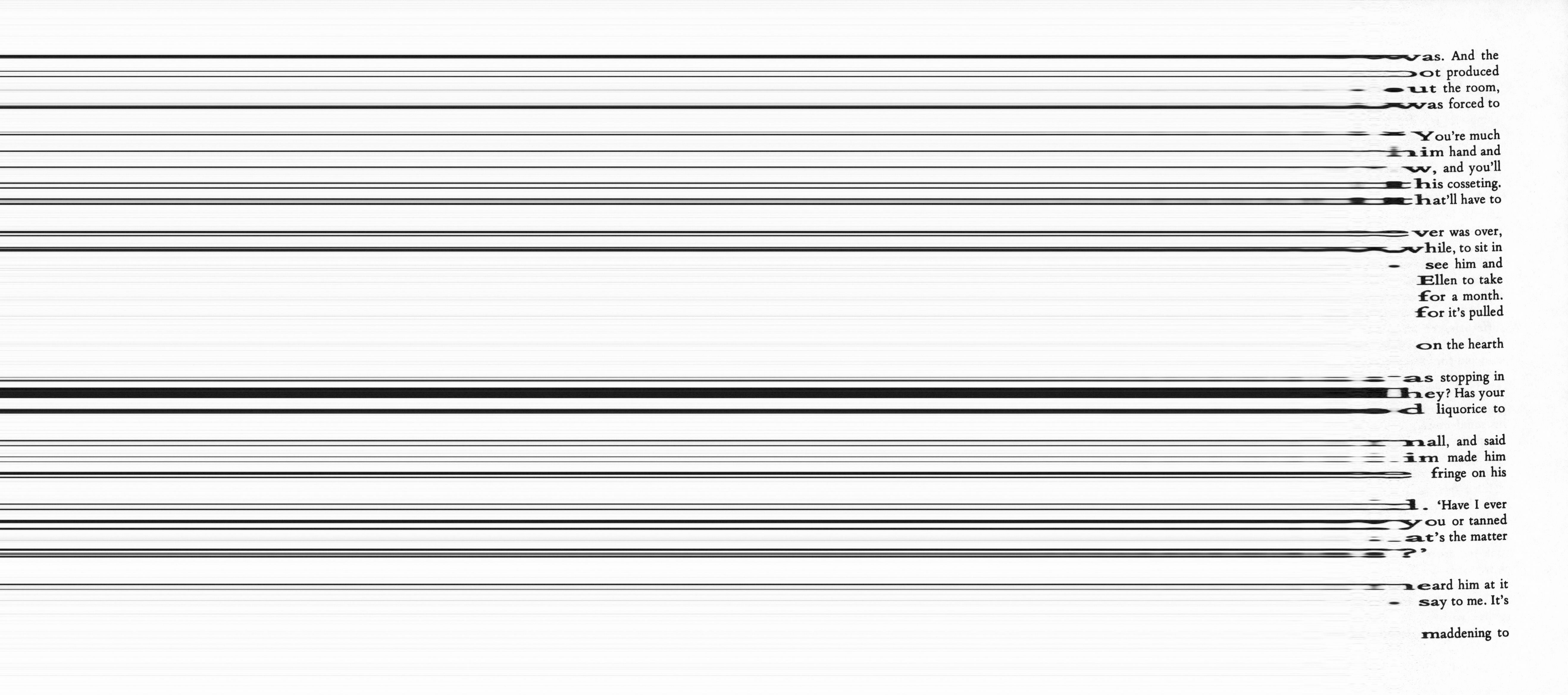

as. And the
ot produced
ut the room,
vas forced to

You're much
im hand and
w, and you'll
his cosseting.
hat'll have to

ver was over,
hile, to sit in
see him and
Ellen to take
for a month.
for it's pulled

on the hearth

as stopping in
hey? Has your
d liquorice to

nall, and said
im made him
fringe on his

. 'Have I ever
you or tanned
at's the matter
?'

eard him at it
say to me. It's

maddening to

Richard. He jeered an
making a fool of hersel
And although she trie
of her ministrations in
thing. If John had be
chair had been move
sucking a cough lozen
to say. And the more
shrank into himself as
fault with everything.
and the boy's coughing
Cough-cough-cough!
only does it to see me

Often, Ellen's own t
so extreme was the pr
Richard's face and rem
found new patience an
sufferings, trapped un
foul water, breathing f
cold and for fear of dro

The effort of will th
dear. He was a man wh
given it in exchange fo
his mind and dark fanc
escape in the brandy bo
eyes at these times had
them.

Ellen felt she could
made him suspicious, a
out he almost always fl
the table and hurled he
took the dress she was
skirt. 'Now you've reall
he said, and walked out,

She hated this strange
to live with. But alway
been and prayed that s

to see his son. He never even asked how he was. And the sight of Ellen preparing egg custard or arrowroot produced such irritation in him that he would stride about the room, flinging open cupboards and drawers until she was forced to take notice and ask what he was looking for.

'It won't interest you, will it?' he would say. 'You're much too full of your lambkin up there, waiting on him hand and foot! He's making a fool out of you, you know, and you'll never be able to do nothing with him after all this cosseting. You'll have spoilt him rotten and *I'm* the one that'll have to put it right!'

At the end of a week the worst of John's fever was over, and on the ninth day he was allowed up for a while, to sit in a chair beside the fire. Dr Reed came in to see him and brought him a monkey-on-a-stick. He advised Ellen to take care of him and keep him away from school for a month.

'Keep him occupied,' he said, 'but gently so, for it's pulled him down.'

Richard, coming in from the mill later, stood on the hearth with his back to the fire and looked at his son.

'So you're up, then, I see! I thought you was stopping in bed for good. Have you had your curds and whey? Has your mother made you comfy? Sweets to suck and liquorice to chew? I shouldn't like you to go without!'

John, still weak and shivery, sat, very small, and said nothing. His father's tall presence beside him made him cower in his chair. His fingers plucked at the fringe on his rug.

'Why do you flinch like that?' Richard said. 'Have I ever raised my hand to you? Have I ever cuffed you or tanned your hide?' And to Ellen he said irritably: 'What's the matter with the boy? Why don't he never speak to me?'

'It hurts him to talk. It makes him tired '

'He talks to you, though, right enough. I heard him at it when I came in. But he's never got nothing to say to me. It's like as though I wasn't there.'

The attention she gave the little boy was maddening to

Richard. He jeered and scoffed repeatedly and said she was making a fool of herself, allowing the child to run her around. And although she tried to be unobtrusive, performing most of her ministrations in his absence, he always noticed everything. If John had been given a change of clothes; if his chair had been moved close to the window; or if he was sucking a cough lozenge; Richard was sure to have something to say. And the more sarcastic he became, the more the boy shrank into himself as though deaf and dumb. Richard found fault with everything. The dumbness, he said, was insolence, and the boy's coughing got on his nerves.

Cough-cough-cough! Lord Almighty! How much more? He only does it to see me vexed!'.

Often, Ellen's own temper was in danger of breaking out, so extreme was the provocation, but when she looked into Richard's face and remembered him as he had once been, she found new patience and remained calm. She thought of his sufferings, trapped underground for sixteen days, drinking foul water, breathing foul air, unable to sleep because of the cold and for fear of drowning.

The effort of will that had kept him alive had cost him dear. He was a man who had lost his soul, as though he had given it in exchange for his life. There were dark places in his mind and dark fancies had taken root there. He sought escape in the brandy bottle and made matters worse, and his eyes at these times had the shifting shadows of madness in them.

Ellen felt she could have helped him, but any tenderness made him suspicious, and whenever she tried to talk things out he almost always flew into a rage. Once he overturned the table and hurled her work-basket into the fire. Once he took the dress she was mending and tore the bodice from the skirt. 'Now you've really got something to mend, ent you?' he said, and walked out, slamming the door.

She hated this stranger that she and her son were obliged to live with. But always she remembered the man he had been and prayed that some miracle would restore him to her.

*   *   *

John recovered eventually and went back to school, but two weeks later he was at home again for the Christmas holiday.

'Seems it's all holidays for you!' Richard said. 'I shall have to find you something to do.'

When the doctor sent his bill, Richard dropped it in Ellen's lap.

'You can pay that.'

'How can I?'

'I dunno how. That's up to you. I said you'd be sorry for calling him in.'

'Very well,' Ellen said.

She went to Rainborough the next day and sold the cameo brooch that her Uncle John had given her on her eighteenth birthday. When she had paid the doctor's bill she still had fourteen shillings left, and she put the money into a jug on the top shelf of the dresser.

'Well?' Richard said at suppertime. 'Did you pay the doctor's bill?'

'Yes, I called at his house.'

'Where did you get the money from? Out of the week's housekeeping?'

'That goes nowhere. You should know that. I had to sell my cameo brooch.'

'You'll have had a bit left over, then.'

'Yes. I thought it would buy some extras for Christmas.'

But when she went to the jug again her money was gone, and when she spoke to Richard about it he merely shrugged.

'It came in handy, that fourteen shillings. Say I borrowed it as a loan. I'll pay it back when business gets better, though when that'll be it's hard to say.'

Whereas in the past he had wanted the best for his wife and son, now he grudged every penny she spent. John's clothes had to be turned, and his boots had to be bought second-hand. Even food was difficult, for Richard grumbled at the amount of flour she used and doled it out to her, so much a week, never allowing her into the mealroom. He gave her no extra money for Christmas and if Jerry Trussler had not called as always, bringing a twelve-pound goose, they would have had no Christmas dinner.

'I've got no money for extras,' Richard said. 'This has been a bad old year. You must manage as best you can.'

'You've got money to spend on brandy,' she said, 'but none to buy your son a present.'

'The boy is spoilt enough already. He's getting too full of hisself by half.'

Christmas that year was the saddest Ellen had ever known. There was no softening in Richard's manner; no show of cheerfulness for the child's sake, nothing to set the day apart except what she herself could contrive. Richard went to the mill as usual and spent the morning tarring the luccomb. He was up at the top of a ladder when a few people from Water Lane passed on their way to the church in Dingham.

'Don't you know what day it is, Mr Lancy?'

'Yes, it's Thursday!' Richard said.

Ellen, in the kitchen, cooking dinner, gave John little tasks to do and tried to create a festive feeling. She got him to climb on a high stool and hang sprigs of holly on the beams. She gave him the apples to peel for sauce. She allowed him to baste the roasting goose, growing brown and crisp-skinned in the oven of the range. He was happy enough in his quiet way, until his father came in to dinner.

Richard as usual had little to say. When he did speak, it was only to grumble at the church bells, ringing in Dingham and Sutton Crabtree and three miles away in the abbey at Rainborough.

'They've been at it all the morning and that's a noise I can't abide. Dothering, dothering, in my head, all the time I was up that ladder. The ringers must want something to do!'

'It *is* Christmas, after all.'

'D'you think I don't know?'

Ellen, talking cheerfully, remarked on the tenderness of the goose.

'Aren't we lucky,' she said to John, 'that Mr Trussler should be so kind, giving us a goose at Christmastime?'

'Kind? Why kind?' Richard said. 'I reckon he owes me something, don't he, seeing I gave him one of my donkeys to carry on his smelly trade?'

That afternoon, when Richard had shut himself in the mill, Ellen and John sat in the kitchen and roasted chestnuts at the fire. The nuts were small. She had picked them up in the woods at Spinnam. When they popped open and flew out into the hearth, John laughed and clapped his hands. But then, suddenly, even as he laughed, his small face crumpled and he was in tears. Sobs shook him. He bowed his head. Ellen took him in her arms.

'Don't cry, don't cry,' she said to him. 'Why, I was going to sing some carols! Favourites of yours, like "The First Nowell", and I shall need you to tell me the words. What about "I Saw Two Ships"? You know how I get in a muddle with that. How can I sing it without your help?'

'*Three* ships,' he said, drawing back to frown at her.

'Three? Are you sure?' And she wiped his eyes. 'I do believe you're right,' she said. 'But where were they sailing to, those three ships?'

'Everybody knows that!'

'I suppose they were sailing to Sutton Crabtree.'

'Silly!' he said. 'It was Bethlehem.'

'There! I told you I always got in a muddle. What a good thing it is that you know the words.'

But although she could comfort him in the end, and even bring back the laughter again, secretly she was afraid. What of next Christmas? she asked herself. What would their lives be like by then?

* * *

After Christmas, the weather worsened. 1880 came in cold. There were several days of hard frost. One morning, when Richard had some beans to grind, the waterwheel was frozen up. He laid a plank from the footbridge to the wheel, resting it on the edge of a paddle, and went across with a big kettle of boiling water, to thaw the ice surrounding the axle. But the axle, frozen, had warped a little, and the waterwheel, after less than a quarter turn, caught against the mill wall. Richard, swearing angrily, put the plank across again and set to work with hammer and chisel.

It was not easy for him to reach from the plank, and he was about to climb up the wheel when he saw John watching him from the garden.

'Ent you got nothing better to do than stand there gawping at me?' he said. But when the boy would have turned away, Richard called him back again. 'Come round here. You can give me a hand. You're a lot smaller and lighter than me. This here job is just right for you.'

Half an hour later, Ellen, going in search of John, found him crouched on the waterwheel, struggling with hammer and cold chisel, chipping at the brickwork of the wall where the rim of the wheel had caught against it. Richard, on the plank, was peering between the wheel and the wall, shouting instructions, but the little boy, his hands blue with cold, could scarcely lift the heavy tools and more often than not the blows of the hammer went astray.

'Lord Almighty!' Richard said. 'Can't you do no better than that? Get the chisel against that brick and keep tapping until it chips.'

'I can't!' John said, with a little sob. 'I can't do it! It's too hard. I shall drop the hammer in a minute.'

'You do, that's all, and see what happens!'

Ellen ran forward onto the bridge and cried out to Richard to bring the boy down. He glanced at her over his shoulder and muttered something under his breath. Then he turned to the boy again and put up his arms.

'You may as well come down, I suppose, for all the use you are up there! Come on, come on, I ent got all day! You'll have to come down further'n that or I can't reach you.'

Inch by inch, the boy moved towards him. Crouched as he was on the ice-covered paddles, he was terrified that the wheel would move and that he would be borne down into the stream, where the swift white water ran full pelt. He was paralysed with cold. His fingers were stiffened, twisted like claws, clutching the heavy hammer and chisel.

Richard took hold of him, under the armpits, and carried him back along the plank. He swung him over the rail of the bridge, into Ellen's waiting arms.

'Here, take your chilver, he's no use to me! I'll have to do the job myself.' He snatched the tools from John's hands and turned towards the waterwheel. 'He don't even try to help me, that boy. All he does is snivel and cry.'

'He might have been drowned!' Ellen exclaimed, pressing the child against her body. 'Supposing the wheel had begun to turn? Have you got no sense at all?'

'The wheel wouldn't shift as fast as that. If it had I'd have tumbled in myself.'

'The boy is frozen through to the bone. Have you no feeling left for him? Can't you see him suffering?'

'Then get him into the house, woman, instead of standing there ranting at me! And take that empty kettle with you. I've finished with it for today.'

Ellen left him and went indoors. She put John to sit in a chair by the stove and wrapped her shawl around his shoulders. Now and then a shiver shook him, but he was quite silent and sat in a trance, staring into the heart of the fire. When she spoke he seemed not to hear her. His face was shuttered, unreadable, the eyelids drooping, hiding the eyes, the lashes shadowing the pallid cheeks. He was shut up inside himself. Even she could not reach him.

* * *

Richard got the waterwheel turning at last and all that afternoon he was grinding bean-meal. But the day was full of accidents and his mood grew blacker with each delay. He was using a runner stone that was very old, worn to a mere two inches, and during the day it split across with a loud crack. He lost two hours putting on a new stone. Then the pulley in the loft became jammed, putting the sack-hoist out of use, and when he went up to see to it he found that the rafter had given way, eaten by worm, which meant another hour's work.

He did not come in for his midday dinner, nor for his supper at five o'clock, and Ellen, worrying about him, went into the mill with a plate of bread and cheese and pickle.

'You ought to eat. You'll make yourself ill, working so hard in this cold weather without proper food inside you. You can surely find time for bread and cheese.'

'No, I don't want it. Take it away.' He was weighing sacks of meal. He spoke to her without looking up. 'And don't come pestering me again.'

'Perhaps if I were to leave it here – '

'D— you!' he said, swinging round. 'Didn't you hear what I said to you?' And he struck the plate out of her hand, so that it fell to the floor and smashed. 'Get ouf of my mill and leave me in peace! I'll *tell* you when I want to eat!'

'Very well,' Ellen said, stooping to pick up the scattered food. 'I only hope you won't drink tonight, that's all. In your present mood, and not eating, who knows what it will do to you.'

Richard picked up a ten pound weight and raised it in his hand as high as his shoulder. He took a sudden step towards her.

'Are you going or not?' he said.

'Yes, I'm going,' she said quietly, and looked at him with steady eyes. 'But I won't be threatened, Richard, even by you. Let it be understood between us.'

'Won't?' he said, not meeting her gaze. 'That's your favourite word, seems to me! I get it twenty times a day!' But he turned back to the weighing-machine and lowered the weight onto the ledge. 'Just get out, that's all,' he said. 'Just get out and leave me be.'

Ellen went back into the house. She had not been afraid of him, rounding on her with the upraised weight. She had never for an instant felt herself to be in danger because something of the past remained between them and in facing him she had made him ashamed. Yet now she was trembling. Now she was very close to tears. For the violence was there, in his mind. She had seen it, ugly, in his eyes, and had sensed how destructive it could be.

She put John to bed early that night and sat with him until he slept. She herself stayed up till ten. Richard was still shut in the mill when she went to bed. She left his supper on the table.

* * *

She was wakened by the slamming of the back kitchen door, and as she lay, listening, she heard him being sick in the yard. Then the door slammed again, shaking the house, and after a while he came stumbling up the stairs and into the bedroom. He set his candle on the chest by the bed. Ellen lay with her face to the wall.

'Are you awake?' he said, touching her.

'I couldn't be anything else but awake, after the noise you've been making downstairs. Did you eat the supper I left for you?'

'I hadn't the stomach for it, Nell. It's too late for eating. It's past one o'clock.' He sat on the bed with his face in his hands. 'Nell, I feel wretched. I reckon I'm ill.'

'I'm sorry to hear it,' Ellen said.

'Ah, I know, you *sound* sorry.'

'You know what it is that makes you ill. The cure is easy. It's in your own hands.'

'I dunno what you're on about. I've been doing my accounts.'

He took off his boots and threw them into a far corner. He stood up and undressed and slung his clothes over the bed-post. He blew out the candle and got into bed.

His breath on her face was hot and sour, smelling of vomit,

and she moved away from him even further, seeking the coolness of her pillow. His hands thrust their way to the front of her body and worked at her with ungentle fingers until, in some pain, she fought against him.

'Richard, please, I beg of you! Leave me alone. I'm very tired.'

'You're always tired! It's just an excuse. What about thinking of me for a change? You never want me nowadays.'

'How can I want you when you come to me in this condition? Have you no pride in yourself any more? Can't you see what's happening to you?'

'*Will* you turn round to me?' he said. 'Or must I make you?'

He clutched at her nightdress and dragged it up over her stomach. His hands went roughly down to her thighs, thrusting against the tender flesh.

'No!' she said, and struggled against him. 'No, I will not, and you shall not make me!'

'Won't? Won't? That's all I hear! You go against me the whole time! But who's the strongest of us two? Who's in the right of it, you or me?'

'You're drunk and disgusting,' Ellen said, 'and you make me hate you, behaving like this.'

'Drunk, am I? Is that your excuse?'

'Yes! You are! Your breath is loathsome!'

'Then get out!' he said, and began pushing her out of the bed. 'If I'm so disgusting to you, woman, you can d— well get out and sleep elsewhere! Why should I let you share my bed? What do you do to earn the right to be called my wife? Nothing whatever, so just get out!'

His knees were in the small of her back. His hands were pressing against her shoulders, pushing her over the edge of the bed.

'Are you getting out of here? – Are you?' he said. 'You'll be sorry if you don't!' He brought up his feet and kicked at her spine. 'Are you getting out, then?'

'Yes,' Ellen said, 'I'm getting out.'

She slid from the bed and stood for a moment shivering. In the dark, she could not find her slippers. The floorboards were cold under her feet. She went to the door and took her knitted shawl from the hook. She drew it over her head and shoulders. Her hand was on the sneck of the door when Richard lumbered out of bed. He snatched at the shawl and pulled it off her and as she moved to go out of the door he took hold of her nightdress at the throat and tore it down from top to bottom. Ellen stumbled and the door swung open against the wash-stand. The pitcher and basin fell with a crash, and water flooded over the floor, wetting her feet.

The noise woke John in the room next door. He came out onto the landing, peering fearfully round the rail. Ellen went to him at once. She felt him trembling, close against her, as she led him back towards his room. Richard moved suddenly and blocked the way. His face, seen dimly in the starlight, had an ugly intentness. He was breathing heavily through his nose.

'Where d'you think you're going?'

'I'm taking John back to bed. I shall sleep the rest of the night with him.'

'Oh no you won't!' Richard said. 'I shall decide where you sleep tonight!' He was pushing her towards the stairs.

'Don't you dare hurt my mother!' John cried in a shrill voice. 'Let go of her! Just leave her be!'

'Down you go, you and him both!' Richard shouted. 'I've had as much as I can take!' And he pushed them in front of him, down the stairs. 'Go on, get a move on, I've had enough! I'll show you who's master in this house!'

On reaching the kitchen, he unbolted the outer door and flung it open. Outside, beyond the porch, the night was stilly cold, the sky splintered with frost-bright stars above an earth steeped in silence and darkness.

'What are you doing?' Ellen asked. 'Would you put us out?'

'I said you'd be sorry, going against me all the time! Now you'll see that I meant every word!'

'Are you insane?' she exclaimed. 'On a winter's night? Do

you mean to kill us?'

'It was you that chose to leave my bed! You can d— well leave my house altogether!'

'You can't do such a thing to us!'

'We'll see about that! Oh, yes, we shall see!'

Roughly, he pushed them towards the door, where the frosty night awaited them, reaching for them with cold embrace. Ellen resisted and little John, throwing himself against his father, struck at him with both fists.

'Surely you'll let us put on some clothes?'

'Clothes I paid for? No, I will not! You can think yourself lucky you ent stripped bare!'

'For heaven's sake, Richard, listen to me! Doesn't it mean *anything* that you and I are man and wife? It's only since you had that bad time—'

'You're no wife to me!' Richard said. 'Setting yourself and the boy above me! Going against me at every turn! I've had more than I can stand and we'll d— well see how you get on without me! Go on, get out, I've had enough!'

He was indeed mad, Ellen thought, and she knew she ought to pity him. But as he thrust them out of the house and she heard him bolting the door against them, she felt only hatred and bitterness and knew she would never be able to forgive him. Her hands went up, two puny fists, knocking helplessly at the door, and she shouted to him through her angry tears.

'We shall never come back to you after this! Richard, do you hear what I say? We shall never come back to you! Never! I swear!'

There was no answer. The millhouse was silent as the grave. She stooped and lifted John to her naked breast, settling him there, inside her nightdress, wrapping the two torn halves around him. She sheltered him as best she could, her arms completely encircling his shoulders, and he in turn, with his arms round her neck and his legs gripping tightly round her waist, gave his warmth to the front of her body.

* * *

Underneath her naked feet the frost was sticky, so that with every step she took, each foot was released with stinging reluctance. The cold struck upwards into her legs, tightening the muscles and twisting them, till the pain of cramp was almost more than she could bear. Her body, too, was clenched tight, the flesh cringing upon the bones, and as she walked she moved the upper part of herself from side to side, with a swaying motion, inside her nightdress, thus creating a rub of warmth as the coarse flannel moved on her skin. But the cold was killing. Her face and skull were splitting with it. She began to feel light-headed.

Inside her nightdress, her child was a close-clinging burden upon her, taking warmth from her breast and giving it back as he stirred against her.

'Mother?' he said, murmuring. 'Where are we going?'

'We're going to the village. Another few yards and we shall be in the main street.'

'What'll we do there? Where shall we go?'

'I'm hoping we'll find a place to shelter.'

'In somebody's house? Will they take us in?'

'Hush, now,' she whispered to him. 'Hush, now, there's a good boy. I'm trying to think.'

But the truth was that she knew no better than he what would become of them that night. She was drawn to the village because it was her only hope; because she and her child would surely perish unless they found shelter from the cold. Yet now that she was here, among the houses, their silence and darkness terrified her, for what would the people sleeping behind those doors and windows say to her if she roused them up? What claim had she on their goodwill? What had she ever said or done to win their friendship?

Had there but been a single light burning in one of those cottages, it might have been easy. A light would have been a sign to her that God, through some wakeful villager, was stretching out a merciful hand. But the houses slept, hunched up black against the stars, silent as death in the bitter cold, their doors and windows sealed in darkness. And she walked on, with the unthinking obstinacy of despair, tightening her arms about her child.

'Mother?' he said, against her throat. 'Shall we get there soon? Somewhere indoors? I don't like it out in the cold.'

'Just a little way on,' she said to him. 'Not much further. We'll soon find a place.'

'What place? What place? It's a long way.'

'Try to be brave,' she said, pressing her face into his hair. 'Try to be brave, for my sake.'

The road was now running steeply downhill, turning a little towards the left, and in another hundred yards or so she came out onto the green, where stood a curving row of cottages, the church, the smithy, the shop, the inn. This was the last of Dingham village. Beyond the green lay open country. Ellen knew she could go no further.

Chapter Seven

Will Gale, the blacksmith, had been drinking with friends in Sutton Crabtree. It was no new thing for him to be coming home in the small hours. Nor was it strange that he should loiter on the green. For he was a man who, much as he loved company, especially when the drink was flowing, could still enjoy these late hushed moments of the night, when he and the shadowy gliding owl had the darkness to themselves.

His little cottage, adjoining the smithy, was merely a place where he ate and slept. No one but he had crossed its threshold since his parents had died in 1870, and the place was nothing but a shell. The smithy, of course, was a different matter. He brought it to life at six o'clock every morning when he lit his fire in the forge, and all day long it rang and resounded with the noise of work and the comings and goings of horses and men. But the cottage was nothing. He could never bring that to life. And he always delayed going in, for out of doors on a fine night there was at least the company of stars.

Looking across the open green he smiled to himself, because fancy tonight was playing him tricks.

'Good night!' he said. 'I surely can't be as drunk as that! What did Lovell put in my ale?'

There was a movement. A pale figure. A woman, white-clad, crossing the green, vanishing into Draycott's cartshed.

'Lumme!' he said. 'I must look into this! There's something funny happening here.'

The cartshed was open along the front, its roof supported on four pillars. At the back of the shed, behind the carts, lay a tumbled litter of hay and straw, and Ellen was on her knees among it, trying to pile it up in a bed that would give some protection to herself and her child. When she heard heavy footsteps crunching the frosty track outside, she swung around with a little cry, covering herself with her torn nightdress and pressing John closer still. Will, a dark shape against the sky, stood with one arm about a pillar, peering in between the carts. He could see her kneeling among the straw. He gave a little tipsy laugh.

'What the devil! It *is* a woman. My luck has changed and no mistake! No need to be frightened, whoever you are! It's only Will Gale from the smithy there. I daresay you know me well enough?'

Yes, Ellen thought, she knew him all right. Fate had sent her another drunkard.

'Why don't you speak?' Will demanded. 'Who are you, poking about in there, and what are you up to at this time of night?'

Swaying a little he stepped inside. He struck a match and

held it before her and in its brief yellow flare he recognized her and saw her plight.

'Why, it's Mrs Lancy and her boy! Whatever's happened to you, my dear, to bring you out in such a fashion? What're you doing scrabbling in there?'

'There was an upset,' Ellen said, but it was some time before she was able to speak again. She was in the grip of a terrible rigor. Only by keeping her teeth tight-clenched could she still the spasms that shuddered through her. 'There was an upset. With my husband.'

'You mean you're running away from him?'

'Yes. No. He turned us out.'

'Turned you out? In this bitter weather? Without no proper clothes on nor nothing? Why, bless my soul. that's murder, that is! It's the wickedest thing I ever heard. You can't stop here. You must come home with me.'

He took off his jacket and put it on her, drawing it round till it wrapped both her and the child in her arms. He turned up the collar behind her neck and fastened the buttons down the front, and the warmth of it, after the flaying cold, made her shrink as though she would swoon.

'Steady a minute,' Will said, and his voice seemed to come from a great distance. 'Steady a minute, I'll give you a hand. You can't move. The cold has got you. Just leave it to me, I'll soon get you home.'

It was true, she could not move. Her legs were paralysed with the cold. She could not have raised herself from the straw. But Will bent over her and the child and lifted them into his strong arms. The night's events had sobered him. He managed a perfectly steady course across the green to the smithy cottage. And there, in the kitchen, he wrapped them in a cocoon of blankets and sat them in a chair by the hearth. He then lit a fire in the old iron range and gradually, as the light spread, she saw that John was watching darkly, his eyes just visible above the enveloping folds of the blankets.

'It's all right,' she whispered. 'It's Will Gale, the smith. He's taken us in, out of the cold. We shall be safe enough here for the night. We'll be all right, John. We'll be all right.'

Whispering thus to the child at her breast, she felt hot tears begin to fall, and, being too weak to brush them away, she bent her face to the rough blankets. Will saw, but said nothing. He made himself busy at the stove. Soon he had milk growing hot in a pan. He poured it into two mugs and gave it to them, and all the time, while they drank, he kept heaping wood onto the fire, till it filled the stove and roared up the chimney. He took the empty mugs away and sat in the chair opposite. He began talking.

'I thought you must be a ghost at first, when I saw you out there on the green. And you would've been, too, if you'd been left in the freezing cold! – You'd both've been ghosts by morning for sure! What does Lancy think he's up to, turning you out on such a night? You may have quarrelled, you and him, but there's *nothing* excuses his doing that. Why, you and your boy there, you would've died!'

He leant forward across the hearth and lifted her feet, wrapped in the blankets, onto the step of the brass-topped fender. He threw a lump of coal on the fire and sat back again, wiping his hand on his corduroys.

'Mind you,' he said, 'you don't have to tell me about it if you don't want to.' Looking at her, he scratched his jaw. 'What happens between a man and his wife is a private matter, certainly, and it's nothing to do with the likes of me. But a man who can do a thing like that –! Why, if you and your boy had died of cold, he'd have found hisself on the end of a rope. But you don't have to tell me about it if you don't want to. I shan't press you. I'll hold my tongue.'

'There was a quarrel,' Ellen said. 'I can't really say more than that.' With the heat of the fire bringing her body to life again, she was full of pain. The waves of warmth ebbed and flowed in her blood and every so often, drowningly, she felt her senses slipping away. She looked at Will with eyes that ached. 'There was a quarrel. That's all.'

'Is it likely to mend itself?'

'No, no. It's past mending.'

'I should d— well think so too! A man that can do a thing like that—! Is he all right, the little boy? He ent said a word since he came in. Seems he don't think much of me. I reckon he's wondering who I am.'

'He's all right. He knows who you are.'

'Not surprising he's quiet, is it, after what he's been through tonight? Of course, I know Dick Lancy ent quite right, since his accident that time, but for him to do a thing like that – '

'Perhaps, if you'll let us, we can sleep by the fire here, and tomorrow I'll think what I must do next.'

'Stop by the fire? What, sleep in that chair? You'd be a lot better sharing my bed.'

'I'd rather stay here,' Ellen said.

'Lumme!' he said. 'I didn't mean share in that sort of way. I meant you and him. You two together can have my bed and I'll have the room above the smithy.' Pausing, he gave a little laugh, then passed a hand across his face as though to wipe the laugh away. 'Share!' he exclaimed. 'What a thing to say! As though my luck would change like that – ' He broke off again, scowling fiercely, and stooped to throw more coal on the fire. 'You don't want to take no notice of me. It's just the way I talk, that's all. It don't mean a thing. Just close your ears.'

For a while he was silent, his big broad face, black-jawed, black-browed, resting on the knuckles of his fist. Then he leant forward across the hearth and laid his hand on Ellen's knee.

'I shan't take advantage. You needn't think that. I'm a rough sort of chap, the way I talk, but I wouldn't harm you or try nothing on.'

'If you did I should kill you,' Ellen said, and her voice, though quiet, was so full of angry vehemence that Will recoiled, withdrawing his hand. 'If you did I should kill you,' she said again.

'Ah!' he said, staring at her. 'Then I can't say I haven't been warned, can I?' And after a little while he said: 'Well, if you're going to stop here by the fire, I must stop with you, that's all!'

'I'd sooner you left us by ourselves.'

'I'm stopping here, to keep up the fire. It wouldn't do for you and your boy to get yourselves chilled again, twice in one night. Are you comfy, you and him? Warm enough in them there rugs? Then just you lie back and go to sleep and don't worry about nothing else. I shall look after you. Bible oath!'

So Ellen lay back in the Windsor chair, her head against the hanging cushion. John, on her lap, was almost asleep, lying perfectly still at her breast, wrapped with her in the warm blankets. And after a while, with the heat of the fire stinging her eyelids, she also slept, slipping into a midway world where, although exhaustion sucked her down into a whirling pool of darkness, she was at the same time always aware of the leaping, living fire in the stove and of Will Gale reaching out now and then, moving quietly, feeding the flames.

Something happened to Will that night, watching over the woman and child. Something touched him and changed his life. For these two, through their sleeping faces, became so intimately known to him that they took possession of his mind. He was only a young man, but he had no wife or family, no relations in the world. This cottage of his was nothing to him. Just a place where he ate and slept. He was rather a lonely man, once he closed the door. But by the end of his vigil that night, guarding the sleep of this mother and child, he felt the place belonged to them. He couldn't imagine it empty again. Everything he had was theirs, and they in turn belonged to him. Their two lives were in his keeping.

They, of course, having been asleep, did not share his feeling of intimacy, and in the morning when they awoke he was still a stranger to them, or at least a man they hardly knew. When he made hot porridge for them, they took it shyly, as though in his debt. They did not know, as he knew, that their lives and his were already linked.

* * *

Having given them breakfast and eaten his own, he brought a big stoneware bowl to the table and filled it with steaming hot water for them to wash. He put out a scrubbing brush and soap and hung a towel to warm at the fire. He also brought a great pile of clothes – corduroys, waistcoats, stockings, shirts – and a workbasket full of needles and threads.

'I ent got no women's clothes. Nor no clothes for boys neither. But if you're handy with your needle, you can maybe cobble up the things you need, just to make do for the time being.'

'Yes. Thank you. You're very kind.'

'What do you aim to do, after?'

'I think I must go to Cheltenham. I'm hoping I might find work there and some sort of lodging for John and me.'

'It's twenty miles to Cheltenham. You can't walk there without good shoes. You'd better stop here a day or two and then maybe I can get you fixed up.'

'I've got no money to buy shoes.'

'Then I shall have to lend you some.'

'I don't want my husband to find me here.'

'Then it's up to you to lie low. Keep as quiet as you can and if anyone knocks don't answer to them. The front door is bolted so you're perfectly safe. There's the back door into the smithy, of course, and I shall come in and out that way, but nobody else ent likely to and they can't anyhow without they pass me.'

Will put his hand on John's head and ruffled his hair in a teasing way.

'How about you, young fella?' he said. 'Can you keep quiet as a mouse so's nobody knows you're here at all? Of course you can! I'd no need to ask. You're the quietest chap I've ever seen.'

'John will be quiet enough,' Ellen said, 'but what if something is said in the smithy?'

'I shan't let on. No lections of that. But now I must go and open up. I'm late already. Just look at that clock.'

Before leaving he showed her the larder, telling her she must help herself.

'I take my dinner at The Old Tap. Archie Shaw gives me bread and cheese. I'd better go on as usual, otherwise it'll cause a stir, so you stay snug and warm in here and see that you eat to keep up your strength.'

Will went through into the smithy and opened up the outer door. His helper, Jim Pacey, was on the step.

'You're slow off the mark this morning, Will. You been making a night of it, drinking with Lovell at Sutton Crabtree?'

'Been sleeping it off,' Will agreed. 'It's a good house, The Post Horses. They don't sling you out till you've had enough.'

All through the greater part of that day, although many people came to the smithy, nothing was said about Ellen Lancy. Nor was she mentioned at The Old Tap. But towards the evening, about half past six, Ted Gore the carrier drew up outside, delivering a load of iron, and when Will went out with Jim Pacey, Ted had a small knot of people around him.

'The Mad Miller's been after me, asking me if I've seen his missus. Seems she's gone off with their boy in the night and nobody knows where she might've got to.'

'Gone off?' said Will. 'What, Mrs Lancy? Good gracious me!' He began unloading the bars of iron, flinging them down on the frosty ground. 'Why should she have done that?'

'According to Lancy, she ent only left him high and dry, but she's took all his money and left him broke.'

'She won't get far, then,' said Billy Jukes, 'if she's carrying all the miller's money!'

'Supposing there's somebody with her, though? Some other chap that she's gone off with?'

'Why, is somebody else missing from Dingham?'

'Not that I know of, but it might be a chap from some other district.'

'On the other hand,' Will said, 'he might not exist.'

'She surely wouldn't go off alone?'

'I can't see her with another man. Not Mrs Lancy. She ent the sort.'

'They're often the worst, them quiet ones. They're often the ones that give us a shock.'

'Are they, Ted?' said Simon Shaw. 'You seem to know a lot about it. How many shocks've you had that way?'

'I don't know nothing about the woman, save what Lancy hisself was saying, down at Pex Bridge a while ago.'

'Then if I was you,' said Alfred Meadows, 'I'd take it with a pinch of salt.'

When Gore had gone and all the iron was stowed away, Will began clearing up in the smithy. Pacey watched him cleaning his tools.

'You're stopping early today, ent you? What about old Temple's drill?'

'He can't sow seed in this weather. Any time will do for that drill. You get off while the going's good.'

Pacey left and Will bolted the door behind him. He hung his apron on its hook and went through into the kitchen. For the first time in almost ten years, firelight and lamplight welcomed him there, and the kettle was steaming on the hob. It was not much of a cottage, he thought, but it *had* been once in his mother's time. Now this woman and her child, by their presence there, had made it into a home again.

* * *

Ellen had spent the whole day sewing. She had cut up the clothes Will had given her and had made breeches, jacket, and shirt for John. She had made a corduroy skirt for herself, from an old pair of trousers, and a long-sleeved blouse from an old flannel shirt. Undergarments she made from a sheet and boots for them both from an old leather jerkin. And for most of the day, while she worked, John sat with her at the kitchen table, going quietly through the needlework basket, sorting out the old loose buttons, the tangled wools, the reels of cotton, and laying them out in tidy rows.

Sometimes he sat, perfectly silent, his hands together in his lap, content to watch her as she cut and measured and pinned and stitched. And when she tried some garment on him, he stood quite still in front of her, obediently raising an arm when told, or holding a fold of cloth in place while she made some adjustment. The two of them shared a sort of exhaustion and were quiet together, drawn extra close in an understanding that needed no words, passing between them as it did in each warm touch and each slow, comforting glance.

Once, when wandering round the untidy kitchen, he drew a finger along the dresser and showed it to her, black with dust.

'It's rather a dirty cottage, ent it, mother?'

'Men are not fussy when they live alone. And it seems the smoke gets in from the smithy too. Can you smell it? I can.'

There was a scullery and passage between the kitchen and the smithy, but the smell of the smoke got in all the same, and so did the noise: the cling-cling-clink of iron on iron, the trampling of horses now and then, and sometimes the voices of men upraised. The smithy yard was a busy place. John wanted to peep from the kitchen window. He raised a hand to the drawn curtain.

'No!' Ellen said. 'You mustn't look out! Nobody must see you here. D'you want your father to come for us?'

The boy's face became deathly white. He returned to his place at the kitchen table, and sat very still again, as before. Sometimes, when Ellen looked at him, his stillness and quietness hurt her heart. It was all wrong that a child should be so mute and grave. And she had added to his fear.

When Will came in, there was a change. John was amused at himself in his new clothes, and he walked about for Will to see them, showing off his square-toed boots and worsted stockings, his knee-length breeches and fawn flannel shirt, and, best of all, the shiny brass buttons on his jacket.

'I remember them buttons,' Will said. 'They come off a weskit I had years ago. You look pretty smart in em, don't you, eh? Have you seen yourself in that old mirror? You ent? Laws! Then I'll have to show you!'

Will took the mirror down from the wall, dusted it with

a sweep of his arm, and held it for the boy to see.

'You're smart enough for two or three! Just look at them boots! I never did!' Will put the mirror back on the wall and looked at Ellen, who stood at the table, winding up the cotton reels and putting them back into the basket. He surveyed her newly made skirt and blouse. 'Your mother looks smart, too, don't she? She must be a clever needlewoman to get you both dressed up like that, out of them cast-offs I brung down this morning. I'll have to get her to sew for *me!*'

He went to the fire-place and took a big frying-pan from a hook. He set it on the trivet on the stove and went to the cupboard for a bowl of dripping.

'You been all right in here today, lying low and keeping mum?'

'Yes,' Ellen said, 'we've been all right.'

'Seems your husband's been out looking round a bit for you. I reckon he's wondering where you've got to. He's putting it about that you've upped and left him, and he says you've took his money, too.'

Pausing a while, the bowl in his hand, he saw that they were watching him.

'Ah! I knew that'd make you stare!' he said, and dropped a lump of dripping into the pan. 'That riled me no end to hear the story he's putting about, knowing he turned you out of doors without a stitch of clothes nor nothing, on a freezing cold night like it was last night. Why, you could be dead in a ditch some place, for all he knew any different about it.'

Ellen, making the table tidy, said nothing. She brushed threads and remnants into her hand and threw them into the ash-can.

'It was Ted Gore who told it to me. Me and one or two others, that is. I never said hardly nothing at all but if that'd been Lancy hisself standing there, telling such a lying tale, I'd have had to throw it back in his face.'

Busy with a knife at the kitchen range, he soon had sausages frying in the pan, with onions, potatoes, parsnips and turnips, all cut up and jumbled together, filling the place with their savoury smell.

'You hungry, John? So am I! I'm just about ready to eat that chair! How d'you like your sausages? D'you like em laughing and splitting their sides?'

So boisterous were Will's ministrations with his knife that one fat sausage flew out of the pan and rolled across the rusty stove. He snatched it up quickly and hurled it back, and, licking his greasy finger and thumb, looked at John with a nod and a wink. The little boy watched, a faint smile touching his lips, and a faint gleam coming into his eyes.

'That's not the proper way to cook.'

'Ent it? Why not? What's wrong with it?'

'It's not the way my mother does it.'

'Well, tomorrow maybe she'll cook for us, and we shall have something worth eating, eh? Like meat pie with gravy? Or maybe a stew? I'll have to mind my p's and q's and then perhaps she'll agree to do it.'

Ellen set out the knives and forks and placed three plates to warm on the stove. She warmed the teapot and made the tea. Will took a huge crusty loaf from a crock and hacked it into two-inch slices. He sent them skidding across the table. In the same rough fashion he dished the supper onto their plates, one sausage for John, two for Ellen, and three for himself, together with the sliced vegetables, fried crisp and brown.

'Eat up, young tucker,' he said to John, 'and one day you'll be as big as me.'

'Can I come into the smithy tomorrow and see you bending the hot iron?'

'Not in the daytime,' Will said. 'That'd be all round Dingham in two shakes of a ram's tail. But tomorrow night, when I've shut up shop, I'll take you in and show you what's what.'

'We must be gone by then,' Ellen said. 'We ought to leave first thing in the morning and slip away before it's light.'

'You can't walk to Cheltenham without proper boots.'

'You did say you'd lend me a sum of money.'

'So I will! And gladly too! But – '

'If we can get as far as Runston, I can buy boots for both of us there, and we'll be all right the rest of the way. I'll pay you back as soon as I can.'

'You can't make a little boy like John walk all that way, Mrs Lancy, ma'am. You can't. It's unheard of. It is, that's a fact. And what if you don't find a lodging there? Supposing you're stranded in the town?'

'I know, I know!' Ellen said. 'But that's a chance I've got to take!' She would not show her fear in front of John. 'I must hope for the best, that's all.'

Will shovelled food into his mouth and munched it loudly. He washed it down with a draught of tea.

'I'll tell you what!' he said, passing his mug for her to fill. 'I reckon you're better stopping here!'

'No, no! We can't do that.'

'Why can't we, mother?' John asked. 'Why can't we stop here along with Will?'

'It's out of the question,' Ellen said. 'We must get away as far as we can.'

'Away from Dick Lancy, you mean?' Will said. 'But I should look after you, you know. If he was to come buzzing round after you, I'd soon send him packing, never fear.'

'No. It won't do. I must get away.'

'Well, wait until Friday at least,' Will said. 'I go into Runston myself on Fridays, to do a bit of this and that, and no one'd think more'n twice about it. I could borrow Draycott's horse and cart and take you to Cheltenham myself. We could leave before light so's nobody sees you, and buy what you need on the way, like you said. So how's that for a proposition? Better than walking, I'll be bound!'

'You're very kind to us,' Ellen said.

'Right, then, it's settled! Friday, first thing. And then if you don't find a lodging there, you can come back with me in the cart again.'

'I *must* find a lodging. And I *must* find work.'

'Yes. All right. It's up to you. We'll see what happens, anyway. Friday ent very long to wait. It's only three days, it'll soon go by. I know it's hard on you and the boy, having to skulk in here all day, but if you can stick it out for three days – '

'Yes, we can stick it,' Ellen said. 'We're very grateful, my son an I.'

'I know the place is none too clean. It's a pigsty in here, I grant you that. Worse, in fact, cos pigs get mucked out a sight more often than I get mucked out in this here cottage. And that goes hard on a woman like you, having to stick in such a place.'

'A woman like me. What sort is that?'

'House-proud,' he said, cleaning his plate with a piece of bread. 'I remember that time I came to the mill and brought Dick Lancy home to you, the place was as clean as a new pin. It was a palace and you was the queen. You warnt too pleased at having your husband brought home drunk. The way you spoke to me that time and the way you showed me out of the door – '

'Yes, I remember,' Ellen said. 'You called me a shrew.'

'Did I?' he said. 'Oh glory be!' And, looking at John, he made a face. 'That was the ale talking,' he said. 'It does that, you know, when I've had enough. It takes over and talks with tongues. I can't get a word in, myself, oftentimes, on account of the ale got to have its say.'

'Then why drink it?' Ellen asked, and was at once ashamed of herself for presuming on his good nature. 'Take no notice of me,' she said. 'I had no right to say that.'

'You're right all the same, I shouldn't ought to do it,' he said. 'But it's thirsty work, being a blacksmith, and where else should a man go to be with his friends if it ent to the inn? Still, I shan't be going tonight, however. I'm going to be busy airing the bed in the spare bedroom and finding some linen for you to sleep in.'

'We can perfectly well sleep in the chair.'

'Whose house is it, I'd like to know? You'll sleep upstairs

and no nonsense about it. You can both of you help me to get it ready.'

Will pushed his empty plate aside and cut himself a slice of bread. He spread it with honey and bit into it with strong white teeth. He looked across the table at John who watched him, wide-eyed, astonished to see a slice of bread vanish so quickly, in three or four bites.

'You got to be firm with womenfolk, John, otherwise they do as they like. You got to show em you mean what you say.'

So Ellen and John slept that night in a warm featherbed, between twilled sheets and woollen blankets, with a stone hot water bottle at their feet, and if everything was not as clean as Ellen in the past would have expected, such was her gratitude that she hardly noticed.

* * *

The following morning, with John's help, she swept and cleaned the kitchen. It was not easy, confined as they were, unable to open the doors or windows, but Will, coming in to see how they were, marvelled at the change in the brick-nogged floor, scrubbed and ruddled; looked into the larder, where clean pots and pipkins were ranged neatly along the shelves; and stooped over the kitchen stove, pretending to look at himself in the dark-gleaming slab, now blackleaded to perfection.

'The place ent looked so spick and span since my old mother was alive and ruled the place like a proper tartar. She took a pride in it, just like you, and woe betide my dad and me if we walked in here with dirty bootses. I reckon that'd warm her heart, if she could see it nice again, after the mess I let it get into. I reckon she'd shake you by the hand!'

That day in the smithy, always a favourite gathering-place, especially in winter, Will's customers talked about Ellen Lancy.

'She still ent been found. Nor the boy neither. The miller's been asking everywhere but it seems like they've vanished without a trace.'

'Funny, ent it?' said Jonah Middling, one of the grooms from Dinnis Hall. 'Just a year ago, pretty exactly, Lancy hisself was gone missing, with nobody knowing where or why, and now it's his missus and boy the same. Seems queer to me. Seems like there's something fishy in it.'

'Fishy's the word,' said Ben Tozer, the carter from Neyes. 'There's one or two folk think Lancy hisself has got them locked up in the millhouse down there. Well, he's queer enough for anything, ent he, these days? D'you know what he said to me last harvest-time? He said I warnt to water my horses no more when crossing the ford at Biddy's Dip cos it took the water and slowed down his wheel. He did! Mortal fact! And he meant it too!'

'Touched,' said Middling. 'Dangerous too. You never know which way he'll jump. If his wife *has* left him and took the boy, I dunno that I blame her, nohow. I reckon he's brought it on hisself.

Over supper that night, when his day's work was finished, Will repeated the gossip to Ellen and saw how she blenched at her husband's name.

'Looking for us? Are you sure? Is he going from house to house?'

'Well, he's asking questions everywhere, and knocking at one or two places, it seems. And somebody saw him out at Skyte, poking about in the hedges there. He knows you can't have got very far, well-nigh naked as you was, and he knows there's only two things could've happened to you. – Either you asked for shelter some place or else you're lying out dead of the cold. I reckon it's got him rattled a bit, and serves him right, too, after what he done to you.'

'You mustn't blame him too much. It's not his fault that he does these things. It's something that happened to his mind when he was trapped underground all that time. He was a good man up till then, and you must make allowances.'

'If you say so, of course. But he knows what he's doing, right enough, and it's no good your asking me to think kindly thoughts about him or remember him in my prayers, cos I shan't and that's flat. It's too soon since I saw you and John out there, scrabbling about in Draycott's cartshed, trying to make yourself a bed in the straw.'

For a little while he ate in silence. Then he spoke again.

'You ent changed your mind by any chance? You ent thinking of going back to him?'

'No, no. I shall never do that. Not now the break has come. I couldn't bear to go back now. We must get away, John and I, and start a new life by ourselves.'

'Friday ent long to wait,' he said. 'All you got to do is lie low here and build up your strength against the future. Strikes me you'll need it, come what may, for that's a hard old world out there, you know, for a woman struggling all alone.'

* * *

But although she remained close in the cottage, and took good care that John should be quiet, their presence there was soon suspected. Will's neighbours around the green observed that his chimney smoked all day, and Mrs Beard, in the next cottage, whose bit of garden ran with his, swore she had heard a child coughing. The door, when Mrs Jennet tried the sneck, proved to be locked, and that was a strange thing indeed, for nobody living on the green ever locked their doors during the daytime. There was also a smell of good home baking which no door or window, however tightly closed, could prevent from escaping, and Will Gale, surely, said Mrs Beard, had never been known to make pastry?

'You got company, Will?' asked Tommy Breton, coming into the smithy to light his pipe.

'Company? What makes you ask?'

'Something my missus said to me, that she heard from your neighbour, Mrs Beard.'

'You listen too much to that missus of yours. You should get her a nosebag and strap it on.'

'You *are* still single, I suppose? You ent took a wife on the quiet, like, just now lately, these past few days?'

'Not unless it was while I was drunk.'

'Nor another man's wife by any chance?'

'No, Tommy, not even yours!'

There was some laughter among the men gathered round the forge, and a few ripe jokes accompanied the departing Tommy, but Will was aware, as he worked on, that his customers eyed him with sharpened interest.

'Was there anything in what Tommy said?' Bert Franklin asked in a casual way.

'Don't talk to me now,' Will said. 'I got to concentrate on this here plough.'

They took the hint and left without asking further questions. Will and Jim Pacey, for a few minutes, had the smithy to themselves. Jim was a man of fifty odd. He had worked with Will for sixteen years. They had a good understanding together.

'You muzzled their snouts in here, right enough, but they'll soon make up for it outside.'

'I know. My ears are burning like them coals.'

'Seems you've got yourself into a pickle of some sort. What're you going to do about it?'

'I dunno. I got to think.'

When Will went out at dinnertime, crossing the green to The Old Tap, a small group of neighbours, men and women, stood gathered under the oak tree, gazing at the smithy cottage.

'All right, Will?' asked Ralph Jennet.

'Why shouldn't it be?' Will said.

'I been racking my brains,' Ralph said, 'but I can't for the life of me think why your curtains is drawn across the window all day.'

'It's to stop the sun from fading the carpet.'

'Hah! Since when've you ever had a carpet?'

'Since when've you ever had a brain?' Will said.

In The Old Tap, when he walked in, the customers there became silent, and Archie Shaw, as he filled Will's tankard at the barrel, spoke loudly enough for them to hear.

'Do you want your bread and cheese today, Will?'

'Why shouldn't I want it? Are you short?'

'I just got it into my head that somebody – I dunno who – might be getting your dinner for you at home.'

'A good chunk of Cheddar, that's what I'd like, and the crustiest part of a loaf,' Will said. 'If not I'll settle for Double Gloster.'

For once he ate in a corner, alone, and left as soon as his meal was finished. He returned to the smithy and went through into the cottage. Ellen and John were at the table, drinking the last of their mutton broth. He pulled out a chair and sat down with them.

'Our secret's out, all over the village. They know I've got somebody here with me and they're pretty sure they know who it is. It's only a question of time before one of em goes and tells Dick Lancy.'

Wearily, Ellen put down her spoon. She half glanced away, as if he were to blame. John looked at them each in turn, his eyes darkly questioning, full of thought.

'I should've known better,' Will said. 'You can't keep secrets on this green.'

Ellen turned and looked at him.

'What am I to do?' she asked.

'This evening I'm going up to Neyes to pick up Draycott's horse and cart. He said I could have it at six o'clock. You get yourselves ready by that time and I'll take you to Cheltenham straight away instead of tomorrow like we planned. I don't see there's nothing else we can do, unless – '

'Unless what?'

'Unless you stay on and face him out.'

'No,' she said, 'I must go.'

'Right you are. It's up to you. I'll root out some coats to keep you warm. It's going to be nippy, travelling this evening after dark, but I'll get you there, safe and sound, and help you to find some place to live. You leave it to me. I'll sort it out. If we get a move on at six o'clock, you should be safe in

Cheltenham by the time the gossip's got around.'

* * *

But in fact it was already too late. The gossip had gone right through the village and had reached Richard Lancy at Pex Mill. At half past two that afternoon the smithy was filled with villagers. Will looked around and counted fifteen. Some were there on genuine business. The carters from Whitestone had come for their drill. But most were there on some pretext or other, such as wanting a poker straightened out or begging a shovelful of fire from the forge. Outside the smithy, other loiterers stood in groups, and all round the green, although the day was bitterly cold, elderly cottagers stood at their doors.

'By the deuce!' Jim Pacey muttered. 'You'd think the circus was coming through.'

'I reckon it may be,' Will replied.

'Shall I chase this lot out and lock the door? Shall I put this hot rivet on Sue Breton's bum?'

'What, and waste good metal?' Will said. 'I'd sooner get on with the job in hand.'

A little after three o'clock, young Barney Roberts came running in to say Dick Lancy was on his way.

'I seen him coming up past Tanner's. He's got a shotgun under his arm. He's coming here as sure as fate. My mother asked and he said yes. He said he'd got business with Will Gale.'

'Did you hear that, Will?' asked Billy Jukes. 'The miller's coming and he's got a gun.'

'Yes, I heard,' Will said, and, straightening up from the seed drill, turned towards Barney Roberts. 'Is the miller's shotgun loaded, boy?'

'Laws, I dunno!' Barney said. 'How should I know a thing like that?'

'Trust that mother of yours,' Will said, 'to send you here with half a tale.'

'It's no laughing matter,' Ralph Jennet said. 'I don't like

the sound of it, not one little bit. He's after you, Will, be sure of that.'

'You came to see some fun, didn't you? You and all these others here?'

'Not a shotgun, no,' said Tommy Breton, looking round in search of his wife. 'Somebody ought to go and stop him. Reason with him. Take it away.'

'Tommy, lad, the job is yours!'

'Ent you afraid, Will?' asked Fred Byers. 'The miller is mad as a March hare. He's used that shotgun once before. Supposing he was to use it again?'

'You'd better all clear out of the way.'

'Ent you afraid, Will? Not even a bit?'

'I'm too busy trembling to be afraid.'

'Know what he's coming for, do you, Will? Know what business he's got in mind?'

'He certainly ent coming to bring me a bag of flour.'

'Then what're you going to do about it?'

'I reckon I'm going to let him come!'

Will bent over the seed-drill again and went on working as before, hammering out the red-hot rivets that Jim Pacey pushed through the holes in the flange. But although his back was towards the door, he knew when Lancy appeared there by the sudden quietness of the crowd and the way they parted, giving way, leaving a space around the anvil. He flattened out the last rivet and plunged the drill-section into the trough, where the water sizzled and boiled up white. He put the section on one side and turned with his hammer in his hand.

Richard came forward, steady-paced, and confronted Will across the anvil. His long, handsome face, with its fine bones, had the slackened look of the man who drinks, the features blurred by thickening flesh, the skin inflamed with an angry redness. And although he stood face to face with Will, his gaze slid away repeatedly, as though he disliked the glare from the forge. His shotgun lay in the crook of his arm. He allowed the muzzle to rest on the anvil. Will saw that both hammers were cocked.

'Is it true, what I hear, that you've got my wife and son?'

'Supposing it is?' Will said. 'They're safer with me than they are with you.'

'Oh, I daresay she's told you some tale about me, making me out to be this and that! But I don't call it safe for her to be living in with you here, a man that's enticed her away from home, along with my son only five years old.'

'You're a liar!' Will said. 'You was the one that turned them out and these listeners may as well hear about it. *You* turned them out in the small hours on Monday night with next to nothing hardly on. No shoes on their feet, nor coats to wear, only their nightclothes and nothing else! *You* locked them out of their own home on a night that meant death, so cold it was, and for all you knowed or cared about it, they might both be dead and in their graves.'

'If she told you that, it was just a tale!'

'I ought to know – I was the one that found them!' Will said. 'They was both near naked and just about froze to the very marrow, so don't talk to me about tales, man! *I* saw them. *I* took them in. If it wasn't for my doing that, you would be up for murder by now, and you'd find yourself on the end of a rope!'

'You're as big a liar as my wife. It's you that's enticed them away from me. No one will believe what you say.'

'The folk here today will make up their own minds who's telling the truth. They know you and they know me. It's up to them to decide for theirselves.'

'Are you going to let me see my wife?'

'I dunno that she wants to see *you*.'

'I'm her husband. I've got my rights.'

'You gave up your rights when you turned her out.'

'D— you!' Richard shouted, and took a step or two past the anvil, towards the door leading into the cottage. He was breathing heavily, through his nose, and in the smoky-red glare of the forge it was easy to see that he was sweating. 'If you don't let me past – '

'You're all in a sweat,' Will said. 'I shouldn't go too near that fire if I was you. You're that full of brandy, you'll go up in flames.'

'That's rich, that is, coming from you! – The biggest soak for miles around!'

'At least I drink where folk can see me. I don't soak in secret and then take it out on my wife and child. And I stick to good clean honest ale, not spirits and such, that rot your guts.'

'I've had enough of wrangling with you!'

'Then all you got to do is get out of my smithy.'

'I ent leaving,' Richard said, 'without I take my wife and son.'

'They'll never come with you,' Will said. 'You're wasting your time and mine too.'

'Then fetch them out for me to see, and let her tell me so herself.'

'Do you think I'll do that,' Will asked, 'when you're standing waiting with a gun?'

'What, this?' Richard said, and, raising the shotgun gradually, he pointed it at Will's stomach. 'I brought this for you, not for them. You're the one that's enticed them away. You've got them in there, my wife and son, and won't even let me speak to them. There's many a man been killed for less and folk would say you'd asked for it. A wife-stealer's no loss to the world. A wife-stealer's dirt and deserves all he gets. Any husband would say the same.'

Slowly, as though enjoying himself, he raised the shotgun higher still, till the muzzle was pointing at Will's chest. The people watching became very still. Only Jim Pacey twitched a little and muttered something under his breath. He was standing close and could see Richard's finger on the trigger. He sensed the excitement in Richard's mind. Will sensed it too. He was trying to think of something to say.

'Well?' Richard said. 'Who's sweating now?'

'I am!' said Will. 'I'm sweating pints. Is it loaded, that gun of yours?'

'Both barrels. A full charge.'

'Then hand it over to Pacey here and I'll fetch your missus out to you.'

'So you're ready to bargain after all?'

'I said I'd fetch her. I didn't say you could take her away.'

'That ent for you to decide,' Richard said. 'She's my wife, not yours. Her proper place is with me. But fetch her out by all means and let us hear what she's got to say.'

He surrendered the gun to Jim Pacey, who carefully lowered both the hammers. Will cast a glance around the smithy and saw that the crowd inside had grown. He went to the door leading into the cottage.

* * *

'Richard? Here?' Ellen said. She turned to John and drew him close. 'In the smithy, do you mean?'

'Turns out we're too late. Somebody told him where you was. So he wants to see you and take you home. He won't take no for an answer from me. He wants to hear you say it yourself.'

'Can't you get him to go away?'

'I reckon it's better to face him out.'

'That's what you wanted, isn't it? Are you satisfied now you've got your way?'

'I reckon it's better to clear the air. He's been spreading lies about you. Now's your chance to answer him back, and there's witnesses to hear the truth.'

'Witnesses?' Ellen exclaimed. 'Am I appearing before the Bench? Would you play magistrate over me?'

But gradually her anger died. She composed herself and thought deeply. After a while she nodded assent. She and John followed him into the smithy. The crowd by now had almost doubled, and people were pressing in at the door. She was a public spectacle, but it was too late to turn back now. She felt John's hand tighten on hers and saw that Richard was coming towards them.

'Well, Ellen?' he said to her, and his tone was so gentle that it came as a shock. 'Ent it time you came back home?'

Ellen stared, unable to speak. This, if she let herself be deceived, was the old Richard revived from the past, a tender, loving husband to her, a devoted father to their son. But, looking into his shadowy eyes, she saw beyond the gentle smile to the dark, unloving hardness behind.

'Ellen, come home,' he said again. 'This ent very well done in you, dragging our son about like this, living under another man's roof. You bring him home where he belongs.'

He put out a hand towards his son, as though to touch him on the head, but John shrank away, behind his mother, and Richard's hand fell to his side.

'There, now,' he said reproachfully, 'you've even turned my boy against me.'

'We're not coming back to you,' Ellen said. 'Nothing on earth will change my mind.'

'I'm willing to try and make amends. I know I've done wrong, I grant you that. But a man and his wife must stick together. Neither one has got a right to go running off with somebody else.'

'Don't try and twist the truth, Richard. You turned us out on a winter's night, with only our nightshirts on our backs, and we should have perished in the cold if it hadn't been for Will here, finding us and taking us in.'

'So you better prefer to stop with him? You set him above your own husband?'

'Will and I are nothing to each other. I hardly knew him before Monday night. He gave us shelter, that's all, and tomorrow we shall be moving on.'

'You don't expect me to swallow that!'

'It's the truth, every word, and you know it as well as I do.'

'Are you coming back with me or not?'

'No, Richard, I am not.'

'Well, you've had your chance!' Richard said. 'If that's the way you answer me, I wash my hands of you, good and all. But my boy John is a different matter. You've got no right to take him away. He's coming back to the mill with me.'

'Never! Never!' Ellen exclaimed, and little John, looking out at his father from the safety of his mother's skirts, cried shrilly: 'Go away and leave us alone! We're not coming back to you! No, we are *not!*'

'Aren't you? Richard said.

'You've had your answer,' Will said, 'so now maybe you'll take yourself off and leave me a chance to get on with some work.'

'I'll tell you this much!' Richard said. 'You'll never get work from *me* again! Any ironwork I've got, I'll go to Lovell at Sutton Crabtree.'

'I daresay I'll manage,' Will said.

'You ent heard the last of it!' Richard said. 'Do you think any good will come to you, stealing my wife and son from me? I reckon you'd better think again!'

Will spoke to Jim Pacey.

'Give the miller his shotgun,' he said, 'and let him take hisself back to the mill.'

'All right. Just as you say. But I reckon I'd better empty it first, just to be on the safe side.'

Jim, with the shotgun under his arm, pushed his way to the door of the smithy. He drew the hammers and fired both barrels into the air, and the two shots echoed around the green. He turned to Richard, who had followed him, and handed over the empty gun.

'You want to take care with that old piece of junk,' he said. 'It kicks worse than Joe Hooper's mare.'

Richard stood in the open doorway, looking at Will, who was seeing him off.

'It's as well your helper's emptied this gun or I might've been tempted to shoot you yet. But one thing, blacksmith, I promise you! – I'll pay you back, somehow, one of these days, for coming between my family and me! I'll pay you back if it takes twenty years!'

Shouldering the gun, he strode away, up the track that ran round the green. Will and Jim Pacey went back to the forge, and Jim at once began working the bellows, blowing up the dying fire. Ellen and John had gone back into the cottage. Will addressed the crowd in the smithy.

'All those who've got work for me are welcome to stay. The rest of you can clear off home. The raree show is over for today. If you stop much longer, I'll pass round the hat! Come along, neighbours, get moving, please! How can I work if I can't swing my arm?'

Reluctantly, the crowd moved out. They stood about, talking, on the green. Only a few now remained in the smithy, among them the carters from Whitestone Farm, and one of these, who was new to the district, spoke to the other in a low voice.

'Is there always such goings on in this here village?'

'Laws, no!' said the other man. 'It's mostly no more than once a week!'

*　　　　*　　　　*

When Will went in to speak to Ellen, he found her sitting all alone, her hands lying idle in her lap. The shabby curtains had been drawn back from the windows, and for the first time in three days, daylight came into the cottage kitchen: dull grey daylight, for it was nearly half past three, and the winter dusk was coming on. Ellen sat straight-backed in her chair, staring into the fire in the stove. She was thinking of Richard and the change that had come to spoil their lives.

'Where's the little un?' Will asked.

'He's out in the garden, talking to your neighbours over the fence. It's the first time he's been out of doors for three days. Now that it's known we're here with you, it doesn't matter any more.'

'I've been thinking about that.' He sat in the chair opposite and studied her face in the light of the fire. He saw that her eyes were full of sadness. 'Now the secret's out like you say, there ent so much hurry for you to move on. Any old day will do for that. You may as well take time to think.'

'I don't seem able to think,' she said. 'I seem to have lost the power completely.'

'Then why not let me decide for you? There's no need for you to move on at all. Strikes me you're better stopping here.'

'For good, do you mean? I don't think I can.'

'It's only common sense to me. Seems as though it was meant that way, as though we was throwed together on purpose, like. You and young John without no home. Me with a home and no one in it. Seems to me it's common sense.'

'Live here with you, in this cottage, when Richard is only a mile away, out at the other end of the village? Have you thought what people will say?'

'They'll think the worst. They always do. And that'll be harder on you than me cos it's always harder on the woman. I've got a tough hide and it's no odds to me what people say, but if you can't take it, we'll think again.'

'Richard threatened to shoot you. I heard him say he'd pay you out.'

'He can't do nothing. What can he do? I can look after myself all right. I'm big enough. I ent a dwarf.'

'Why should you have to bear his threats? And all the gossip there's bound to be? It's hardly a fair return for you, after being so good to us.'

'That's my decision, ent it?' he said. 'If I don't mind, that's up to me.'

'I don't know. I just don't know . . . '

'You stop here. That's the best thing to do. Cheltenham ent the place for you. Think of having to look for work, going among a lot of strangers, you with the little un to support. Does it seem better than stopping here?'

'No, it's not that,' Ellen said. In truth, the world seemed a frightening place, beyond the boundary of the village. 'It's just a question of right and wrong.'

'I'll tell you what, just give it a try! A month or two, say, and see how it goes. Seems you can't say no to that. Seems to me it's common sense.'

'All right,' she said. 'We'll give it a trial as you suggest and see how we all get on together. It's a bargain between us. We'll see how it goes.'

There was immense relief for her in having come to this decision, even though she still had doubts, and when she looked across at him, it was with a brighter, clearer glance.

'Right so!' he said, slapping his thigh. 'It's a bargain between us, like you say, and we'll work it out to suit both sides. You don't need to be afraid no more. I'll look after you from now on. You and young John, you're all right with me, and the first thing I aim to do for you is to get you fixed up with some proper clothes.'

'You're very good and generous. I don't know why you should be so good. I shall never be able to pay you back.'

'I dunno about that,' he said. 'A bargain's a thing that works two ways. There's more than one party involved in it. It's all a question of give and take.' Leaning forward across the hearth, he put out a hand and patted her knee. 'You'll pay me back all right – in your own way.'

Ellen stiffened and drew away.

'I'm not sure that I know what you mean.'

'Why, getting the house to rights, of course! Mollying for me and getting my meals! I've let this cottage go to the bad, but that ent to say I like it that way, and I shall expect to see a change now that you're stopping here with me.'

Will rose from his chair and stood for a while with his hands in the waist of his leather apron. The expression on his big broad face was half offended, half amused.

'What did you think I meant?' he said. 'Did you think I'd got thoughts of a different kind? That I'd take advantage and try it on? I reckon you've got a suspicious mind.'

Before she could answer, the back door burst open and John came in, red-faced from the cold and with a dewdrop on his nose.

'Well, young fella?' Will said. 'Your mother and me have been having a chat. I've been saying she ought to stop here, at least for the time, to see how it suits. So what's your opinion on the matter? Do you say go or do you say stay?'

'I want to stay,' John said, 'and be a blacksmith the same

as you.'

The boy's face was eager, expectant, full of trust, and he looked up at Will with bright-shining eyes. Ellen might still have her doubts, but her son had none.

Chapter Eight

A few days later the Christmas holiday came to an end, and John began going to school again. The children plied him with endless questions. The older ones were rather sly.

'Who does your mother like the best? Will Gale the smith or the Mad Miller?'

'What does she call herself nowadays, Mrs Lancy or Mrs Gale?'

'How many wedding-rings has she got? Does she wear them on either hand?'

John, in his innocence, merely stared. He thought them silly to ask such things. But other questions made more sense.

'D'you think Will Gale would mend my skates?' Lukey Strudwick asked one day.

'He would if I asked him, I daresay.'

'*Will* you ask him, then, for me?'

'I might,' John said carelessly, 'so long as you lend me a loan of them.'

There were many advantages, he found, in having the blacksmith as his friend.

Will, in the smithy, also had to endure questions. He answered them all with a smile and a shrug.

'Mrs Lancy's still with you, I see, Will. I thought you said she was moving on?'

'We came to a sort of agreement together. She's stopping here to keep house for me. As long as it suits her, anyway.'

'Has she any idea what she's taking on?'

'What about Will?' said Billy Jukes. 'Has he any idea what *he's* taking on, seeing she's another man's wife?'

'First the miller, now the smith,' said Tommy Breton, thoughtfully. 'I wonder why she always chooses a man in an apron?'

'I can soon tell you that,' said Ralph Jennet. 'It's so's she can wear the breeches herself. You can see she's that sort by the way she carries herself and all. I'd sooner Will than me by gum! I should think she's a tartar and no mistake.'

'Now see here,' said Will, straightening from his work at the anvil and admonishing Ralph with his long-handled hammer, 'Mrs Lancy is keeping house for me, and so long as she goes on doing that, I shall ask you to speak of her with respect.'

'Why, surely, surely,' Ralph agreed. 'That's only reasonable, ent it, Tommy?' And then, in a sly way, he said: 'Is she a woman that deserves respect?'

'*I* think she is,' Will said.

'Well, you know her better than we do,' said Ralph, 'so we'll just have to let you have the last word.'

Afterwards, alone with Jim Pacey for a while, Will laughed ruefully.

'You can't get the better of that lot. I should've known better than waste my breath.'

'You can't stop people talking, Will, especially when they got a talent for it. You just got to let it drip, that's all, like it was a shower of rain.'

Once, when Will was alone in the smithy, the vicar, Mr Eustead, called on him.

'It's wrong of you, Gale, to have Mrs Lancy living with you. It's scandalous. You should send her away.'

'Mrs Lancy is my housekeeper. There's nothing wrong

between her and me.'

'All the same, you are playing with fire.'

'I'm used to that, being a smith.'

'This is *hell* fire,' the vicar said.

'Then maybe I'll save a bit on coal.'

The vicar, tight-lipped, stalked out of the smithy. He hardly spoke to Will after that. And Will, who had until then been a bellringer, received a curt note under his door, saying that he was no longer needed, for his place had been taken by Albert Jukes.

More and more, as the spring weather came, Ellen was turning out the cottage, scrubbing the rooms from top to bottom, taking down the dirty curtains and hanging them up again, washed, ironed, and crisply starched. Will hung a clothes-line between the two fruit-trees in the garden, and for days on end, wet blankets thumped in the boisterous wind, and clean white sheets bellied out like sails. The cottage was soon as clean as a pin. Gleaming windows let in the light. And Will, whenever he had a moment to spare, was busy with a paintbrush, outside and in.

'She's certainly stirring you up, ent she, your Mrs Lancy?' said Charlie Beard, from next door. 'Your mice is all coming in to us, to get a bit of peace and quiet.'

'Then mind and be sure to treat them right. They've had nothing but kindness all these years.'

'It don't seem hardly fair on you, a bachelor chap like you are, to have a woman running you round.'

'I ent complaining,' Will said.

'Well, I daresay you get something out of it, to make it all worth-while,' Charlie said, 'but it strikes me you're a bit of a fool, saddling yourself with another man's wife, not to mention the shaver there.'

Will was painting his window-frames, and John, on a ladder against the wall, was watching ready to hand him a rag if the paint went over onto the glass.

'This young shaver,' Will said, 'is coming into the smithy with me, or so he reckons, anyway, as soon as he's old enough, of course.'

'He should be a miller by rights,' Charlie said, 'seeing that's his father's trade.'

'No!' said John, his chin jutting. 'I *won't* be a miller! I shall be a smith!'

*   *   *

Whenever Ellen went shopping now, she was served with a cold courtesy by the grocer, Whitty, and the butcher, Styles; and only Jerry Trussler, delivering fish at the door, treated her with the same old friendliness as before.

'Herrings, Mrs Lancy, ma'am? They're the best you can buy and every one is full of roe. You'd better take a good half dozen. Will likes his herrings. You take my word.'

The villagers rarely spoke to her. Most of them went to a lot of trouble to step aside and avoid a meeting. One or two would merely nod. And those who did speak, during the first few weeks at least, did so only to express disapproval, as on a day in early March, when she was walking along Dip Lane, taking Will's boots to the cobbler, Mustow. A group of women followed her, calling out again and again: 'Get back to your husband, where you belong! It's Lancy you're married to, not Will Gale!'

Ellen walked on with burning face and did her best to close her ears, and although the scene was twice repeated in the week following, she went on her errands just the same and held her head defiantly erect. She never turned towards the women or answered them by a single word.

'She thinks herself somebody, don't she, by gum? Living with Will Gale the smith like that, yet giving herself such mighty airs! And her poor crazy husband at the mill, going downhill all the time for want of someone to care for him. It's a disgrace and that's a fact.'

It was certainly true that the change in Richard was more marked than ever nowadays. He crossed the green once, on his way to Rillets Farm, and Ellen, who happened to be at the window, saw how shabby he had become and how badly he slouched as he walked up the track. From behind he looked an old man and his hair, which had only been streaked before, was now as grey as a panful of ashes.

There were many stories told about him and his strange behaviour. Every week brought something new. He had been quarrelling with the bargemen when they passed through the lock upstream from the mill. He accused them of stealing his chickens and eggs. He had slung a rope across the river, tied to a tree on either side, and when a barge had come along after dusk, a man had been swept clean off the deck. His mates had rescued him just in time. They had threatened Richard with a hiding but he had locked himself in the mill, and they in the end had gone on their way, cutting the rope and taking it with them.

He never let anyone into the mill now. His customers, such few as there were, had to leave their grain outside the door, and their meal, when ready, was put out at once to await collection. Michael Bullock of Rillets Farm complained that his bean-flour was spoilt by rain, and he took the matter to a court of law. Richard was ordered to make good the loss and pay a fine of two pounds. He paid the fine in penny pieces, poured out onto the table in the courtroom, but he never reimbursed the farmer, and the mill lost another customer.

'The man's off his hinges, no doubt of that,' Fred Byers said to Bob Dyson. 'I can't really blame that missus of his for leaving him the way she did.'

'According to some, she didn't leave him. It was Lancy hisself that turned her out. But the strange thing is, to my mind, that she should take up with Will Gale the smith. She was always a superior sort of woman. I can't get over her doing that.'

'She's only his housekeeper, so they say.'

'He's a man and she's a woman. It's not like a couple of old maids that've set up together to share their grub. Something'll come of it, no doubt at all, and that'll end badly, it always does.'

Bob Dyson was sorry about it. He had always admired Ellen Lancy.

* * *

One day when John was returning home from school with three other boys who lived on the green, his father came out of Ainsley's malthouse, and they met face to face in the narrow lane. John stared, going white with shock. He edged away and prepared for flight.

'Don't you know me?' Richard asked. 'Ent you got nothing to say to me? I'm your father. You know that.'

'No!' John said, in his shrill voice. 'You're not my father any more! Will Gale's my father and I'm his son!'

And, putting his head down like a bull, he charged past Richard and ran down the lane, followed closely by his friends. He thought his father would chase after him, and he ran home as fast as he could, there to shut and bolt the door.

'What's the matter?' Ellen asked.

'My father!' he said. 'He's after me!'

Ellen went to the window to see, but although she kept watch for an hour or more, Richard did not come to the cottage that day.

He was not often seen about the green, but once, when Will was shoeing a horse, he came to the open door of the smithy and stood for a few minutes looking in.

'Seems he's keeping an eye on you,' Jim Pacey remarked.

'He'd be better keeping an eye on his mill, instead of letting it go to rack and ruin,' Will said. 'Go to the door, will you, Jim, and see what he's up to out there.'

'Just going round, that's all. I reckon he's calling at the shop.'

Once Richard came very late at night, in the small hours, about three o'clock. He came to the cottage itself this time and hammered loudly on the door until Will leant out of the window above.

'You got my wife in there with you? Keeping her close, are you, warming your bed?'

'Your wife is in a bed of her own. Now shut your row and get back home. D'you know what time it is, standing there, waking the whole blasted village?'

'If I can't sleep, why should *you?* I want to know what you've done with my wife!'

'She's safe enough. You leave her be. She ent coming back to you if that's what you think.'

'I don't want her! Oh, no, not me! Not if she came to me on her knees. But I ent forgot what you've done to me, enticing my wife and son away, and one of these days I'll pay you out!'

He knocked several times at the cottage door, and the noise he made echoed all round the green, bringing one or two people to their windows. Eventually he went away. The next day was Sunday and in the morning, when Will stood 'airing his lungs' on the green, his neighbour, Mrs Beard, setting out for church, stopped and waited for Mrs Jennet.

'Good morning, Margaret. How are *you?* I hope you slept – when you had the chance? No, I couldn't get off again, not after that. And this little bit of a green of ours was always such a *quiet* place.'

'It will be again,' Will said, 'when you two women have done yaffling.'

Over breakfast, when he went in, Ellen was quiet and preoccupied. The night's disturbance worried her. After a while she said so to Will.

'I ought to go away from here. Away from Richard, as far as I can. It's all wrong that you should have to put up with this. The unpleasantness of it. The threats. The talk. Why should you bear it? It's all wrong!'

'I ent complaining,' Will said.

'I ought not to stay here, month after month. I really should be moving on. It's time I stood on my own two feet.'

'You stop as you are. You're all right with me. We get on all right, the three of us? You're comfy, ent you, you and John? There you are, then! Where's the sense? Why, John's got ideas about being a smith. I reckon you ought to think of him.'

'No, we can't stay!' Ellen said. 'Not if Richard is going to do this, coming knocking at your door, disturbing you and making threats. We must think of going. Yes, we must!'

But some time went by and Richard did not come knocking at the door again, and Ellen and John stayed on in the cottage.

* * *

Every moment, whenever John could slip away, he was sure to be in the smithy, watching Will and Jim at work. The iron heating in the fire, changing shape under the hammer, hardening again in the cooling-trough, had a fascination that never failed. Whenever horses were being shod, he would stand watching tirelessly, and, although he was only five years old, he seemed to divine the significance of every single thing he saw.

Once, when Jim Pacey had gone on an errand to Cockhanger Farm, Will was shoeing a mare alone, and John, standing by, was watching him. Will, with the mare's first forefoot on the stand, was about to remove the old shoe, and when he reached out for chisel and buffer, John handed them to him out of the box. Will said nothing at the time, but secretly he was impressed, and afterwards mentioned the matter to Ellen.

'He's quick on the uptake, your boy John. If he does take up smithing, later on, he's going to be good at it, no doubt of that.'

Will was very good with horses. He knew all there was to know about them and rarely, if ever, caused them pain. One day, shoeing a docile gelding from Neyes, he allowed John to come quite close and showed him the parts of the upturned hoof.

'This here in the middle we call the frog. It's spongy, you see, like a leather pad. Then all around here's what we call the horn. The outside layer is pretty tough and that's where we always put the nails.'

John, leaning over the gelding's hoof, made a face and wrinkled his nose.

'Hoo! Ent it smelly?' he exclaimed.

'Most people's feet is smelly,' said Will.

'Mine ent smelly,' John said.

'Well, they would be,' said Will, 'if you was a horse.'

'Can I feel the hoof and see what it's like?'

'Certainly. You go ahead.'

Will let the boy feel the gelding's hoof and then gave orders to stand away.

'I'm going to try seating the hot shoe, so you get back and stand by your mark.'

'But I want to see!'

'You can see as well from there. It ent safe for you to come too close. And the burning will make your eyes smart. Now do as I say and stand back or I shan't let you into the smithy at all.'

Will could be very firm when he chose, and at these times his word was law. But his nature was always so easy-going that the boy, for the most part, twisted him round his little finger. When John wanted a metal hoop to trundle around with a little stick, Will had to make him one in the smithy, and when Davy Bullock's trolley broke, Will had to put a new axle on it and hammer out the wobbly wheel. It was a great convenience to John, having the blacksmith as his friend, and he revelled in the importance it gave him. 'Don't worry, I'll take it to Will. He'll fix it all right – if I ask him to.' So Will melted lead for fishing sinkers; cut up pellets for catapults; and supplied old horseshoes for playing quoits; and Ellen, seeing how her son took advantage of him, sometimes put in a word of protest.

'You shouldn't do everything he wants you to do. He's a lot too free in the way he asks for this and that.'

'I was just the same when I was a boy and my father was in the smithy,' Will said. 'I'll soon let him know when I've had enough.'

'I don't want him spoilt,' Ellen said. 'He's rather full of

himself just now.'

* * *

John at this time paid little attention to his mother. Her restrictions irked him; he thought himself above such things; and often, as the days grew long, he stayed out playing till after dark. What the older boys did, he thought he could do, and when his mother scolded him, he tried out a few of the new words learnt in the farmyard at Rillets or Neyes.

'Buggle the time! What do I care? Why should I go to bed at seven? Let me see the flaming clock!'

Sometimes when she was busy baking he would swagger into the little kitchen, kicking at the floor with his new boots because he liked the noise of his 'hobs', and would snatch the wooden spoon from its bowl to lick the cake-mixture, under her nose. Often, at bed-time, he hid himself up in a tree in the garden or climbed on the roof of Charlie Beard's shed, and when she went to call him in, would answer cheekily, defying her.

'Nell! Nell!
You must not yell!
If you do
I'll tell on you!'

Will soon became aware of the way John defied his mother, and one Sunday morning, when they were out on Roan Hill, sitting not far from Tinker's Pond, he took the little boy to task.

'You shouldn't ought to cheek your mother like you been doing so much lately. It grieves me a lot. Why do you cheek her and play her up?'

John was ashamed and hung his head. He hated Will to think badly of him. But there was a sense of grievance in him and it came out in an angry burst.

'She treats me like a little boy!'

'*Does* she?' said Will, in great amazement, and his eyes became very blue indeed. 'Laws!' he said, solemn-faced. 'And you getting on for six years old!'

'She tries to make me say my prayers!'

'It's not only little boys that say their prayers. I say them myself when I get the time.'

'Do you?' said John, much struck. 'D'you say "Our Father" right through to the end?'

'I always *used* to say it through. I should never have grown so big and tall if I hadn't always said my prayers.'

There was a little silence between them. John plucked a grass and chewed its end. He spat out the fragments between his teeth.

'What else must you do,' he asked, off-hand, 'to make yourself grow up tall?'

'For one thing, you got to eat your greens. Greens is good for you. Carrots, too. They help to make good strong muscle. But you shouldn't suck no lumps of sugar . . . '

'I didn't! I didn't!' John exclaimed.

'. . . nor you shouldn't tell no lies . . . '

'It was only one or two lumps, that's all, that fell on the floor and got all dirty.'

'. . . but the worst thing of all a boy can do is when he don't respect his mother . . . '

'I *do* respect her,' John said. 'I do. Honest. Cross my heart.'

'I daresay you do, but how is she to know that, when you're always saucy and don't obey? How can *anyone* know it, hearing the way you talk to her? It's only *small* boys that cheek their mothers and small boys grow up to be *small men.*'

John's head drooped again, and there was a brightness in his eyes, which Will pretended not to see.

'Well, now, young fella, I reckon we've sat here long enough. Shall we go on to the top of the hill or round the pond and home by Neyes?' Will got up from the mossy stone and dusted the seat of his Sunday trousers. His little lecture was at an end. 'If we go round by the pond,' he said, 'we must keep an eye open for the treasure.'

'What treasure?' John said.

'The tinker's treasure,' Will said. 'They say the tinker hid it here, somewhere close by the old pond, and nobody's never found it yet.'

'Is it golden sovereigns?'

'I dunno. Nobody knows. But I shouldn't think it was gold, somehow, cos tinkers ent so rich as that. Tin, perhaps, or copper, maybe, but I wouldn't reckon on finding gold. Still, we'll keep a look-out, you and me, and maybe we'll find something, who can tell?'

They walked together down the track.

* * *

There was a definite improvement in John's behaviour after that and Ellen knew it was due to Will. He and the boy were good friends and often on a Sunday afternoon they rambled about on Roan Hill, 'keeping an eye out for the tinker's treasure' or stalking the fallow deer in the woods.

'You ought to come with us sometimes,' Will said to Ellen. 'It'd do you good to get out a bit.'

But Ellen was reluctant. She shook her head.

'Why not?' he said. 'You never go nowhere, only the shops.' Then he thought he understood. 'You think we'd look too much like a proper family, going out, the three of us? But does it matter how it looks? The villagers talk whatever we do. You may as well please yourself.'

'I'd sooner not ask for trouble,' she said. 'They're beginning to accept it now, I think, and I would like to keep it that way.'

'All right,' he said, 'it's up to you.'

Once every four or five weeks or so, Will went to Runston to see the ironmonger there, to order his stock and meet other blacksmiths for a gossip. He made a day of it, looking round the market shops, and drinking afterwards at The Swan, and always, when he returned home, he had some 'surprise' for Ellen or John. Once he brought her a beautiful shawl of dark red silk with a fringe around it, quite the richest, costliest thing she had ever seen.

'What's up?' he asked, as she opened the parcel and took out the shawl. 'Don't you like it?'

'It's lovely,' she said. 'But I can't wear it. You must take it back.'

'Maybe the colour ent right for you? I could always change it for another. There was plenty of different colours there.'

'It's too extravagant,' she said. 'You're much too generous and I can't accept it.'

'I know you need a shawl,' he said. 'I seen you unpicking that old knitted rug. I heard you say you'd be making it up – '

'I know what I said. I have only to mention this or that and out you go to get it for me. I shall never say anything, ever again! I shall button my mouth and bite off my tongue.'

'You say it!' he urged. 'You just say whatever you need. I ent short of a shilling or two and as for this shawl – '

'Who have you ever seen in Dingham wearing a shawl such as this?' she said.

'You think folk'll talk and make too much of it the way they do? You're right, of course. I should've thought. But it's only this once. Won't you try it on?'

'No, I'm wrapping it up again, straight away.'

'All right. I'll take it back. But I'm sorry about it all the same. That red would've suited you just about fine.' Sadly, he watched her wrap up the shawl. He saw that she was not to be tempted. 'What'll I get for you instead?'

'Just ask for your money and pocket it.'

'That'll only go on drink.'

'I don't mind where it goes, so long as you don't spend it on me.'

'You'd sooner see me catching stars!'

'If it makes you happy, by all means.'

'I'm happy sober and I'm happy drunk.'

'Yes,' she said, and smiled a little. 'You're the happiest man I've ever known.'

When she had first agreed to stay with Will, she had worried about his drinking habits, and, for John's sake, she had been afraid. What madness possessed her, she asked herself, that, having escaped from one drunkard, she should deliver herself and her son straight into the hands of another? But Will, however much he drank, was always good-humoured, always kind, and after a while she no longer worried. Foolish he might be, and noisy at times, but he had never quarrelled seriously with anyone, nor did he ever neglect his work. However late his revels lasted, the smithy would open the following morning as usual, and any piece of work that had been promised for such-and-such a time would be completed on the dot.

The worst sin ever laid at his door was that, when he had drink inside him, he was apt to say outrageous things. Once, encountering the respectable Mrs Batty, big in the body with her seventh child, he called out in the village street: 'Been at it again, Mrs Batty, my dear? Some people never learn! You should try putting salts in the old man's tea!' Another time, coming out of The Old Tap, he espied the vicar across the green, and he said something terrible. And there was the night when he and Frank Coe, another bachelor like himself, drank a whole cask of home-brewed ale in Frank's cottage and made such a noise, singing and playing the concertina, that Mrs Thurrop got out of bed and knocked on the wall with her candlestick. Will went out and called through the keyhole of her door. 'Shut up your knocking, you silly old flowerpot, you, or I'll come in there and give you what for.'

And always, afterwards, meeting these same people when he was sober, he would give a slow sheepish smile, then pass his hand across his face as though to wipe the smile away.

'It was the ale,' he would say to them. 'You've got to blame it on the ale.'

But although he often said things to make the girls and women blush, no mother feared for her daughter with him, or ever had cause, one way or the other. He was all talk, as they said, and it meant nothing. The brown jug had always been wife and mistress to Will Gale.

'Ah, but what about him and Mrs Lancy?' people were

asking nowadays, and, 'What indeed!' others answered.

* * *

There were some fine hot days in July and August that year, and in the evening, when Will had extra work in the smithy, he would stroll up the green every half hour or so to get his tankard filled at The Old Tap. And those neighbours of his who sat on the bench surrounding the oak tree would be sure to call out some teasing remark.

'Why don't you have a hogshead in the smithy, Will, and save your bootleather, to-ing and fro-ing?'

'That'd get warm in the smithy, Fred, and besides I like to air my lungs.'

'Where's your Mrs Lancy, then? She ent indoors on a pretty evening like this, is she?'

'She's sitting out in the back garden.'

'Don't she like our company?'

'The question is, do you like hers?'

'I dunno. I never spoke to her in all my life.'

'Exactly so,' Will said, 'and I call that unfriendly, I do, that's a fact.'

But a few were speaking to Ellen now. Bob Dyson had come to the door one day and given her a dozen eggs, and Sue Breton had sent her little boy to ask for the loan of a cupful of sugar.

'Soon you'll have Mrs Beard stopping by to tell you about her bunions,' Will said, 'and then you'll have really been let in!'

In the garden behind the smithy cottage, Will had cut down the breast-high grass, clearing a space about ten yards square, and here in the evenings Ellen brought a chair and her needlework and sat in the golden evening sun, between the overgrown currant bushes and the sweet-scented roses gone half wild.

'Sewing? Sewing? You're always sewing!' Will exclaimed, going out to her, pint-pot in hand. 'And when you're not sewing you're knitting, crocheting, or making rugs!'

'It occupies my mind,' she said.

'It don't stop you thinking, I don't suppose?'

'Not altogether.'

'Do you think about *him*?' Will asked. 'That husband of yours, down at the mill?'

'Yes. I think of him as he was before, in the early days, when we were first married and everything was happy between us.'

'I dunno that it's very wise, dwelling on the past like that.'

'Would you have me think of him only as he is now, behaving so strangely, so – '

'You may as well say it! – The man is mad and we both know it. There's no point in beating about the bush.'

For once he seemed brutal, almost as though he wanted to hurt. He stood for a moment watching her, then emptied his tankard and wiped his mouth.

'It's no good looking back on the past. You've got your life to live, same as anyone else. It's no good whiling it away like that, looking back on days gone by, cos there's no kind of miracle can bring them back.'

'Do you think I don't accept that?' she said. 'Do you think me such a fool?'

Will gave a shrug and went back to the smithy.

* * *

One evening in late September, Will went out to the back garden and found Ellen at work with a spade, trying to dig the tussocky ground.

'Here, what're you up to, for goodness' sake? You'll kill yourself, digging there. That ground ent been touched for ten years or more. Breaking it up ent no job for you.'

'Mr Dyson has given me some cabbage plants and Mrs Jennet has promised some seeds. Peas and beans, I think she said, and they ought to go in fairly soon if we're to have them next spring and summer.'

'So they shall!' Will said. 'But I'll do the digging, if you please. I ent much of a gardener. My dad and mother looked after that and I've let it go since they died. But I'll soon get it digged for you, and you can do the sowing and planting.'

He took the spade and started at once, slicing at the tussocks of couch grass and sending them flying to one side. Ellen gathered them up with a fork and carried them to her bonfire nearby, and all the time as they worked together, he was watching her with a sidelong glance.

'Spring and summer! That's what you said. Sounds like you think you'll still be here. Settling down, like, feeling at home.'

'Perhaps I'm feeling too much at home, taking things too much for granted,' she said.

'That's the way it ought to be. You can take things for granted as much as you like.'

'If ever you change your mind,' she said, 'you must tell me at once and no nonsense.'

'Right you are, it's a bargain,' he said. 'I'll send you both packing, you and your boy, and turn you out of doors in the cold – '

Stricken, he came to a sudden stop.

'Laws! What a thing to say!' he said. 'I need grubbing out. I do, that's a fact. And I ent even tipsy so there's no excuse.'

But Ellen merely smiled at him and her face in the shade of her straw hat was perfectly happy and serene. His joke had not hurt her. The past was beginning to bury the past.

'It ent very likely I'll want you to go – you feed me too well for one thing,' he said. 'You see that there's buttons on my shirts.'

'You may want to marry, one day.'

'Me? Never! No lections of that!'

'Why not?' Ellen said. 'You're a young man. You can't be much over thirty.'

'I'm thirty-three. But that's nothing to do with it. Marriage is a lottery, so they say, and I reckon the day my number was called, I must've been sleeping it off some place, or else making too much noise to hear. Besides, I'm happy as I am!'

Leaning forward on his spade, his hands clasped one over

the other, covering the handle, he looked at her with a straight steady stare, and his eyes, reflecting the evening sky, were a clear and vivid shade of blue.

'You and me and young John,' he said, 'we get along pretty well together, and that's the way it's going to stay, spring and summer, rain or shine, peas and beans and spring cabbage!'

Within a few days, the whole garden plot was dark brown, double-dug, trodden and raked, the surface soil a tilth of fine crumbs, ready for Ellen to sow her seed. Will was at hand, watching her, nodding approval at everything she did, ready to offer help if needed.

'I can see them beans in flower in my mind already. *And* I can smell the scent of them! There's no scent so sweet in all the world. As for the cabbages, well, you can't accuse them of smelling sweet. But the thought of them, sappy and green and fresh, why, my mouth is watering for them already!'

He strolled among the currant-bushes, now pruned down to the very bone, and with dung from the smithy around their roots, and returned to the edge of the seedbed.

'Spring and summer!' he said again, watching her as she put in the seed. 'I like the way you said that.'

Chapter Nine

However hard Ellen worked, keeping the cottage cleaned and scrubbed, she could never quite get rid of the smell of the smithy, even when the two doors between were kept firmly closed. There was always a hint of it in the air, a faint smokiness hanging over everything, and Ellen knew without fail when a hot shoe was laid on a hoof.

One morning when Will had been into the cottage in a hurry, he left both doors ajar behind him, and Ellen, coming in from shopping, found the kitchen full of smoke. Newly laundered clothes, hanging on the airer, were all covered in black smuts, and so were pastries cooling on the table. She went through to the smithy and called out to Will.

'I *wish* you'd remember to close these doors! The whole house is full of blacks!'

She closed both doors on that side and opened the others to let out the fumes. The smeech, she knew, would hang for hours.

Will, in the smithy, had to endure the inevitable teasing. Ben Tozer was there and so were the grooms from Dinnis Hall.

'Seems as if housekeepers is pretty much the same as wives, the way you get it in the neck, Will. The next thing you know, she'll be stopping you going to The Old Tap.'

'Not with a thirst like mine,' Will said.

'You ent there so much as you used to be, however.'

'Maybe he's got something better to do,' Tozer said thoughtfully, 'or maybe he's thinking of signing the Pledge.'

'Maybe I'm tired of the folk there,' Will said, 'with their everlasting nodding and winking.'

But his tone and his glance were just as good-humoured as usual. No one ever got a rise out of Will, even when they worked at it.

It was certainly true that he spent less time at the inn these days. A couple of pints and a game of skittles were just about his limit now and sometimes indeed, as winter came in and the days shortened, he stayed at home the whole evening, chatting to John after supper, telling him stories about the smithy, and perhaps seeing him up to bed. Afterwards he would sit by the fire, occupied with some small task, such as scraping the soot from the old kettle or mending the leg of a kitchen chair. Ellen noticed the change in his habits and one evening she mentioned it.

'I hope you don't keep away from the inn just because of me,' she said.

'I was there on Monday,' Will said. 'I go when I want to, never fear.'

'You used to go every night, either here or Sutton Crabtree. You used to stay till they closed the doors.'

'It's a fine thing, I must say, when a man gets nagged for *not* drinking!'

'So long as you're not denying yourself.'

'I don't need to go to the inn now I got someone to chat to at home. Besides, I'm too busy nowadays.' And he held up the new potato-masher that he was making out of wood. 'There's no end to the jobs a man has to do when there's a woman in the house.'

'I hope I *don't* nag you,' Ellen said.

'A man likes a woman about the place, to keep him in order and say what's law. I should live like a pig if it warnt for you. You saw this place when you first came. A man needs nagging and that's a fact.' He paused in his work of smoothing the masher and looked at her with a little smile.

'Not too much of it, of course! Just a pinch now and then, like salt with meat.'

* * *

Winter set in early that year and was bitterly cold. One day in November, Mrs Beard slipped and fell on the ice outside her door, and Ellen went out to help her up. She took her into the smithy cottage and gave her a cup of hot sweet tea. She washed her grazed hands and face, and, before taking her home again, threw ashes over the slippery ice. She went to the shop for Mrs Beard's 'arrants' that day and the old woman became her friend.

'To think I ent spoke to you all this time!' she kept saying, again and again, and Will, on hearing the story from Ellen, said: 'She'll soon make up for it now, I'll be bound!'

Most of the people living nearby were speaking to Ellen by Christmas time, and once, when little John had a cold, Mrs Jukes called in with a bottle of home-made cough-syrup and a ha'penny bag of boiled sweets. Not that she approved of Ellen even now. She thought she ought to make that clear.

'Poor little boy,' she said sadly. 'It's not his fault. We can't blame *him*.'

On Christmas Eve, at four o'clock, work stopped for an hour or two in the smithy, and many of the neighbours from around the green, not to mention a few from elsewhere, came in to sing carols around the forge, led by Will's cheerful baritone. It was something of a custom, and mulled ale was served to all who came, and this year, as a surprise, Ellen took in a huge dish piled up high with hot mince-pies, a sight that was greeted with a loud cheer.

Will was delighted at the way she contributed to his festive party, and when she had set the dish down on the anvil, he took hold of her and whirled her round in a little dance. The watchers sent up another cheer, and little John, clapping his hands, shrieked with over-excited laughter to see his mother swung off her feet.

Ellen herself was not best pleased. She was too well aware

of the glances cast in her direction. But she stayed and joined in the merry-making and helped to pass round the mulled ale, heating in an enormous pan at the forge. She was rather shy in this gathering. She had never been used to a lot of people. And they were equally shy with her. But towards the end Billy Jukes, who was rather drunk, came up to her and bowed low.

'Mrs Lancy, ma'am, when you've got a mind to swap husbands again, you might be kind and consider me! Will ent such a fool after all and it strikes me he knows what he's about!'

'Billy, be quiet!' his wife said, and edged him away, angrily.

Ellen said nothing, but, looking up, saw that Will was watching her, over the rim of his steaming tankard.

Later that night, in the cottage, he helped her to fill John's stocking.

'It wasn't very wise,' she said, 'to dance me round as you did in there, with all those people watching you.'

'You don't want to mind about Billy Jukes. He don't mean no harm, not really, you know.'

'He only says what the rest are thinking.'

'We knew it was going to be like that. We made up our minds we'd ride it out.'

'It makes me angry all the same, when there isn't a shred of truth in it.'

'You mean if there *was* some truth in it, you wouldn't mind so much?' he said.

Ellen glanced at him sharply, but he was intent on what he was doing, packing an orange and some nuts into the foot of John's stocking. It seemed he did not expect an answer.

'It's you I mind about most,' she said. 'After all, I have chosen to live apart from my husband, and that's a sin in the eyes of the world. But you've done nothing wrong at all and for your sake I mind what they say.'

'Then don't!' he said bluntly. 'I can fight my own battles.'

Ellen looked at the toys he had laid out on the table. A tiny clasp-knife. A catapult. A packet of chalks. A rubber ball. And a tin pea-shooter, with a bag of peas.

'I'm not sure that I like these things.'

'You don't have to like em. They're meant for John.'

*   *   *

Christmas Day was very cold, with a grey wind blowing out of the north. In the morning, after breakfast, while Ellen was busy cooking the dinner, Will took John for a walk on the hill, to look for a good stout Christmas log.

'But we've got a whole heap of logs in the house! And a whole heap of coal as well.'

'We must have a proper Christmas log, it's a sort of tradition,' Will said. 'My dad and me, in the old days, we always came out on Christmas morning, to look for a proper Christmas log. So you keep your eyes skinned, sharp as sharp, and if you see a likely log – '

'There's one!' said John, going forward into the wind. 'Over there, under that tree.'

'So there is! And just the job! Nice and old and daddocky, so's it'll burn up nice and bright. I reckon I'd better carry that. It's a bit big for a chap like you.'

As they went down the track again, snow began falling thick and fast, a cold white blindness enveloping them. Will took hold of John's hand and the two of them stumbled down the hill, across the pasture at Neyes Farm and out onto the green again. They ran the last fifty yards or so, arriving breathless at the cottage, and bursting in with a great deal of noise, laughing and puffing and flinging about, shedding wet snowflakes everywhere as they hung their coats in the back-place to dry, bustling to the fire with outstretched hands and asking when dinner was going to be ready.

The kitchen smelt of roasting goose, savoury sage – and – onion stuffing, and potatoes sizzling in the fat. And Ellen, in the act of setting the table, paused to give them warm spiced wine.

'You two!' she said, as they quietened down. 'You'd think there were six of you, racketing in.'

'We're hungry enough for six,' Will said. 'We're hungry enough for umpteen!'

After dinner, when everything had been cleared away and the table had been pushed back, they drew up their chairs around the hearth, and, wearing the paper hats from their crackers, sat toasting themselves at the big fire. Will took up the Christmas log and made to heave it into the stove, but in doing so he appeared to drop it. It fell with a heavy thud in the hearth; the old rotton wood split open wide; and there, among the soft splinters, was something that glinted in the light.

'There's something in it!' John exclaimed.

'Is there?' said Will. 'Fancy that!'

'Whatever is it?'

'I dunno. You'd better look.'

John got down in front of the fender and put his fingers into the log. The two halves of it came apart and lo, fallen out upon the hearthstone, were six brand new pennies, shining bright, winking and twinkling in the glow of the fire. John's eyes opened wide. He picked up the pennies one by one, and, sitting back on his heels, looked first at his mother, then at Will.

'It's the tinker's treasure,' he said, in a hushed voice.

'Why, so it is!' Will agreed. 'Would you believe it? In that old log!'

'How did it get there?' John asked.

'Ah, now, I wonder! I do indeed!'

'*You* put it there! I can see by your eyes!'

'Me? Why, lumme! What makes you think that?'

'Did he, mother?' John demanded. 'Did he put them in the log?'

'Yes,' Ellen said, 'I'm sure he did.'

'And supposing I did?' Will said. 'What d'you think of your treasure, then? Have you looked and seen the date? They're next year's pennies, new as new, that've never been spent yet, not even once, and can't be neither till New Year's Day. See the date on them? What's it say?'

'1881,' John said, turning each penny in his hand.

'Right so. Next year, like I say. And the queen on em, smart as smart!'

'Where did you get them?' Ellen asked.

'I've got a friend in the bank at Runston. He let me have them, special favour. And come next Saturday, New Year's Day, I'll take John into the town and he can spend them at the fair. How'd that be, young fella, then? Would you like to spend them at the fair?'

John nodded, bright-faced and bright-eyed. He sat with the pennies clasped in his hand and leant against his mother's knees.

'I like Christmas,' he whispered to her. 'I wish it was Christmas every day.'

Ellen, putting her hand on his head, looked at Will sitting opposite.

'You spoil this boy of mine,' she said. 'Yes. You do. You spoil us both.'

Will, with his blue paper crown over one eye, stooped and put the log on the fire. It burnt up like tinder and lit their three faces in its glow. Outside, the wind was blowing hard, and snow was beginning to fall again.

* * *

Sometimes, during the winter evenings, when she and Will sat together, he would fold his paper and put it aside and sit scarcely moving in his chair, watching her as she knitted or sewed.

'What are you thinking,' she asked once, 'when you sit so silent by the hour?'

'I dunno. You got me there. About the smithy, I suppose, and the job I'm doing for Mr Lord. I'm mending a back-boiler for him and I was remembering how my dad and me first made it for him twenty years ago.'

'You still miss your parents very much.'

'We was good friends, the three of us. They warnt all that old when they died and the way it happened, so sudden, like – '

'Tell me about it,' Ellen said.

'I was over at Brooks on a job. My father was in the smithy alone, working as always, clink-clink, and all of a sudden he collapsed. My mother found him lying there. Nobody knew his heart was bad. She tried to lift him and strained herself, and what with the shock and everything, she followed him in less than three weeks. They was all I had in the world. When they were gone, there was nobody. Only the smithy, that's all, and this here cottage, left to me.'

'You're a very solitary man.'

'Not now,' he said, looking at her. 'I've got you and John to think about now, and one day, perhaps, if all goes well, the smithy and cottage will go to him.'

Ellen, who was making a rug, allowed it to fall into her lap. 'You can't look as far ahead as that. John is only six years old. Anything could happen by then.'

'I hope not, by golly! What sort of thing?'

'You might get married and have a few children of your own.'

'That old song of yours again? Seems you're determined to find me a wife! Have you got anyone in mind! It ent Nolly Byers by any chance?'

'Who's Nolly Byers?'

'Fred's sister. She's fifty odd. A nice enough girl in her way – '

'I wish you'd be serious for a change.'

'I ent getting married. I'm serious enough about that.'

'Very well. I'll say nothing more. But I don't know why you should set your face against it so.'

'Don't you?' he said, looking at her. 'You ought to know. It's simple enough.'

For a moment he seemed to be challenging her. There was something different in his mood. But it was his gaze that fell away first.

'What I mean is, you're a pretty good manager. The way you do things suits me fine. I should be pretty hard to please if I was to start looking round for a wife.'

Abruptly he rose and walked to and fro about the kitchen. He returned to the hearth and looked at the clock.

'Will, what's the matter?' Ellen asked.

'Nothing at all. Why should it be? I was thinking of going for a drink, that's all. Would you like me to bring you anything back?'

'No, thank you,' she said, and resumed her work with rag-strips and hook.

A few minutes later, looking across at his empty chair, she felt that she had driven him away.

* * *

The new year came in and brought hard frosts. The horse-pond at Rillets Farm was frozen across from rim to rim, and one afternoon, the carter's boy, dared by two or three of his friends, drove his horse and cart onto the ice. When he was roughly half way across, the ice broke with a loud crack, and horse and cart were in the water, badly stuck in the deep mud. Michael Bullock sent for Will, and he spent half an hour in the pond, with the icy water up to his armpits, half lifting, half coaxing the horse from the mud, while other men hauled on a rope round its neck.

No sooner were horse and cart delivered safely from the pond then someone came running to fetch Will because Mr Rissington's bull had got out and was trampling all over the vicarage garden. Will got home at six o'clock and stood steaming in front of the fire.

'Aren't you going to change your clothes?'

'No, I've got work in the smithy,' he said.

'Why is it always you,' Ellen said, 'that gets called out at times like these?'

'I'm a big strong chap, that's why,' he said. 'I know that bull of Rissington's. It was me that put the ring in his nose. Why shouldn't they come to me about it?'

'They take advantage,' Ellen said. 'Because you're always so willing to help, they take advantage, all of them.'

'You may be right. But if one takes advantage, like you say, then why not another and all the rest?'

'You mean I do the same myself?'

'I never said that. I never did.'

'You thought it, however. I saw you smile.'

'You don't know what I was thinking. That was private, in my head. A man's mind is his own affair. It's the one place in all the world where he can be safe from nosey parkers.'

He took the bread and cheese she brought him and ate it, standing as he was, filling his mouth and chewing quickly.

'You women!' he said. 'You'd like to know us through and through, but that'd never do at all. My thoughts are my own, such as they are, and you shan't know them except when I choose.'

'It's perfectly true, anyway. I do take advantage. I know that. You've been so good to me, and you ask so little in return.'

'You keep house here and look after me. I don't see that I could ask much more.'

'You know what I mean.'

'Do I? Perhaps!'

'Will,' she said, touching his arm. 'I've seen the way you look at me – '

'Have you?' he said in a harsh voice. 'Then I must stop it, mustn't I?'

'Why are you in such a difficult mood?'

'We're different sorts of people, you and me,' he said, and, having finished his bread and cheese, he wiped his hand across his mouth. 'You've only got to hear us talk. The way we say things. I ent your sort.'

'You mustn't belittle yourself,' she said.

'That's what I tell myself sometimes. After all, you married Dick Lancy, didn't you, and I reckon I show up better than him?'

'Don't say things like that, Will. Richard was always a good man, until that accident turned his mind.'

'And you still love him, I know that. The man he was,

anyway. You're still a faithful wife to him, and I've got no right to look at you.'

'That's what the world would say to us. But why should you do so much for me and get so little in return? I know I can never pay you back but at least – '

'No! That's right! You can't!' he said, and moved away suddenly, so that her hand fell from his arm. 'I wouldn't want you to try, neither!' He went to the door and opened it. He spoke to her over his shoulder. 'I shall be working late tonight. Don't sit up and wait for me. I'll get what I want when I come in.'

At eleven o'clock he was still working. Ellen went through into the smithy and stood beside the glowing forge. The smeech of it made her eyes smart, and she stepped back a little, watching him work. He was making two new ploughs, identical in every respect, and was beating out the two new coulters, laid out together on the anvil. He did not look up when she came close. His sweat-moistened face was closed against her.

'Will,' she said, 'what is the matter?'

'Nothing,' he said, and went on working without pause.

'I've never seen you in this mood.'

There was no answer, only the noise of his hammer-strokes, with the chink-chink between as he turned each coulter with his tongs. She drew her shawl across her breast.

'Why are you treating me like this?'

'It's what you said to me, that's all! About your owing me this and that, and about your wanting to pay me back. As though I was someone who'd sent in a bill!'

'I didn't mean it like that. I put it badly. You misunderstood.'

'I don't want paying for what I've done! I'd have done it for anyone, not just you!'

'Yes,' she said, 'I know that.'

'Being so kind!' he said, scoffing. 'Offering yourself to pay a debt! What sort of man do you think I am?'

'It seems I can't talk to you in this mood. I shall leave you to take it out on the anvil. Your supper is ready whenever you want it. I'm going to bed and I'll say goodnight.'

He gave no answer, and she left him working.

* * *

It was sad and strange and almost unbelievable that two people could live so close, coming and going under one roof, and yet be such a distance apart. There was so much they knew about each other: the face of each, the man's, the woman's, was so familiar to the other, betraying feelings, thoughts, fears; yet still they were strangers, a barrier between them, and even while they talked together, as they had to whenever John was there, each took refuge in an inner silence.

'We've been here a year now, in your cottage. John and I were discussing it. A year tomorrow, to the very day.'

'A year? Is that so? Ah, it would be, you're right. The calendar says so if nothing else . . .'

Meaningless words, tossed between them for the sake of the child, who looked from one to the other with a worried, suspicious frown.

That winter was very severe, snow and frost coming by turns, and in the blizzard that blew all night on January the twenty-fourth, sheep at Neyes Farm and at Eddydrop were buried in snowdrifts fifteen feet deep. Will, in demand as usual, worked all day on the twenty-fifth, helping young David Rissington to dig out his flock. He then worked on throughout the night, repairing two snowploughs for the haywarden, and early next morning, when a message came from Mr Draycott, he went immediately after breakfast to help with the buried flock at Neyes.

'Must you go?' Ellen said. 'Surely the Draycotts can manage together?'

'They're three men short, absent sick. They need all the help they can get. Don't keep dinner for me. I daresay I'll get a bite at Neyes.'

He was gone all day and returned home at nine that

evening. He had been on his feet for forty hours, and, strong as he was, the weariness of it showed in the slow, sluggish way he removed his coat, in his heavy stillness as he sat in his chair beside the fire. He drank the tea Ellen gave him and passed his cup to be refilled. He looked at her through half-closed eyes.

'You ent going to scold me again, I hope, just cos I've been helping a neighbour?'

'No,' she said, quietly. 'I learnt my lesson the last time. Did you get the sheep out safe and sound?'

'Every last one,' he said, 'and that was a hundred and thirty-five.'

'What would you like for your supper?'

'Nothing, thanks. Old Draycott fed me like a king.'

His mood of the past few days was gone. He had driven himself to the point of exhaustion, and his bitterness had been purged away.

'I ought to go and shave by rights, instead of sitting taking my ease. I must be as black as that there hob.'

'Sit and be peaceful. You've earnt your rest. You're not indestructible, you know, and you've worn yourself out these last few days.'

'It ent very easy to wear me out. I'm a bit lapsadaisical, that's all, but I ent worn out. Oh dear me no!'

But as the warmth of the fire worked over him, gradually he began to nod. Soon his chin was on his chest and he was asleep, snoring gently. Ellen, in the chair opposite, sat quite still and studied him. She felt she knew him through and through.

He was a man who would answer any call for help. Nothing she said would alter him, and she smiled to think that she had tried. His face, with its broad cheekbones and blunt chin, had stubbornness in every line, and his straight black eyebrows told the same tale. His mouth, for all its readiness in smiling, could close as tight as a mussel-shell, and to anyone who read the signs it meant he was set on his own course and woe betide those who tried to turn him aside. He was a good man, Ellen thought, and he was obstinate in his goodness.

He awoke with a start and sat up straight in his chair. 'I wasn't sleeping if that's what you think!'

'Yes, you were. I've been watching you.'

'Well, dozing a bit, I grant you that.'

'You really ought to go to bed. You haven't slept for I don't know how long.'

'That's too good a fire to leave,' he said. 'I was always one for a good fire. Just to be sitting here like this is all the rest I want or need.'

But as he leant back in his chair again, his head against the hanging cushion, she could sense the aching tiredness in him as though it throbbed in her own bones, and, getting down on her knees beside him, she began untying his bootlaces.

'Here, what're you doing?' he exclaimed, and leant forward, trying to stop her. 'You ent a skivvy, to wait on me!'

But she merely pushed his hands aside and went on picking at the leather laces. They were tightly tied and still damp. She had some trouble, untying the knots.

'I'm something worse than a skivvy, I think, from what you said the other night.'

'Don't remind me what I said! I reckon I was in a mood.'

'You've got a right to say what you think.'

'I was just hitting out at you. Don't ask me why. It was a mood.'

'You thought I was offering myself to you without any tenderness or love, as payment for your kindness to me. You scorned being paid in such cheap coin.'

She had got the laces undone at last and now she drew off the heavy boots. She placed them beside the hearth to dry. She put his slippers on his feet, and remained where she was, sitting back on her heels, her dark green skirts spread out around her, her hands together in her lap.

'I don't blame you for hitting out, but I'm not really as bad as that.'

'Don't rub it in to me, what I said.'

'We should be able to understand each other by now. We know each other pretty well, if only we are honest about it.'

'I dunno so much!' he said. 'Know each other? I ent so sure!'

'Is it so hard to understand?'

Her face, reflecting the glow of the fire, had a delicate warmth in it and was tilted towards him, the shape of nose and chin outlined, the hollows in her cheeks very softly shadowed. Her dark brown hair, drawn so smoothly over her ears, had flecks of golden light upon it, and the same fire-flecked light was in her eyes.

'Well?' she said. 'What are you thinking?'

'I'm thinking about the night you came, when Lancy turned you out of the mill. You warnt too happy, taking shelter here with me, and you said if I ever touched you – '

'Yes, I remember what I said.'

'You said you'd kill me, didn't you? And you looked at me in such a way, I reckon you would've, given the cause. "Glory be!" I said to myself. "I wonder what she thinks I am!" But that was a whole twelve months ago. I ent so pert about it now. And I've come pretty close to getting myself killed, once or twice, since that night a year ago. So don't be too sure about knowing me. You've got no idea what goes on in my mind. I'm only flesh and blood, you know. I'm only a man like any other.'

'And I'm only a woman,' she said. 'You don't make allowances for that.'

'I made a vow from the very start that I'd always treat you with respect – '

'Perhaps you treat me with too much respect.'

'Ah, no, you mustn't say that! I don't like to hear you say such things.'

Will leant forward a little way and put out his hands. They were big, scarred, work-hardened hands with square knuckle-joints and square-tipped fingers, and, looking at them, he shook his head as though to say, 'What hands! What hands!' But the touch of his fingertips on her face was gentle, loving, rather shy, and she looked at him with fearless eyes.

'What've you been saying to me?' he asked in a voice she could barely hear. 'Ellen? Have you really thought?'

For answer, she turned and kissed his hands.

Chapter Ten

Their son, Peter William, was born in December, 1881, a black-haired baby, the image of Will. At his baptism, after Christmas, the vicar stood as far away as he could from Will and Ellen, refusing to look them in the eye, and as soon as the ceremony was over, he hurried out without a word. There was no congregation in the church. He had told the village to keep away. Only the godparents, Bob Dyson, Jim Pacey, and Mrs Beard, were there with Will, Ellen, and little John.

'Don't take no notice of *him*,' said Bob, jerking his thumb after the vicar, and Jim Pacey, sour-faced as ever, said: 'Just wait till the next time Rissington's bull gets into the vicarage garden again!'

Little John, now seven years old, was delighted at having a baby brother, and every day, coming in from school, he went at once to the cot in the corner to see if Peter was awake. One day, however, he seemed perplexed and turned to his mother with a frown.

'Why is he always sleeping, sleeping? Is there something wrong with him?'

'No, of course not,' Ellen said. 'Babies always sleep a lot.'

'You sure there's nothing wrong with him?'

'Quite sure. Why do you ask?'

'I only wondered, that's all. On account of his being . . . oh, I dunno . . .'

'Have they been saying things at school?'

'They're always saying things,' he said, and then, in a sudden angry burst: 'Somebody called him a little b——d! Bobby Tozer it was said that. Why should people call him names? It's a bad thing, ent it, what they said?'

'It's because Will and I are not married. Some people will say things like that. But there's nothing wrong with your baby brother. Not in any way at all. And the best thing is to take no notice of what people say. They'll soon get tired of it if you ignore them.'

'I'm not going to let them call our Peter bad names!'

'Well, don't go getting into fights, or you will have to answer to me.'

'I shan't fight with Bobby Tozer. He's bigger than me. He's nearly ten. I'll have to wait a bit for that.'

'Good!' Ellen said, cheerfully. 'I'm glad to hear it. You've got good sense.'

But often she felt deeply ashamed of what the boy had to bear for her sake. She spoke about it to Will, alone.

'They are the ones that will suffer,' she said, nursing her baby at her breast. 'John now and Peter later – they'll have to bear the brunt of it all, because of what I've done with my life.'

'You ent done nothing. What've you done? It's just the way things've gone for you.'

'I've chosen to live with you like this. I've brought this baby into the world. I must take the blame for what I've done.'

'Not by yourself,' Will said. 'We've both done wrong, you and me, in the eyes of the village, anyway. I know how you feel. I feel the same. But I wouldn't change it, even so.'

Sitting on the edge of his chair, he leant forward across the hearth and touched the baby in her arms, poking at one tiny hand till it closed in a fist about his finger.

'We can't very well send him back, can we? Not now he's made hisself at home?'

'No, nor I wouldn't want to,' she said, and held the baby closer still, till it suckled sleepily at her breast. 'He's the best of babies. He is indeed.'

'No regrets, then?' Will said.

'Not on that score. None at all.'

'Me neither. Not a jot.'

In the smithy, sometimes, his customers tried to get a rise.

'How does it, feel, Will, being a father?' Billy Jukes asked one day.

'You should know. You got enough kids of your own.'

'Ah, but I'm a lawfully married man. My boys ent b——ds. They're just little sods. Having them warnt no fun at all. It was just like pinching a pot of jam out of your own larder, like.'

Fred Byers, watching Will as he shaped a shoe on the beak of the anvil, shook his head regretfully.

'I knew you'd land in a peck of trouble when you gave up going to the inn and took to stopping at home in the evenings. There's many a good drinking man that's gone to the bad along that road. You should've stuck to your pint-pot of ale. It's a lot less costly in the end.'

'Costly? Rubbish!' Will said. 'Peter will come in the smithy with me. Him and John, the two of them, they'll be a support in my old age.'

Will was proud of his baby son. He would bring him into the crowded forge and show him off to his customers, and he was determined from the start that the boy should be accepted there. At the same time he took great care that John should never feel left out. He saw to it that the older boy got as much attention as the younger one. There would be no cause for jealousy if *he* had anything to do with it.

One day, when John was in the smithy, Mr Preedy of Town End came in. He rapped Will with his riding-crop and said in his loud hallooing voice: 'How's this famous boy of yours that I'm always hearing so much about?' And Will, with his hand on John's shoulder, said: 'Both my boys is doing fine.'

* * *

One day in the summer of 1882, someone knocked at the smithy cottage, and Ellen went to the door with her baby in her arms. The man who stood there was thin-faced and hollow-eyed, with a shock of grey hair and an untidy beard, and it needed an effort on Ellen's part to realize that this was her husband, Richard Lancy.

'Don't you know me, Nell?' he said. 'No, maybe you don't. It suits you better to forget I'm still alive, don't it?'

'What do you want?' Ellen asked.

'I came to wish you well,' he said, looking at the baby in her arms, 'and bestow my blessing on you both.'

'You don't expect me to believe that?'

'The way I see it is this,' he said. 'Now that Will Gale has given you a b——d son, you can spare me my own son back again, seeing he's all I've got in the world.'

'No! Never!' Ellen said.

'Then you'll be sorry, I promise you! One of these days, sure as fate, you and Gale will get paid out!'

'Richard, can't you leave us alone?'

'Why should I?' he said. 'I've got a score to settle with you and him and I shan't rest till I've settled it!'

He slouched away across the green and turned into the main road. Ellen watched till he went out of sight. At the smithy door, Will also watched. He came to Ellen and touched her arm.

'What did he want?'

'He was asking for John.'

'You look a bit peeky,' Will said. 'You'd better go in and sit down.'

'It gave me a shock, to see him again. He looks even wilder than before. It frightens me, Will, the way he's always threatening us.'

'He just likes to stir us up. He can't do nothing. It's just his talk.'

'I don't know. I wish I were sure.'

'He's made threats before and it's never come to nothing yet. You go indoors and take it easy. There's nothing for you to worry about. He just likes to stir us up.'

'Yes,' she said, 'I daresay you're right.'

But she worried about it all the same and sometimes, in dreams, she saw Richard's face as she had seen it long ago when he had walked in his sleep at the mill: blank, expressionless, blind-eyed, but with a queer intentness in it. She saw him walking, a grey ghost, moved by whatever it was that had taken the place of his own soul, stealing quietly into the room where she and Will slept.

'What is it? What is it?' Will would say. 'You been having that dream again? There's nobody there, I promise you. Richard ent coming to do us no harm. You've been dreaming again, that's all.'

Will's strength and gentleness kept her safe and comforted her. He never for an instant shared her fears.

'I shall look after you,' he would say. 'And look after myself as well. Lancy can't hurt us, I promise you that.'

Often her fears were for little John, lest his father waylay him after school, but as time and its seasons passed by, these fears were pushed to the back of her mind. If John saw his father in the distance, as he did now and then in summertime, he would turn and run off in the other direction, and always, whatever temptation there might be from the other boys, he kept well away from the old mill.

'I ent going *there*! Oh, no, not me! I'd sooner fish upstream at Chack's.'

* * *

John, in his bedroom over the smithy, awoke every morning to the noise of iron striking iron, and went to sleep every night with the tune of it chinking in his dreams. The sounds of the smithy were music to him. The smell of horses and their dung, of hot iron and coalfire smoke, were the very breath of life itself. He longed for the day when he could take his place with Will.

'When can I start work in the forge?'

'The moment you've done with your lessons at school.'

'Mother says I must stop till I'm twelve.'

'That'll soon go,' Will said. 'You'll turn yourself round one of these days and find the years've gone like a flash. Why, look at young Peter, the way he grows. It's only five minutes since he was a baby cutting his first tooth. Now he's talking and walking about and weighs a hundredweight on my scales.'

'D'you call that *talking*?' John said.

But Will was right about time passing. It went on wheels, there was no doubt of that, and every six months or so, when he put the two boys to stand at the wall, the marks would show how much they had grown.

'Peter will never catch up with me! Not if he grows and grows and grows!'

'He might do,' Will said, 'when you're both men.'

'Well, he'll never be as old as me, anyway.'

'No, that's true, he never will. There's seven years and three months between you and nothing will ever alter that.'

John, looking down on his little brother, was nevertheless protective towards him, helping him to cut up his food, fastening his buttons and bootlaces, and speaking up in his defence when Ellen scolded him for some misdeed. He could never bear to see Peter crying and once, when the little boy was ill with chicken-pox, John drank his nasty medicine for him, morning and evening for three days, before Ellen found out about it.

Peter, developing fast, was soon aware of the power his tears had over John. Whenever he wanted a pick-a-back ride, or a share of John's liquorice strings, or a story read to him at bedtime, he had only to cry to get his way. John once relinquished his best blood alley and six white commoneys to stop Peter's tears, only to find afterwards that Peter had dropped them down the drain.

'You shouldn't give in to him,' Ellen said. 'I don't spoil

him. Neither does Will. You must be firm and say no.'

John did his best, but Peter's tears made him miserable, and always in the end he gave in. Until a day in September, 1885, when he said no and meant no. John had a small spyglass that Will had given him for his birthday. It was a miracle to John and he prized it above all other things, for with it, as he rambled about, he could watch the birds of the air in their antics as though they were only a few yards away.

'No, you can't have it, you're much too young. You'd only break it. The answer is no.'

Peter cried and howled in vain. John for once was adamant and kept the glass in a secret place. But he felt uncomfortable all the same, especially as Peter, in his rage, ran blindly against the table and hurt his head.

'I hate you, John! I think you're mean! I hate you and hate you! I think you stink!'

'Hate away,' John said, with a great show of indifference, but he felt uncomfortable all the same.

* * *

Watching the flight of wild birds was a thing he never tired of, and as he grew older it occupied more and more of his time.

'Come along, John,' Will would say, when he took the two boys out on Roan Hill, 'Peter and me is wanting our dinner.'

But John would be watching a hovering kestrel as it hung without moving on the air. Through his spyglass he saw how very still it was. He would count the seconds while it hung.

'I dunno how they do it,' he said. 'I dunno how they manage it, stopping so still in the air like that, with scarcely a bivver in their wings.'

'I daresay they've practised a bit,' Will said.

He himself knew nothing of birds, although he was full of sayings about them.

'When you see a rook by itself, it's a crow!' he would say, and, whenever he saw a woodpecker: 'There goes the mean old baker's wife!' Geese going over meant a storm and the

Seven Whistlers or Curly-whoos might just mean the end of the world. 'There's six of them flying about, you see, all on the look-out for one more, and when they find him, the old folk say, this world of ours will come to an end.'

'Will it really?' John asked.

'I shouldn't worry if I was you. The world will last long enough for you to come into the smithy with me!'

'And me? And me?' Peter said.

'That's right, the pair of you!' Will said. 'And shan't we see the sparks fly then!'

When Peter, aged four, began going to the village school, in the room above the butcher's shop, John held his hand all the way there and kept an eye on him during lessons. That same spring, in 1886, a new school was built at the north end of Dingham, with two separate classrooms in it, a playground with drinking-fountains, and a handsome gate with a stone arch above, on which were engraved some words.

'What's it say, John?' Peter asked.

'As-the-twig-is-bent-shall-the-tree-grow,' John said, reading slowly.

'What twig?' Peter asked. 'Is it Mrs Tanner's stick that she canes us with when we're naughty?'

'Don't be silly. Of course it's not. It's only us older ones that get the cane.'

'Then what's it mean, about the twig?'

'I expect it's something out of the Scriptures, that's all.'

John was worried because in this big school Peter would be in a different room and he would not be there to protect him. He called all the younger children together and showed them his fist.

'If anyone calls my brother names, they'll get what-for, so just watch out!'

But Peter, from the first, was very well able to fight his own battles, and often it was the other children who came to John asking for help.

'Your Peter's a bully. He punched my nose. Just cos I wouldn't let him share my oneses.'

'Then it's up to you to hit him back. I ent got time to worry over you little uns. You run along and buck yourself up.'

John, during his last year at school, was something of a leader with the other boys of his own age, and was always up to some sort of mischief. Once, when Mr Rissington left his horse and cart on the green, John and his followers sneaked up and loosened the traces, so that when Mr Rissington returned and gave the ribbons a little twitch, the horse moved forward without the cart and he was pulled clean out of his seat. On another occasion, after dark, the boys put soap down the well on the green, and when the pump was used in the morning, bubbles issued from the spout and Mrs Naylor's bucket was soon full of suds. Often the whole village was up in arms at once, because John and his band of desperadoes had been busy and had left a trail of havoc behind them. They removed knockers from cottage doors, released frogs in church on Sunday, and changed Mrs Parker's line full of washing for that of her neighbour, Mrs Pie.

'That'll be a good thing when John Lancy starts work in the forge,' people were always saying to Will. 'Sooner the better. He wants wearing down.'

* * *

On the day he left school John, with three other boys, raided old Mr Draycott's orchard and carried away as many apples as each could tuck inside his shirt. The apples were green and John, having eaten one and found it sharp, took the rest home to his mother so that she could make a tart.

'Where did they come from?' Ellen asked.

'The orchard at Neyes,' John said.

'Then they must go back there, straight away. You must see Mr Draycott and give them back.'

'I can't do that! He'd very likely tan my hide.'

'It may well be what you deserve.'

'Just a few apples? Glory be! What a tarnal fuss for a few apples!' And he watched her putting them into a basket.

'They ent even worth eating!' he said. 'Besides, I warnt the only one. There was three others along with me. I bet *they* ent got to take them back!'

'I'm not their mother. But I am yours. And you're taking these apples back at once.' Ellen, facing her angry son, saw rebellion in his eyes. 'I don't want my son to be a thief.'

'I ent a thief! No, I am *not*! Scrumping ent thieving. It's just a lark. You've got no right to say such a thing!'

'It seems you don't care to be called a thief?'

'No! I don't! And I won't have it!'

'Then you shouldn't be one,' Ellen said.

'All this fuss!' John exclaimed. 'What if I say I ent going?'

'You *are* going,' Ellen said, 'and don't think to deceive me for I shall see Mr Draycott afterwards and make sure you've done as you're told.'

John snatched the basket out of her hand and stamped angrily to the door. He knew this unyielding mood of hers. His life would not be worth living until she had seen her order obeyed. But that he should have to face Mr Draycott, that stern old man with the fierce white brows!

'The sooner you go,' Ellen said, 'the sooner it will be all over.'

So John went out across the green, up the track leading past the cartshed, and round to the back door of the farmhouse. As it happened, old Mr Draycott was just coming out of the big barn, and behind him came Hannah, his granddaughter, a girl of about John's age, hugging a puppy in her arms. That John should have to face Mr Draycott was bad enough, but that Hannah should be a looker-on was too unfortunate for words, and under her steady, critical gaze he felt himself growing as red as the turkeycock in the yard. She thought herself somebody, this girl, because she had left school at ten to keep house for her father and grandfather, and old Mr Draycott encouraged her, saying she kept them both in hand.

'Well, boy, and what's this?' The old man looked at the basket of apples. 'You selling something?'

'I've been in your orchard. I took these.'

'Speak up, boy, speak up! Let's hear it plainly, whatever it is.'

'I took your apples,' John said, 'and my mother told me to bring them back.'

'Did she now! And who is she, this mother of yours, who means you to be an honest man?'

'Mrs Lancy,' John said.

'Ah, yes, I know you now. John Lancy. Yes, of course. And what've you got to say for yourself, John Lancy, apple thief?'

'I reckon I'm sorry,' John said.

'So you should be! So you should!'

The old man took the basket of apples and emptied them into a barrel nearby. His face, although it seemed severe, with its white whiskers and flaring brows, had a certain humour in it, and his eyes especially seemed to laugh. He spoke to his granddaughter, standing by.

'What shall we do with him, eh, Hannah? Are we to let him off scot free?'

'If I had my way, he'd get a whipping,' Hannah said.

'What, after he's brought the apples back?'

'He's always in trouble of some sort. It was him that rode Mr Grey's pony and got him all muddy that time.'

'At least he obeys his mother, though. I reckon he ought to have some reward.'

'H'mph!' Hannah said, and looked away, fondling the puppy in her arms.

'What about you?' the old man said to John. 'What do you reckon you deserve?'

'I dunno,' John said, and gave a slight shrug. The old man, he felt, was having him on.

'Well, I shan't whip you as Hannah suggests, but I'll let you do me a favour instead. She's just going to take the goats to the green. You can go with her and give her a hand. How's that? Does it seem fair?'

'I dunno. I suppose so.'

The old man took Hannah on one side, and something passed from his hand to hers. John pretended not to see. He stood with the basket on his arm and stared at a wagtail on the roof. The old man took charge of the tiny puppy, and Hannah walked across the yard.

'Come on, you,' she said to John, and he followed her round the end of the barn, into a field that was part oat-stubble and part beans. 'Leave the gate,' she said, tossing the words over her shoulder.

'So you'd have me whipped, would you?' he said.

'Yes, I should. It's what you deserve.'

'Your grandfather don't agree with you.'

'My grandfather is much too easy-going.'

'I can see that,' John said, 'by the way he lets you speak to him.'

The two nanny goats, one white, one brown, were tethered on the oat-stubble. Hannah pulled one tethering-rod out of the ground, wound the rope in a loose coil, and held it like a halter, close to where it encircled the goat's neck. She stood waiting while John did the same with the other, then she led the way down the stretch of stubble, taking the shortest route to the green.

But John's goat refused to move. It dug its feet into the ground, pulled hard on the rope, and, putting its muzzle into the air, knuckered at him, showing its teeth.

'I thought you was supposed to be strong!' Hannah said, waiting for him.

'I don't want to choke her, do I?' he said.

'No fear of that. Try pulling harder. She's playing you up.'

But although John pulled with all his strength, the goat merely yielded a step or two and once again came to a halt.

'It's because she don't know you,' Hannah said.

'She *will* know me in a minute!' He held up his fist.

'Don't you hit her! Don't you dare!'

'Glory be! As though I would!'

'I'll hurry on with Rosalee, then perhaps Belinda will follow.'

Sure enough, when Hannah walked on with the white goat, the brown goat followed with a burst of speed, and John, completely taken by surprise, was pulled stumbling along behind it. The tethering-iron fell on his toe, the coil of rope slid from his arm, and his feet got caught in its many tangles. He fell headlong, onto his face, and the empty basket, round-bottomed, went bowling merrily down the slope. So that by the time he reached the green he was breathless, bruised, covered in mud, and very thoroughly out of temper.

When they led the two goats onto the green, several children gathered round, and the rumpus they made brought a few neighbours out to watch. Little Peter came out of the cottage, and Will came out of The Old Tap.

'If it ent our John there, acting the goat! And him so thick with Hannah Draycott! Would you believe it? I never did!'

'Don't speak to *me*!' John muttered, still struggling with the tangled rope.

'Don't speak to *him*!' Will said. 'He's doing his knitting and he's dropped a stitch.'

John was looking round for a stone, and when he bent to pick one up, the brown goat, Belinda, butted him hard against the rump, pitching him forward head over heels in a neat little somersault on the grass. The people watching laughed in delight. Will's laughter was loudest of all and Peter, beside him, almost choked.

But John, as he stood, was chiefly aware of Hannah Draycott's superior stare, and rage for a moment blinded him. He felt he could strike her in the face. Then suddenly he was calm. He brushed himself down with a certain jaunty deliberation, retrieved the lost stone, and hammered the tethering-iron into the ground, keeping an eye on the goat and assuming a comical nervousness.

Hannah had already dealt with her goat and now, as John finished, she came to him and held out sixpence.

'My grandfather told me to give you this.'

'I don't want it, thanks all the same.'

'It's yours for helping with the goats.'

'I don't need to be paid for that. I reckon you'd better keep it yourself. – Buy yourself a string of beads.'

John was rather pleased with this. It put Hannah Draycott in her place. But then, as he was turning away, the glittering sixpence fell at his feet.

'*I* don't want it!' Hannah said. 'Why should I want it, for heaven's sake?'

She turned and walked across the green.

'In that case,' said John, to those who watched, 'it'll just have to darn well stay where it is!'

Peter ran forward and snatched up the coin.

'If you don't want it, can I have it?'

'If you like,' John said. 'It's no odds to me.'

He picked up the empty apple-basket and sauntered homewards across the green.

* * *

Soon after that, John's indentures were drawn up, and he was formally bound apprentice to Will Gale, blacksmith, of Dingham Green. On the following Monday, he was at work in the smithy, starting at six o'clock in the morning and going on till eight at night. He considered himself a man now and he was determined to do a man's work. When Will suggested an hour's rest, John only drove himself harder still. He worked the bellows till every muscle quivered and ached; he brought in the coals and got rid of the ashes; he drew and carried supplies of water; and he ran to and fro, fetching new iron from the shed at the back. At the end of that first day, when he sat down to supper, he had barely enough strength left to eat, and Ellen, packing him off to bed, looked reproachfully at Will.

'Must you work him so hard? He's only twelve.'

'There's no stopping him,' Will said.

During his early days in the smithy, John was forever getting grit in his eye, or burning his hands, or dropping iron on his toes. But there came a time when he was so hardened to these misfortunes that he scarcely noticed them any more.

And there came a time, too, when the accidents happened less and less. He had been in the smithy about six weeks. He came to a standstill one afternoon and looked at his hands.

'Just look at that,' he said to Jim. 'Hardly a scratch anywhere.'

'Ah, you're finding your feet, sure enough. You're a lot more nimble than you was.'

'He gets the practice,' Will said, 'keeping out of the way of them goats.'

The two Draycott goats remained on the green till the end of September, and every two or three days or so, Hannah came to take up the rods and move them to a fresh place.

'There's young Hannah,' Will would say. 'Ent you going to give her a hand?'

'Not me!' John said. 'Oh dear me no!'

But one morning when Hannah came, the ground was hard for lack of rain, and she had trouble driving the rods into the turf. John stood at the smithy door and watched her at it. She was using a tiddly bit of stone that anyone with half an eye could see would break in a few seconds. So he went and fetched a sledge hammer and walked briskly across the green. He ordered Hannah to stand back, and, with two clean, swinging blows, drove the rod into the ground. When he stood erect again, Hannah bobbed him a little curtsey.

'Thank you kindly, sir, I'm sure.'

But there was no gratitude in her glance. There was only a bored, superior amusement, as though she thought he was showing off.

'It's nothing,' he muttered. 'You'd have been all day, patting at it with that stone. Let's get on and do the other.'

'All right, but mind you keep out of Belinda's way.'

'D'you think I'm afraid of a d——d goat?'

'Tut,' she said, moving on, 'he's swearing like a grown man.'

When the second rod had been driven in, John shouldered his sledge hammer and would have turned away at once, but Hannah was looking at his leather apron, which, with its ragged untidy fringe, reached almost to the ground, and he saw that she was hiding a smile.

'Something amusing you?' he said.

'That apron of yours is so long, you'll trip over if it you're not careful.'

'I shan't trip over it, don't you worry.'

'The rats've been at it, too,' she said. 'They've made it all ragged at the end.'

John looked her straight in the eye.

'A blacksmith's apron,' he said with scorn, 'is always ragged at the bottom.'

'Tut-tut, he's a blacksmith now,' Hannah said, turning away, 'and there was I, thinking he was only an apprentice!'

John went back into the smithy and met Will's enquiring glance.

'I thought I'd give her a hand,' he said. 'She warnt getting nowhere, fooling about with that bit of stone.'

But it would be many a long day, he added grimly to himself, before he helped Hannah Draycott again.

Chapter Eleven

His work in the smithy was a passion with him and the day he made his first horseshoe he became certain in his bones that he had it in him to be a good smith.

Until then he had had his doubts. There was such a tremendous amount to learn: about the iron in the fire; about the iron under the hammer; about the unity there had to be between eye and brain and hand and tool. It seemed he would never learn these things, and often he railed at his own slowness and clumsiness. But, from the day when he made his first horseshoe, the doubts fell away. He would do it, given time. The fire and the iron would yield their secrets up to him and he would fashion forth those things, from the blades of scythes and reaping-hooks to the shafting and drums of the traction engine, by which men got a living from the land.

That first horseshoe was made for stock. It hung upside down on a nail on the wall. And John, in passing, would give it a tap, setting it swinging to and fro. Sometimes he stopped and took it down, trying the weight of it in his hands, feeling the crimp of its inside edge, squinting at the nail-holes, four and three. And Jim Pacey, catching him at it, would say in his dry old sourpuss way: 'It's a masterpiece. That's what it is. You ought to wear it round your neck.'

But the horseshoe in fact was not very good and John knew it. He had to do better, and better again. He watched Will Gale with hungry eyes and schooled himself to a man's patience.

'If I could only be half like Will . . . ' he said to his mother one day, and Ellen, watching his eager face, smiled at her own innermost thoughts.

For John, after years of imitation, was so like Will in many ways that he might have been his own son. Everything he did, in the smithy and elsewhere, was done with Will's little tricks and manner. The way he rolled his shirtsleeves up and the way he handled a pair of tongs; the way he sauntered out to the green and said he was going to air his lungs; the way he splashed and gurgled and gasped when washing himself in the scullery; even his voice, deepening when he was fourteen, became exactly Will's in tone, and he had the same teasing, easygoing humour.

He and Will worked well as a team. There was a special understanding between them. Even while John was still quite young, not yet fully skilled, Will would ask for his opinion.

'Two heads is better than one, even if it's only two sheep's heads, so come and have a look at this here cart-brake, will you, John?'

And although at first he did it chiefly to encourage John in thinking things out for himself, there soon came a time when the boy's opinion had some value of its own.

'John can *see* things,' he would say. 'He'll be a better smith than me by the time he's through, and when I get to fifty or so, I'll take a little farm some place and let him get on with it in the forge.'

'What about me?' Peter demanded. 'I shall be in the forge too!'

'Why, yes, of course,' Will said. 'You and John'll work together, ding-dong, while your mother and me sit back a bit and raise a few chickens on our farm.'

Peter, as a boy, like John before him, was always hanging about the smithy. Often he had to be driven out forcibly to go to school and on one occasion John had to drag him all the way to the gate. Peter was so enraged by this that he wouldn't speak to John for a week. He was, as his father said sometimes, a powerful and determined sulker. But it was not that he disliked school. It was merely that he liked the smithy better.

'When can I have some iron to work on? When can I have a go with the hammer?' And John, teasing his half-brother, would say: 'When you're tall enough to see over the top of the anvil!' Peter would fly into a passion at this. 'I ent that small! You! I am not! I'll be a better smith than you!' And often as he grew older, repeating what he heard on the green, he would say: 'I'm Will Gale's son. I shall take after him. You ent his son. *You* ent got smithing in your bones.'

John had no answer to make to this. He could not take refuge in pretence, as he had done in earlier times. His brother had him cornered here and made the most of it time and again.

'*Your* father,' he would say, 'is the Mad Miller of Pex Mill!'

John would turn away with a shrug but it was a good

many years before he could hear Peter's jibe without a sinking of the heart. And even then – even when he was a grown man – it still cost him a pang that he could not boast, as Peter did, of being Will Gale's son.

Sometimes he saw his own father here or there about the village. A scarecrow figure of a man whose face, although gaunt, was somehow fleshy and loose-lipped, always dewy with drops of sweat. Whose dulled eyes were never still but seemed always, even when he stopped to talk, to be seeing something that crept or crawled just behind you.

'The way Lancy looks at you,' Jim Pacey said once, 'it makes you feel as if you'd got a lot of snakes coming out of the back of your collar.'

John never met his father if he could help it. Seeing the waggon in the distance, he would contrive to slip away. But a meeting could not be avoided for ever, and one day in the summer of 1891, father and son came face to face, unexpectedly, in Gow's Lane. John by then was nearly seventeen. He was tall, well-made, square-shouldered, strong, and he carried himself with something of Ellen's graceful ease. Richard stood in front of him and looked him over with hungry eyes.

'My Lord!' he said, and his voice had the strained huskiness of the man whose throat has been roughened by drink. 'It's my son John, grown a man. You ent denying you're my son? Cos you did do, once, when you was a boy, and it hurt me worse than you'll ever know.'

He put out a hand and touched John's arm. His fingers moved up to the shoulder, feeling muscle, flesh, and bone. Briefly, he even touched John's face, and John endured it, surprised to find that fear had gone. The revulsion he felt as he looked into the hot-fleshed face and tried to meet the slithering eyes was because he saw his father's sickness. Felt it, smelt it, like a disease. But now he no longer felt afraid. He was a man and had a man's strength and courage. His father, once, had been very strong. Now John could have felled him with a blow. Somehow it made him pity him.

'You ent denying you're my son?'

'No.'

'You're working in Gale's smithy, ent you? I can see by your skin. That ent no proper work for you. It's not healthy. It's not right.'

'I like it,' John said. 'It's what I want.'

'You should ought to come to me. I need your help in running the mill.'

'I better prefer to be a smith.'

'You running off again?' Richard said.

'I've got an errand out at Brooks.'

'Running off! Turning your back! Can't you even stop and talk?' And, following John along the lane, he called out in his husky voice: 'Tell Will Gale I'll be even one day! I ent forgot what he done to me! I'll serve him out and make him pay!'

When John repeated this in the smithy, Will merely shrugged.

'He's been saying that for years. It ent come to much, I'm glad to say. But you'd better not mention it to your mother. It'll only start her worrying again.'

'I reckon he's going downhill.'

'I reckon he is,' Will agreed.

There were still plenty of stories told about Richard's strange and violent behaviour. Only a few weeks before, he had attacked old Jerry Trussler, delivering fish in Water Lane, and had tried to steal old Jerry's donkey.

'I gave you that donkey as a loan. I reckon it's time I had him back!'

There had been an exchange of blows. The parish constable had come and Richard had received a summons. Nothing much had been heard since, but some people said that Richard ought to be put away, and Jerry Trussler was one of them.

'I had to have stitches in my head! Fred'll tell you, he was there. And that ent the same donkey Lancy gave me years ago. This here donkey is only three!'

'Mad as a hatter,' Fred Byers said. 'He really ought to be put away.'

'But he ent never done no one any serious harm, has he, Fred?' said Joe Dancox. 'Apart from Jerry's stitches, that is?'

'Have we got to wait till he kills someone, then, before they ups and puts him away?'

* * *

One day in 1893, as John walked through Dingham on his way to Cockhanger Farm, he came on his father a second time, being teased by a crowd of children.

Richard's waggon stood in the road, and a sack of meal had fallen off. The sack was rotten and had burst open. Three or four boys were kicking it along the road. And while Richard lunged at them, others were at the back of the waggon, rocking it from side to side in the hope of dislodging another sack.

John descended on them in wrath, and, being quicker than his father, made himself felt with a few stinging slaps. Within a minute, the children had retreated to a safe distance, and John was helping his father to rope the sacks onto the waggon.

'You're a good boy, John. I knew you was. You're a good son to me, in spite of it all, and I shan't forget what you've done today. I shan't forget. You mark my words.'

Having secured his end of the rope, he got down on his haunches and began gathering up the loose bean-meal that had spilt in the road, scraping it up between his hands and throwing it into the burst sack. John watched him, ashamed to see him scuffling about, gathering meal and dirt together, and yet unwilling to leave him alone while the children watched from nearby. And after a while he too got down in the road and helped to scrape up the scattered meal, aware that two or three women had come to their doors, to join their jeering, sneering children.

'There, we've done our best,' he said, rising. 'I should move on if I was you.' He wiped his hands on his corduroys.

'Where are you heading for?' Richard asked. 'Maybe I can give you a lift.'

'No, I'm cutting across to Cockhanger Farm.'

'Suit yourself. Suit yourself. But you're a good son to me after all and I shan't forget what you done today.'

Richard drove off along the road and John, with his toolbag slung over his shoulder, took the pathway up to Skyte. He was gone until late in the afternoon, and when he returned to the smithy at five, the story of his meeting with his father had got there before him. Jim Pacey mentioned it.

'Seems you and your dad is getting pretty matey these days, from what Tommy Breton was telling us.'

'The kids was teasing him,' John said, and sought Will's gaze. 'A sack'd fallen off the waggon. I gave him a hand fixing the rope.'

'You don't have to explain yourself to me, John. There's plenty of people, I daresay, who will find it funny to watch how you act when you meet your dad. But you don't want to mind them. They ent worth the paper they're printed on.'

'I couldn't very well pass him by.'

'Of course you couldn't,' Will said. 'You got to do what you think is right.'

Some weeks later, on a rainy morning in July, Richard, with his waggon, drew up outside the smithy door. His mare had cast a shoe, he said, and he wanted John to see to it. He completely ignored Will, who had come out in case of trouble, and addressed himself only to John. He would wait, he said, while the job was done.

It was the first time Richard had come to the smithy on business for twelve years. John was rather at a loss, but, receiving a little nod from Will, he went ahead and did the work. Richard remained where he was, sitting up on the waggon in the rain, his coat-collar up and his hat-brim down. He made no move to get down and help when John took the mare out of the shafts, nor when he brought her back again, but sat hunched, perfectly still, a bundle of rags, apparently lifeless. But when John came round to the side to be paid, he sprang to life perkily and looked down in great surprise.

'Pay?' he said in a loud voice. 'What, pay my own son for

a fiddling little job like that, just putting one shoe on and nothing else? You're having me on, boy. You're pulling my leg!'

John went prickly hot all over. He felt the blood rush into his face. Behind him, in the smithy, all noise of work had stopped abruptly, and as he stood, trying hard to find his tongue, he knew that Will and his customers had come to the door. Richard, having achieved his object, pretended not to see them. As before, he spoke only to John.

'A son don't charge his father, boy. It's one of the perkses between two trades. I wouldn't charge *you* if you came to me with some corn to grind. Nor I don't expect to pay for a trifle of shoeing, neither, not when the smith is my own son.'

'I ent the master here,' said John, 'I'm only the apprentice.'

'You do a good job, though, I daresay?'

'I hope so, yes.'

'As good as your master would have done?'

'I dunno about that, I'm sure.'

'You did the work, not your master, boy. And you surely wouldn't charge your own dad?'

'Look here!' said John. 'Seems I'd better pay it myself.'

But Will stepped forward and stood at his side.

'No need for that, John. Let it go. Like your father said, it's only a trifle, nothing more. If he means to bring his trade here again, well, that'll be another matter. He can settle up at the end of the year.'

Richard looked directly at Will.

'I've got a long score to settle with you already and you needn't think that I've forgot. You stole my wife and son from me and turned them against me all these years, but now my boy is a grown man and I reckon he can think for hisself. We ent enemies, him and me. We're the same flesh and blood. We belong together. And I shall get him back again if it takes me a lifetime, I promise you that!'

He flicked at the ribbons and drove slowly down the road, round the bottom of the green, and back again up the far side, into the main road of the village. John and Will stood watching him go.

'I'm sorry about that,' John said. 'It's all my fault for helping him the other day.'

'Don't worry about it,' Will said. 'He's bound to feel sore, the way things are, and this is his way of getting back at me. It's only a fleabite, that's all. We must just bear it as best we can.'

Ellen, however, on hearing about the incident, was gravely troubled.

'Sometimes I wish we could go away from here,' she said. 'Right away, where Richard can't reach us.'

'Laws!' said Will. 'I shouldn't like that. I've lived in Dingham all my life.'

And young Peter, now eleven, looked at them all with his black-browed scowl.

'Why should we go away from here, just because of Dick Lancy? Who cares a wit for the Mad Miller?' And he turned to John. 'If Lancy wants you so bad,' he said, 'why not go and live with him and help him with running his old mill?'

'Because I don't want to,' John said.

'The mill'd be yours when your dad was dead. Seems to me you haven't thought.'

'That'd just about suit you, wouldn't it, eh?' And John, with a laugh, punched Peter's chest. 'I know how it is with you, my lad! – You want to take my place in the smithy!'

'Not me,' Peter said, with a shrug. 'My own place is waiting for me and I shall be in it come August time.'

'I pity that anvil!' John said, winking at Will. 'We shall see something soon, eh, Will, when our Peter starts work in the smithy?'

'By golly, yes!' Will agreed. 'The sparks'll be flying then, I'll be bound!'

And afterwards, alone with Ellen, he spoke to her about her fears.

'You don't really want to leave Dingham, do you, Nell?'

'It's Richard coming and pestering John. I'm always afraid

of what he'll do.'

'He won't do nothing. What can he do? I know he stirs us up a bit, but it's only a fleabite, that's all. I reckon it's something we've got to bear and it's little enough, all told, compared with how happy and comfortable we all are most of the time, ent it, now?'

Ellen, smiling, agreed with him. She put the matter out of her mind.

* * *

At the end of that summer, Peter started work in the smithy. He scorned staying at school until twelve and Will, for the sake of peace and quiet, gave in and let him have his way. His indentures were drawn up by the lawyer in Runston, and were locked away in Will's iron document-box which was kept, safe from thieves, on a ledge inside the kitchen chimney. And just as Peter's apprenticeship began, John's was drawing to a close.

It was a Saturday in September; a beautiful day, sunny and warm; and at four o'clock in the afternoon, Will called a halt to all work in the smithy. Followed by John, Peter, and Jim Pacey, he led the way out, up the green, to the open door of The Old Tap. There he called for the landlord, Shaw, who, knowing what was expected of him, came out with a gallon jug of beer and a fistful of tankards. The customers also came out and stood around watching as Will, with a certain dignity, took a rolled document from his shirt and gave it into John's hands.

'There's your indentures back again, that was drawn up and signatured seven years ago, all sealed and witnessed in the proper way by the lawyer chap in Runston town. You've served your time in the smithy with me and that there paper's a proof of it. You can go wherever you like with that and any smith will give you work, and I'll say in front of these witnesses that any smith will be lucky to have you.'

John, somewhat flushed, shook Will's hand. It took him a moment to clear his throat.

'I'd a lot rather stop on here.'

'That's what I hoped you'd say, my boy, and that's what we'll drink to, all of us. Now ale all round for everyone so's they can drink to my boy John.'

'Your very good health, John!' the onlookers said, raising their mugs.

'And yours!' said John. 'I'm much obliged.'

As he took his first draught, Peter put a hand under the mug and tilted it against John's mouth, so that the ale sloshed over his face and trickled down his throat and neck.

'Your very good health, John! Mind you don't choke!'

John untied his sweat-rag and wiped the ale from his face and throat.

'I'll give you choke in a minute!' he said. 'I'll put you under that there pump.'

'Oh, he's somebody now!' Peter said. 'Now he's got his indentures and all. It's tuppence to speak to him today!'

'Never mind, Peter,' said Fred Byers. 'You'll have your day, all in due course, and your dad will do the same for you.'

'I know that!' Peter said. 'Tell me something I don't know!'

Standing well away from the group for fear of John's retaliation, Peter drank from his pint tankard, and the older men watched, much amused, as his throat-muscles worked manfully and the tankard was drained to the very bottom.

'Be careful you don't fall in, my lad!'

'You're doing mightily, that you are, for a little tucker twelve years to be!'

Peter set his tankard down and wiped his mouth with the back of his hand.

'Time we was getting back to work.'

'I reckon it is,' Will agreed, but to John he said very casually: 'No need for you to hurry, boy. Have another drink on me and enjoy yourself while you got the chance.'

So John, it being his special day, lingered outside The Old Tap, talking to the Shaws and Billy Jukes and old Byers and Joe Dancox, and making his second mug of beer last. And as he stood there in the sun, one hand in the breast of his shirt, where the rolled indentures lay half-hid, Hannah Draycott came out of the cottage next to the church and walked past on her way to the shop. She carried a basket in one hand and a leather purse in the other.

'Nice day!' said John, nodding politely. 'Makes you feel glad to be alive.'

Something had happened to him today. He felt he could talk to anyone, even Hannah. And she perceived the difference in him. She eyed him warily as she passed.

'Nice day for drinking, seemingly.'

'A man must drink if he's got a thirst.'

'A man?' she said, and walked on.

'I shouldn't stand for that!' said Jukes. 'It's saucy, that is. You should answer her.'

'You're right and I shall,' John said, and, seeing that Hannah had stopped to read a poster on the wall outside the shop, he strolled along and tackled her. 'If I'm not a man, what am I?' he said. 'I surely ent a woman, I hope!'

Hannah turned and looked at him. Her eyes were a clear light shade of brown.

'A pint-pot in your hand doesn't make a man.'

'What does, however? You tell me that.'

'I've got errands to do for my aunt. I've got no time for gossiping.'

'Come along, now, I want to know. I'm turned nineteen and I'm fully growed and I've been shaving for donkey's years. If that don't make me a man, I should like to know what does.'

Hannah was cornered. He had her now. She was wishing she'd never made that remark, and it served her right, he told himself. But she was as cool as ever she was and her voice when she answered was quite unflurried.

'Perhaps a little common sense.'

'You think common sense would make me a man?'

'It would help,' she said, 'certainly.'

'Maybe you're right,' John said. He was enjoying himself today. He had suffered enough from her in the past, but now he was in command of himself and could match her coolness word for word. And he knew, furthermore, that the few men listening were on his side, willing him to win if only because this was his special day. 'The trouble is,' he said, 'how can us men have common sense when plainly you women've got it all?'

He then sauntered back to the grinning group at the inn door, taking his place there, a man among men.

'Now what was we talking about?' he said. 'Ah, yes, the cricket match – '

Behind him, the grocer's doorbell rang, and he knew Hannah Draycott had gone inside. He finished his drink and went back to the forge.

* * *

'Seven years!' Peter said. 'Seven years learning the trade. I shall be an old man like John by then! When am I really going to *start*?'

'I hope you're learning something already,' Will said indulgently.

'Oh, yes!' Peter said. 'I'm learning how to sweep the floor!'

'All in good time,' Will said, handing him the watering-can. 'Rome wasn't built in a day, you know, nor a blacksmith can't be made over-night.'

Peter, at the age of twelve, was exactly the image of his father, and the likeness grew stronger all the time. But although he had Will's face and features, the same straight black hair, the same square build, he had little of Will's easy-going temper, and little of Will's extreme patience.

'Why does it always have to be me that sweeps up the horse-muck and empties the ashes? Why always me and never John? I've already brought in the water, ent I? Why does it always have to be me?'

'The apprentice always does them jobs,' said Will. 'John done his share, by golly, yes, right up to the very day you came. Ah, and he made a lot less fuss about it than you, boy, I tell you straight.'

'Oh, John is a masterpiece, no doubt of that! The sun can't rise in that there sky without he gets the credit for it!'

'I knew he'd be in a mood,' said John. 'He tried my new cap on this morning, first thing, and no one could find him for half an hour!'

'I didn't try your rotten cap! I picked it up by mistake for my own.'

'Here, I'll give you a hand,' John said, and, turning the ashbin on its side, began to shovel out the ash, into the waiting wheelbarrow.

'That's Peter's job,' Will said, 'and you should leave him get on with it.'

'Just this once,' John said. 'He wants to watch you weld them bars.'

'I don't just want to watch,' Peter said. 'I want to help with making them tyres.'

'Well, you can't, and that's flat!' Will said. 'You'll do as you're told and watch, that's all, and see that you don't get in our way.'

Peter, scowling, went to the forge. He took up a pair of long-handled tongs and turned an iron bar in the fire. The red-hot coals were a-tremble with heat, and the iron itself was almost white, pulsing as though with a life of its own. *That* was where a smith's work lay; where he made his mark and showed his skill; and Peter felt the pulse of the iron, the same way he felt the pulse of his heart. The craft of it was in his bones. The knowledge of it was in his blood. It was all wrong that he should be held back like this, day after day, week in, week out. He could show them something, given the chance. Now if *he* was going to weld two bars –.

'Get away from that fire and leave that tarnal iron alone!' Jim Pacey roared, working the bellows. 'How many times've you got to be told?'

'Don't you shout at me!' Peter said. 'I ent going to stand for it! My Lord, I'm not!'

And, shedding his apron as he went, he dashed out of the smithy door. It was not the first time he had stormed out and left his work. They knew he would not be home until after dark, when his family were all in bed, and in the morning, sidling late into the smithy, he would take up the empty water-pails and go without a word to the pump.

'That boy!' Will would say, shaking his head. 'He'll learn, I suppose, but don't ask me when!'

*　　　　*　　　　*

Time for Peter seemed not to move. His first year at work in the smithy seemed the longest in his life. Even the second was not much better, for he was given only the simplest tasks, such as cutting old horseshoes up for tuckers, or cleaning old implements of their rust, or mending the neighbours' pots and pans. These tasks were hateful to him and one day when Pacey gave him a pair of sheep-clipping shears to grind he hurled them into a far corner.

'I'm sick to death of these fiddly oddlies! When am I going to do something worth doing?'

'The trouble with you is, you want to run before you can walk,' Jim Pacey said to him. 'You want to be a frog without serving your time as tadpole.'

'You seem to forget I'm Will Gale's son. My dad, my granddad, and right back for five generations, have all been blacksmiths in this place and all been masters of their trade.'

'Ah, and the line'll likely come to an end with you, lad, the way you're going.'

'What d'you mean?'

'Them cart-springs you mended yesterday and that there hinge you made last week – you should be ashamed of such shoddy work.'

'It warnt worth the labour, that's why. It was just to give me something to do!'

'That's how you learn, boy. That's how you learn. Every job's worth doing if you've got somebody paying for it.'

'Hah! Tuppence-ha'penny down the drain! I won't lose no sleep for that.'

'Jim's right,' Will said. 'If you don't buck up your ideas

a bit, you'll get no jobs to do at all. You must show yourself to be a smith in the making, and there ent much sign of it so far.'

'A smith in the making!' Peter sneered. 'That makes me laugh!'

But he went and retrieved the sheep-clippers and spent half an hour grinding them until, as he said, a man could have shaved with them, easily. He cared very much what his father thought of him. His work showed improvement for a while.

The trouble was that Peter, proud of being Will Gale's son, expected everything to come easily to him. The blacksmith's skill was his birth-right. It should come as naturally to him as walking and talking and drawing breath. He should not have to strive for it, as did the sons of lesser men, nor should he have to be ordered about by anyone but Will himself. When Will was out, he did as he liked, and he tried giving orders to Pacey and John. Pacey merely turned his back, and John laughed at him, saying: 'Right you are, young un! You show us how!'

Whereas John, from the very first, had approached each task with deep suspicion, sensing the problems, prepared for the worst, Peter would rush at it eagerly, thinking to toss off a piece of work with his father's quickness, his father's apparent lack of thought. Perhaps, had he been the only boy, it might have been different, but rivalry was a sharp spur that goaded him and destroyed his judgment. He was seven years younger than John and yet he expected to catch him up. After all, he was Will Gale's son, and John was not.

This was a favourite taunt of his, repeated often over the years, and on one occasion, Peter being by now sixteen, John rounded on him in a moment of utter exasperation.

'Yes, yes, we all know whose son you are! And we all know that it makes you something different from the rest of us, though what that is I don't like to say!'

Peter looked at him with a smile. He was pleased to have stung his brother for once. He made the most of it while he could.

'I'd rather be Will Gale's b——d,' he said, 'than Richard Lancy's son by marriage, and so would you if the truth was known.'

'Yes, well,' John said. His outburst had not been a serious one, but Peter's answer made him ashamed, and he was aware of Will nearby, watching and listening although hard at work. 'Yes, well, you're right there.'

At supper that evening, Peter referred to the incident. He looked at his mother and told her about it.

'Our John's been throwing it up to me that I'm a b——d. You want to watch out for yourself, mother, or who knows what he'll be calling *you.*'

'I shan't call her nothing,' John said. 'That other was just between you and me. I'll say I'm sorry if that's what you want, cos I never meant to hurt your feelings.'

'It's no odds to me,' Peter said. 'It's my mother's feelings that count, not mine.'

'Mother would never have known about it if you hadn't told her,' John said.

Ellen looked at her two sons and under her gaze they became sheepish. She looked across the table at Will and began speaking, quietly, about other things. No quarrel would last long in that household if she had anything to do with it, and within a few seconds, John and Peter were laughing together at her story of the currant cake that had disappeared.

'Where did you find it in the end, mother?'

'Upstairs, in the bedroom, on the bed. And your father's underwear, only just ironed, was in the cake-tin in the larder.'

'Seems like you're getting absent-minded, don't it, mother?'

'Yes,' Ellen said, with a little smile, 'I'm getting old.'

Again she looked across at Will and in the glance that passed between them, as John had often noticed before, there was a deepening of amusement, as though there were something beyond the particular joke of the moment, and only they had the key to it.

Watching his mother's face now and thinking of what she had just said, about getting old, he said to himself: Yes, well, perhaps it was true. She was a woman of forty-four. There were little lines about her eyes, there were traces of grey in her soft brown hair. But she was beautiful, he thought, and the sudden discovery took his breath. He saw her as though for the first time and he thought it must be some trick of the light or some soft fancy in himself. Then he looked from her to Will, and saw by the warmth in the man's eyes, smiling over the rim of his cup, that Will knew, and had always known, just how beautiful she was.

Chapter Twelve

John, growing older, had an extra keen sense of the closeness between his mother and Will. It had always been there from the very beginning: as a child he had warmed himself in its glow; depended upon it; drawn strength and assurance from it. But now, growing older, becoming more and more aware of his own manhood, he sensed the closeness in a different way. He understood it in his bones. He was often caught up in the little currents of humour and tenderness passing between them, and would turn away, smiling secretly to himself, with the warmth slowly spreading and growing inside him.

But afterwards he felt cut off. Alone. Restless. Full of unease. He would go for long walks, squaring up to his own aloneness, fighting a feeling of emptiness that he could not quite understand. Or he would work long hours in the forge, getting rid of his mood on the anvil. Work was the one fulfillable passion. The things he made were the one source of pride. He was a man and knew he had other men's respect. Surely that ought to be enough? He had the respect of women too. There were plenty of pleasant, pretty girls willing to stop and talk to him, with plenty of teasing, this way and that, and no commitment on either side. Why not take life as it came?

With Hannah Draycott, of course, it was different. She could not accept teasing, it seemed, but must always be on her dignity, taking a harmless joke amiss and turning it against you, adding a few extra barbs of her own. He and she were like tinder and spark together, though which was tinder and which was spark it would have been difficult to say.

Once, when John stood gossiping on the green with young Billy Jukes and a few others, Hannah came down the track from Neyes, herding the cows out to the pasture behind the church, for the Neyes fields were much scattered. The cows spread out over the green and began grazing, and the young men watched as Hannah, using a short stick, herded them back to the track again.

'Now there's a sight for sore eyes,' said young Billy Jukes, who, like his father, worked as a cowman at Rillets Farm. 'A prize bunch if ever there was one, especially the roan there, coming behind.'

'I'd pin a rosette on her with pleasure,' said his brother, Chris, admiringly.

'Shapely,' said Scowers, a youth of few words. 'Plenty of milk.'

'It's in the breeding,' said Georgie Byers. 'You can tell it a mile off, can't you, eh? It's wrote all over her, every inch.'

'She's got a nice swing to her, certainly. Style, that's the word, you can't mistake it. You can see it in the way she's swishing her tail.'

'I suppose,' said John, in an innocent voice, 'you are all talking about a cow?'

'Lumme, what else, for goodness' sake?'

'I only wondered, that's all, especially when you mentioned the tail.'

Hannah, coming behind the cows, shot John a glance. It was meant to make him feel very small.

'Nice day,' he said, nodding with exaggerated politeness.

'Is it?' she said. 'Seems to me there are too many *insects* about on days like this.'

'You're right there. The muggy weather brings them out.'

'It's idleness that brings them out.'

'You don't mean me by any chance?'

'Flies *will* sting, won't they?' she said. 'It's their nature to be annoying.'

'I reckon I'm a bit big for a fly.'

'I've seen bigger,' Hannah said, and tapped a cow on the rump with her stick.

'Eh, well, I'm sorry if I've annoyed you,' he said, 'but don't take it out on that poor cow.'

'It'd be a relief,' Hannah said, 'if flies would stick to their own midden.'

'B'zz, b'zz!' John said.

By now she was some little way ahead. The cows were moving slowly on, into the track that led past the church. She rested her stick on the roan's back.

'Seems she's got it in for you,' Billy Jukes said to John. 'I reckon you'd better watch your step.'

'I shall, never fear. I've got a healthy respect for my own skin.'

'You ent afraid of Hannah Draycott, are you, John?'

'Ent I?' said John. 'Well, I dunno!'

The other young men were much amused. They were still laughing when the group broke up. It was a marvellous joke to them that John, six feet tall, with a frame that was all hard bone and muscle, and a fist that could have felled an ox, should be afraid of Hannah Draycott, and the joke had soon gone round the village, enjoyed by young and old alike. John played up to it, in The Old Tap and out on the green. He had only to give a little solemn shake of the head and everyone would be in fits. And the joke, for him, had one great advantage. It took Hannah Draycott by surprise.

It was a day in the autumn of 1897, and John was out on the green, repairing the old iron seat that encircled the oak tree, watched by three elderly men who were waiting to sit on it to eat their lunch. Hannah passed on her way to the shop and Tommy Breton caught her arm.

'What've you done to our poor John, to frighten him the way you have?'

John straightened up, hammer in hand, and looked into Hannah's light brown eyes. For once, there was some uncertainty there, and the sight of it brought him a jolt of pleasure.

'Tell us, John,' said Tommy Breton, 'what is it about this young woman here that's got you shaking like a leaf?'

'Shaking?' said John. 'I ent shaking. Whatever next?' And he held out a hand, fingers stretched, that trembled as though with a terrible palsy. 'That's blacksmith's ague, that's what that is, and I'll thank you not to poke fun.'

'What's your nonsense today?' Hannah asked. 'Some childish jape again, is it?'

'Excuse me,' John said. 'I got business in the smithy.'

'Laws!' said Fred Byers, pulling him back. 'You ent running away, are you, John? What is it about her that scares you so?'

'I reckon maybe it's mostly her tongue.'

'Sharpish, you mean? Well, they're all like that.'

'Not all,' said John. 'There's one or two that're sweet enough.'

'How do you know? Have you had a taste?'

'I can't answer that,' said John.

'He's a good chap, our John,' Fred Byers said to Hannah. 'There's plenty of other girls in Dingham ready enough to be kind to him.'

'There are some girls,' Hannah said, 'who're silly enough for anything.'

'Oh, she's got it in for you, John! There's no doubt of that!'

'The best thing for me,' John said, 'is just to be sure and keep out of her way.'

'That,' Hannah said, 'is all I ask.'

'There!' John exclaimed, as she walked away. 'And you wonder why I'm scared of her!'

The joke lasted a few days and was good for many another laugh. Will got to hear of it in the smithy.

'What's this about you being scared of Hannah Draycott?'

'Oh, that! It's just a joke.'

'There's many a true word spoken in jest.'

'Darnit!' said John. 'I ent *really* scared of her.'

'I reckon our John is smutten on her,' Peter said, knowingly. 'Either that or she's smutten on him.'

John threw back his head and laughed.

'You know all about such things, of course!'

'I know enough not to waste my time getting tangled with girls.'

'I should think so too. At least until you've begun to shave!'

'I been shaving for two whole years!'

'And it still don't make the whiskers grow!'

'At least I ent scared of Hannah Draycott!'

'You got no reason,' John said. 'She don't hardly notice little boys.'

But the joke about Hannah had had its day. John was sick of it, and of her. It was easy enough to avoid meetings and that he now resolved to do. The smithy was busy that autumn and winter. He worked long and hard, day in, day out.

* * *

Peter's work was improving slowly. He no longer let the iron burn, nor did he spoil it on the anvil. He had learnt to think before tackling a task; to consider its needs and guard against problems and sometimes he even accepted advice.

Physically, he seemed to develop in a burst. At fifteen he had been a boy but at sixteen he was a man, and he was determined to be treated as such. He grew no more after that and never attained his father's height, but he was heavier and broader than Will, and somehow, because of this stocky build, he looked a lot older than his years. His face, like Will's, was broad and square-jawed, and his eyebrows were even thicker and blacker, giving him a scowling look. Unlike Will, he rarely smiled, and when he did, as Jim Pacey once remarked, it was nothing more than a show of teeth. Amusement, pleasure, satisfaction, showed as a wicked gleam in his eyes, or was heard as a chuckle deep in his throat. But his smile, as Jim said, meant he was probably hating your guts and thinking of some way to do you down.

In the new year of 1898, Will had an order from Mr Staverton of Dinnis Hall for scythe-blades, billhooks, hay-knives and spades, a dozen of each for the two Hall farms, with two new ploughs and two new harrows. Will was going to divide the work between the four of them, but Peter had his own ideas.

'Why not let John and me do this, half and half of all the items, while you and Jim do something else?'

'All right,' Will said. 'Seems me and Jim can soon retire!'

Peter took immense pains in making his scythe-blades, hooks, knives and spades, and put his initials, very small, on the handle-end of every one. Pacey saw him doing this and gave a little scornful grunt.

'You needn't bother putting your mark cos anyone with half an eye can see which is yours and which is John's.'

'What the heck do you mean by that?'

'I mean exactly what I say.'

'What's wrong with these tools, I'd like to know? Just look at them and tell me what's wrong!'

'They're all right,' Pacey said, 'but you've got a long way to falter yet before your work is as good as John's.'

'You can talk!' Peter said. 'Just a journeyman all your life!'

And he walked out, into the store-shed behind the smithy,

to vent his feelings in heaving iron bars about. There was no love lost between him and Jim Pacey, for Jim made no bones about showing which of the two boys he preferred.

'It's a funny thing,' he said to John once. 'Peter's the spit of Will in looks but as for everything else, well, you're more Will's son than he'll ever be, even though you ent related.'

When it came to making the ploughs and harrows, Peter refused to have anything to do with it. The task had gone sour on him. He told John he had changed his mind.

'Seems my work ent good enough yet. You can d— well do it by yourself. I'm still a new scholar where smithing's concerned – at least according to old Pacey.'

'Why don't we do them together?' John said.

'No, no. You go ahead. I don't want to spoil your work. You're the one with all the skill.'

'D—— all!' John said. 'I'm seven years older than you, boy. I've been smithing a lot longer and I d— well *ought* to be better than you.'

'I suppose so. Yes. Maybe you're right.'

'You expect too much of yourself, too soon. You're only sixteen. I'm twenty-three. You'll catch up in skill in time, but you've got to work at it yet a while.'

'Oh, I shall work at it!' Peter said. 'But I ent going to make them ploughs and harrows. Not till I know I can do a good job.' And then, sincerely, without spite: 'I shouldn't want poor work going out of this smithy, specially not to Dinnis Hall.'

Will at this time was a man of fifty. Old for a blacksmith, he would say, and often he talked of giving it up; of taking a farm of a few acres, somewhere not too far away, and leaving the boys to run the smithy. But he hung on because of Peter.

'I'll see you through your time, boy, and then I'll look round for a little holding. That's another couple of years. You'll have taken up your indentures by then. You'll be your own man, along with John, and the two of you will work in the forge while your mother and me retire to our farm.'

'What about Pacey?' Peter asked.

'Why, he'll stop on with you, of course, so long as he wants to, that is.'

'I'd say he was getting past it, myself. He must be ninety in the shade.'

'Jim's all right,' John said. 'We surely ent going to sling him out.'

'You should start looking out for a farm pretty soon,' Peter said to his father, 'so's you got it in mind when the time comes.'

'You're right,' Will said, 'I shall have to ask questions here and there.

But the months went by, spring and summer, and somehow the questions never got asked. There was plenty of time, Will said, and the day would come soon enough.

'Our John gets about quite a bit these days. He might get to hear of a little place that'll just about suit your mother and me.'

* * *

John often travelled about the district to jobs of work on outlying farms. He would sometimes leave at four in the morning and not return till eleven at night. He liked to get out and about like this, and whenever such work was in the offing he was sure to volunteer.

'Seems you like to get out,' Will said. 'I suppose it's because you get the chance of meeting up with Hannah now and then.'

'Oh no it ent! She's nothing to me.'

'Nobody'd blame you,' Will said. 'Hannah's grown up a fine-looking girl. There's no one to match her for miles around.'

'And don't she know it!' John exclaimed. 'The way she walks past us chaps sometimes, you'd think we warnt human, to see her looking down her nose.

'You young chaps!' Will said. 'You and young Jukes and all that lot, when you stand about in a group out there, have you ever thought how awkward it is for a girl like Hannah going by?'

'There's other girls go by the same. Not all of them give theirselves such airs.'

'In that case,' Will said, casually, 'you'd do better to get yourself tied up in knots over one of them instead.'

'I've told you before – Hannah Draycott is nothing to me. And as for our making it awkward to pass, it'd take more than that to put *her* out!'

But one summer morning, at ten o'clock, when Hannah came round the green as always, delivering the morning milk, John remembered Will's words, and, instead of his usual sarcastic greeting, gave her only a brief nod. He and Peter were out on the green, removing the rusty iron tyres from a set of four waggonwheels, and young Billy Jukes, with his brother, Chris, stood lounging about nearby. They watched as Hannah, with the pony and float, stopping at intervals on the way, made her slow progress round the green, and when she drew up at the Dysons' cottage, and the old lady came out with her jug, Billy Jukes called out to her.

'If I give you a penny, can I have a sup? I've got a throat like a thirsty cat.'

Hannah ignored him. She filled Mrs Dyson's jug from the churn and drove on to the next cottage.

'She's deaf today,' Billy said.

'Offer her tuppence,' Chris said.

'Leave her alone,' John said. He was watching Hannah's face and remembering what Will had said. 'Leave her alone, both of you.'

'I haven't touched her yet,' Billy said.

'Be careful in case she touches *you*!' said Chris.

'I dunno that I'd mind that.'

'Ask if she'll meet you up at the huts.'

'What's the use if she's stone deaf?'

'You might try asking by making signs.'

'No, it's no use. She's taking no notice of us chaps today. We're just the dust beneath her feet.'

'*I'll* make her take notice!' Chris said, and flipped a pebble at the pony's rump.

Hannah had just stepped onto the float when the pony kicked out with both hind feet. She had no chance of taking the reins. It was all she could do to keep her balance and stop the churn from overturning. The pony pulled off with a violent jerk and would have bolted down the road, but John ran forward and took the bridle and in an instant all was well.

'Are you all right?' he asked, as Hannah, in a temper, groped for the reins.

'It's no thanks to you if I am!' she said. 'You and your stupid childish games!'

'I ent bothered about your thanks but Posy here would've been in Runston High Street by now if it warnt for me upping and stopping her.'

'And whose fault was it she started to bolt in the first place?'

'Not mine for sure,' John said.

'I suppose that pebble fell from the sky?'

'Are you calling me a liar?'

'Leave go of that bridle and let me get on. I've lost enough time because of you.'

'I want to know if you think I'm a liar.'

'What does it matter what I think? It was either you or one of them. There's nothing to choose between none of you!'

'It matters to me,' John said, 'and I'm waiting to hear you say you're wrong.'

'I beg your pardon, humbly, I'm sure!'

'I can see exactly how humble you are. It's very nearly making you spit.'

'I've said I'm sorry and now I'd like to get on with my round.'

'I was going to offer a helping hand.'

'Oh, no! You've done enough!'

'All right. Just as you please. It was only a friendly thought, that's all, to make amends as you might say.'

John let go of the pony's bridle and stepped back a little

way. He put his hands in the waist of his apron. The anger still burning in Hannah's face was enough to set light to a bunch of green sticks, but her glance, instead of scorching him, only made him calmer still. This was what happened, he told himself, when a fellow did her a good turn. But he saw the milk that had splashed all over her pinafore and knew that he, in her place, would have felt the same.

'I should simmer down if I was you,' he said, 'or the milk in that churn will be on the boil.'

He watched her move on to the Beards' cottage, then he returned to his work on the wheels. The Jukes brothers grinned at him.

'That was a darn fool thing to do, throwing that pebble,' he said to Chris. 'Supposing the girl'd broke her neck?'

'Why should she, indeed, when you was here to save the day?'

'It *was* a darn fool thing,' said Peter. 'We very nearly had no milk.'

* * *

In November that year, Will was called out to Eddydrop Farm, where the threshing-machine had broken down, and John went with him to help with repairs. The work was done in a couple of hours, but when the thresher was going again, Will, climbing down from the platform, missed his footing and fell against the revolving fly-wheel. His forearm caught against the shaft and the flesh was laid open from the wrist to the elbow. Dr Nathan came out to the farm, cleaned the wound with carbolic acid, and stitched it up on the spot. He told Will to go straight home and to put the arm in a sling at once.

'See that you do no work for a while and give that arm a chance to heal.'

'It's lucky for me,' Will said, 'that I got my two boys to carry on while I take a holiday, ent it, eh?'

That evening, at home, he sat in his chair beside the fire and smoked his pipe like a man of leisure. Peter had fetched him a quart jug of ale and John had brought him an ounce of tobacco, and there he sat, like a bishop, he said, living off the fat of the land while his two boys went back to work in the forge. He was rather self-conscious, wearing the big white calico sling: 'Just like a pudding in a cloth!'; and every so often he would take a peek into the folds: 'I'd say that's just about boiled to a turn!'

Ellen watched over him anxiously and brought cushions to put at his back. She could see that the arm was giving him pain.

'I've always hated threshing-machines – you might have been killed,' she said to him.

'I ent so easy to kill as that. But I'm getting clumsy in my old age, missing my footing like that.'

'Are you quite comfortable now? Is there anything you'd like?'

'I'd like for you to sit in your chair and for us to talk a little while, just the two of us, all by ourselves. That don't often happen nowadays, not since the boys've grown to be men. We can't pack them off to bed no more and have the hearthplace to ourselves, the way we did when they was small. So you sit down there, where I can see you, and let's make the most of it while it lasts.'

'Very well,' Ellen said, and sat in her chair opposite, looking at him in the light of the fire. 'There, I'm sitting, does that suit?'

'Remember them days when you first came? How we sat of an evening, just like this, with little John asleep upstairs? I used to wonder what'd happened to me, a woman and child all of a sudden, under my roof and in my care. Yet somehow I felt it was all meant to be. I felt I'd been chosen to take you in. And whenever I look at you, like I am now, I think to myself, "She's mine, she's mine".'

'Yes. Well. And so I am.'

'I dunno that I deserve the happiness I've got,' he said. 'All I know is, I'd fight tooth and nail to make sure I keep it.'

'You don't need to fight,' Ellen said.

'Just as well, ent it, seeing I've got a gammy arm?'

John, coming into the kitchen a while later, was struck by the way they sat together, with the lamp not yet lit, although it was after eight o'clock, and only the firelight on their faces. He was struck by the way they smiled at each other; by the fact that for once his mother's tireless hands were lying idly in her lap; and although there was silence in the room, he felt himself an intruder there, a trespasser on private ground.

'Your mother's been making a fuss of me,' Will said. 'I shall get to like being laid up if I ent careful.'

'How're you feeling?' John asked.

'Right as rain, boy, right as rain. You just finished in the smithy?'

'I have, yes, but Peter's still at it and will be for hours. He's doing that stove for Mr Grey.'

'Well, draw up a chair, John, and sit yourself down. Get a mug and share my ale.'

'No, I ent stopping,' John said. 'I thought I'd take a walk up the hill and give my lungs a bit of an airing.'

The feeling of trespass was very strong. He suddenly saw his mother and Will as two people with a life of their own. The warmth they created in the home, which he and Peter took so much for granted, sprang from the secret tenderness that a man and a woman shared together. Never in his life had John been witness to caresses between them: their warmth had all been outward-given, filling the house and flowing over the two boys, while their own needs had been met in secret; but now, just this once, he felt he had blundered in where he was not wanted, so he made his excuse and went out into the darkness, leaving them alone together, sitting in the firelight.

His walk took him right to the top of the hill, which was blanketed in descending cloud, and where he disturbed the roosting lapwings who cried out, peewee, before settling again on the ground. He came down out of the cloud and took the footpath across Neyes Farm, over fields of plough and stubble, into the pasture near the house. A light shone in a window there and the dogs barked at him from the yard. His footsteps pounded the steep stony track.

Passing the end of the old cartshed, he almost collided with someone turning in from the green. It was Hannah Draycott, wearing a cape, leading two goats on a short rope rein.

'Whoa, there!' John said. 'Did I give you a fright?'

'You frightened the goats more than me.'

'I remember them goats,' he said, grinning. 'I reckon I'd better keep out of their way.'

'They're not the same ones,' Hannah said, and although he could not clearly see her face, he knew by her voice that she was smiling.

'You remember, then? Although it was such an age ago?'

'*You* remember. Why not me?'

'I've got good cause. One of em went and catched me bending.'

'These two are quiet. You're safe with them.'

'How long *is* it, that other time? Donkey's years if you ask me! Twelve at least, maybe longer.'

'Goat's years,' Hannah said, and they both laughed, making a grey fog with their breath.

The two goats were leaning against them, one against John and one against Hannah. He put out a hand and fondled each of them in turn.

'Funny our meeting like this,' he said, and then, realizing the foolishness of his remark, he became quite dumb, hoping that Hannah would not ask why.

'Yes, it is funny, for I wanted to ask about Will's arm.'

'It's not too bad. So he says, anyway. Did you just drop in at the forge?'

'I did look in, but that's as far as I dared go. Your brother Peter looked very busy, and I didn't like to call at the cottage.'

'Lucky we met, then, chancelike and all. I'll tell Will you was asking about him.'

'Yes, do, and wish him well.'

'You know what I think?' John exclaimed. 'I think we've made history today. It's the first time we've met without having words.'

'We'd better make a note of the date.'

'Red letter day!' he said with a laugh. 'Put a circle round it, eh?'

There was a silence, and he wished he could see the girl's face, but the mist and the darkness were too close, and her loose hood cast a deep shadow. He knew she was smiling, certainly, but what sort of smile might it be, he wondered, and was she mocking him even now? The goats were beginning to stamp their feet. He saw the girl's hands as she shortened the rope.

'Well,' he said, 'I'll say goodnight.'

'Yes,' she said, 'I'd better get on.'

'We're late birds tonight, you and me.'

'Yes. Well. I'll say goodnight.'

'I'll give Will your message about his arm.'

'Yes. That's right. Wish him well.'

'Goodnight!' he called, as she led the two goats into the darkness, and her voice came back to him: 'Goodnight!'

On the far side of the green, a dim light still showed in the smithy doorway, shining out on the squirming mist, and the chink of iron striking iron told him that Peter was still at work. John thought he would look in and tease his half-brother; Peter was a demon for work these days; but as he approached the open door, a man stepped out from the shadows nearby and addressed him by name. It was his father, Richard Lancy.

'I heard a rumour Will Gale was hurt.'

'Yes,' John said, 'he hurt his arm.'

'Nothing more? I heard it was worse. He ent nearly dead, then, the way I was told?'

'Far from it, I'm thankful to say.'

'Ah, the devil looks after his own, so they say. But I'm thankful, too, that he ent dead, cos I've got a score to settle with him and I should be sorry if he was to go and get hisself killed before I'd a chance to pay him out.'

'After all this time?' John said. 'Do you still bear your grudge, after all these years?'

'I'm like the man in the old tale. He kept a stone in his pocket for ten years, turned it over once or twice, and kept it another ten years, to throw at the man that done him harm. I reckon I'm the same sort. I don't forget things, no more than him, and I've got a stone in my pocket, too.'

'Can't you forget it and leave Will alone?'

'I might,' Richard said. 'I might at that.' And in the dim smoky light from the smithy doorway, his grey-bearded face was eager and watchful. 'If you was to come back home with me and help me out with running the mill, I'd say no more against Will Gale and I'd throw my stone away for good.'

John impatiently shook his head. He made as though to turn away.

'The mill would be yours,' Richard said. 'Don't that count for nothing with you? You was born to the miller's trade. It's your proper place, where you belong.'

'My work is here, in the smithy,' John said, 'and my home is here, in this cottage.'

'Home!' Richard said, in a hollow voice. 'And what home have I got, down at the mill? No wife! No son! No company! Nothing to take a pride in at all. *He's* took it all, what I ever had. Him in there behind them shutters. It ent enough that your mother gave him a son of his own. He's still got to keep his claws on *you*! And you wonder that I bear a grudge?'

'He don't stop me coming to you. I'm my own man, I decide for myself.'

'Then you should decide to do what's right. What sort of son denies his own father?'

'You seem to forget you turned us out, my mother and me, that winter's night. I was only a little chap then, but I ent forgot what you done to us, and I reckon you've got no further claim.'

'Now who's the one that's bearing a grudge?'

'I'm sorry,' John said, 'but I ent coming whatever you say.'

'Right so!' Richard said. 'Right so! You've had your chance! You won't get another so easily! I ent got time for coaxing you round. Why the h— should I? My own flesh and blood!'

In his anger, as he talked, he turned away many times, and each time turned back, swinging his arms, until at last he put up his fist in front of John's face.

'You can deny me if you like but just you be sure and remember this! – I've still got a stone in my pocket, ready to throw at Will Gale, and when the right moment comes, he shall have it, you mark my words!'

When at last he had trudged away, John turned and went into the smithy. Peter had stopped work now and was sweeping the floor.

'Was that Lancy's voice I heard? What's he want by any chance?'

'Oh, the usual,' John said. 'About the mill and all that. About what he's going to do to Will.'

'You surely ent worried over that!'

'I dunno if I am or not.'

'He's been singing that same old song for years. He's off his hinges. Cuckoo, that's what. You don't want to take no notice of him.'

'No, well, I don't,' John said, 'but I wish he'd shut up about it all the same.'

* * *

A few days later, Will was at work in the smithy again, obliged to go carefully with the injured arm but refusing to wear the calico sling.

'This arm's got to learn who's master,' he said. 'It'll only get soft if I molly-coddle it overmuch.'

That afternoon, Hannah Draycott looked in at the smithy door, sent by her menfolk to ask about Will.

'I take that kindly,' Will said, 'but are you sure it was really me you came to see?'

'Why, has anyone else hurt an arm?' she asked, and left

without glancing in John's direction.

'Laws!' Will exclaimed. 'Did I say the wrong thing?'

'I dunno, I wasn't listening,' John said.

The following Sunday, after dinner, wearing his suit of dark brown serge and his best shirt with a new white collar, John took his corduroy cap from the peg and brushed it on the sleeve of his jacket.

'Where you off to?' Peter asked.

'I feel like a good long walk on the hill.'

'Shall I spruce up and come along with you?'

'Yes, if you like,' John said.

'No, I don't think so,' Peter said. 'I've got an idea I'd be in the way.'

'If you must be talking rot . . .'

'Strikes me you've forgotten something. You ent got a flower in your coat.'

'Get back to your kennel!' John said, and went out, putting on his cap.

All the way up the steep hill track, along the edge of the earthworks, and down again by the narrow winding sheep-paths, he drew deep breaths of clean air, for that was his purpose in coming there, to rid his lungs of the smithy smoke. The day was a warm one for November, and although he often stopped in his walk, looking down on the village below, all landmarks were hidden under a haze.

'I can't even see Grannie Naylor's bonnet!' he would say if anyone came up the path, and in his mind he heard their laughter. He was full of little jokes today. He could talk to anyone. Anyone at all. He could tell them what was in his mind.

Then, suddenly, down below, Hannah Draycott appeared on the track, coming slowly up the hill. He knew who it was immediately, even though they were some way apart. He knew her by her swinging walk; by the easy way she carried herself; by the dark blue jacket and dress she wore; by the two black sheepdogs at her heels. He knew her by her shining hair.

Any moment now they would meet. He was walking very quickly indeed, the steepness of the hillside lengthening his stride, his boots crunching and slithering on the loose stones of the rough track. He was only a few yards from her and now his feet were refusing to stop. They were bearing him onward all the time; closer and closer; then swiftly past; and he was looking back at her, over his shoulder, a foolish grin on his face, a hand raised in casual greeting.

'I'll be late for tea if I don't watch out! I reckon it must be nearly four!'

If Hannah answered, he failed to hear her, for he was already some way past. But in his mind's eye he could see her face at the moment of meeting: a hint of colour in her cheeks; a shy glance, but perfectly steady; the beginnings of a smile that came to nothing; and surprise when she saw he was not going to stop.

His own face was on fire. He was cursing himself for being a fool. And the moment he was out of sight, screened by a clump of oaks and beeches, he stopped dead, grinding his teeth. Late for tea! What a thing to say! Like a little boy going home in a hurry from Sunday school! And, going up to a beech tree, he struck at its trunk with both his fists.

There was one thing about it, he told himself. If she thought he had come to the hill just on the chance of meeting her, well, she knew better now! But – late for his tea! Surely he could have hit on something better than that!

The fault was Hannah's, more than his. It was something to do with her proud swinging walk; with the steady way she looked at you, her light brown eyes full of unknown thoughts; it was something in the way she smiled. Yes, the fault was hers, for being a woman. There was a certain strangeness in her, a holding out against such as he, even while she walked on the hill, which nobody surely ever did without a reason.

He turned left through the clump of trees, and left again, back up the hill. Hannah by now should have reached the top. She might be looking down from the fort. But instead she was only a hundred yards off, sitting on a log beside the pond, leaning forward a little way and drawing a stick through the weeds in the water. The two sheepdogs lay nearby.

For a while he stood, just watching her, taking time to gather his wits, for he had to think of something to say. But she raised her head and saw him there, and, in spite of the hundred yards between them, he felt he could see her plain as plain. He could see her eyes and their expression: questioning, yet knowing the answer. He could see that her lips were slightly parted: not in a smile but as though she had taken a hurried breath.

For a moment he even saw himself, a dark figure, as Hannah must see him, standing above her, against the sky, and he felt the silence and stillness between them, across the reeds and feathery grasses, touched by the misty autumn sunlight. Removing his cap, he began walking down towards her, and as he went, it occurred to him that he still hadn't thought of anything to say. But now it no longer seemed to matter. Hannah was sitting waiting for him. Words would come if he gave them a chance. And sure enough, when he sat beside her on the log, and stooped to pat each of the dogs, and Hannah took care not to look too directly into his face, talking was not so difficult after all.

'I came back.'

'Yes. So I see.'

'You don't object to my sitting here?'

'No. Of course not. But what about getting home to your tea?'

'Blast the tea! The tea can wait.'

'If you say so,' Hannah said.

'Yes, I do say so. I mean it, too.'

Their glances met just long enough for each to see that the other was smiling. Then they looked at the water again and he watched as she trailed her stick through the weeds.

'What're you hoping for, fishing like that? An old boot?'

'They say there's treasure on this hill. Maybe it's here, in the tinker's pond.'

'No, it ent there,' John said.

'How do you know?' Hannah asked.

'We found it, that's why, Will and me, when I was a young un, six years old.'

And he told her about the Christmas log, with the six new pennies hidden in it, bright and shining in the cracks.

'You must be very fond of Will.'

'I suppose so. Yes. You could say that. He's a good man, you know, even though – '

'Even though what?'

'Well. You know how it is with him and my mother.'

'I've never heard anyone speak against Will.'

'No. Maybe not. It's my mother they speak against, mostly, I think. It's always the woman that gets the blame.'

'That's true,' Hannah said. 'Us women are not allowed to breathe. We're supposed to be saintly all the time.'

'Not too saintly,' John said.

'Just saintly enough to please you men?'

'We've got our ideas, I daresay, on how a woman ought to behave.'

'And we've got our ideas about you men.'

'H'm,' he said, and became silent.

But the silence no longer caused him unease, as it would have done in the recent past. He no longer felt he must say something teasing or manly or smart. It was enough to be sitting with Hannah in the sun, an understanding growing between them, and a certain trust.

He was looking at her all the time now. He was willing her to look at him. For if she faced him and met his gaze, he would learn something important to him. He would see it plainly in her eyes.

'Hannah,' he said, in a quiet voice, and she turned towards him, meeting his gaze. The stick she was holding fell from her hands.

Chapter Thirteen

It was a day soon after Christmas. In the smithy, the Eddydrop horses were in for shoeing, and the two carters, Fossett and Spring, stood near the shoeing-stall, watching Will work. The big grey mare, Jessamy, was having her near hind foot trimmed, and two village mongrels, Tiny and Spot, were running about just out of range, waiting for the parings that fell from the hoof.

The mare was docile; her foot rested peacefully in Will's lap; and he, as he worked with his short sharp knife, caught the pairings in his left hand and hurled them towards the open doorway. The two dogs sprang, snapping and snarling, and each went off with a sliver of hoof, to consume it outside on the green. Will called across the smithy to John.

'Close that door, if you please, John. I don't want them rascals back in here till I've got these horses out of the way.'

John, who was emptying a drum of oil into the oil-trough, failed to hear Will's request. It had to be shouted twice more. Then, red-faced, he shut the door.

'He ent rightly with us these days,' said Jim Pacey. 'His mind goes a-wandering. Don't ask me where.'

'It takes some chaps that way,' said Will.

'What does?' asked John.

'Courting,' said Will, working at Jessamy's hoof with a rasp.

'I dunno what you're talking about.'

'No more don't I, boy. No more don't I. It's just these rumours been going about these past few weeks.'

'Rumours? Hah! You know what you can do with them!'

'Yes,' said Will, 'I can use 'em to light the fire in the morning.'

The two carters were much amused. They watched John as he went to and fro.

'Is he courting in earnest?' Fossett asked. 'Or is he only trying his wings? And who's the girl or can I guess?'

'Ask him yourself,' Will said.

'I can't do that. He might take offence. Some young chaps is funny like that. They keep so close and secret about it, the first thing you know is, they got three kids.'

'I can tell you who it is,' said Peter, turning a horseshoe in the fire.

'You be quiet!' John said. 'And for pity's sake leave them shoes as they are. You're always so tarnal *busy*, boy!'

'It's somebody with an aitch and a dee,' Peter said, enjoying himself.

'An aitch and a dee?' Fossett said, and made a great show of removing his cap and scratching his head. 'Could be anyone, couldn't it?' he said.

'I was never much good at spelling,' said Spring, 'but I daresay the dee'll be an ell before long, eh, John?'

But John, with a shrug, merely walked away. It was a pity, he told himself, that folk could not mind their own business.

Later that morning, when the carters and their horses had gone, and John was shovelling up the dung, a boy came in and gave him a note. Puzzled, he took it to the door to read, while Peter, Will, and Jim Pacey all hung around, watchfully.

'She's sending him notes now,' Peter remarked. 'It must be pretty serious between them, for her to do a thing like that.'

'It's not from a her. It's from a him.'

'Glory be! Whatever next?'

'It's from my father,' John said, and handed the note to Will to read. 'Seems he's bad with the asthma, he says. He wants me to go and stay with him and give him a hand with running the mill.'

In his note, which was scribbled on the back of a bill, Richard asked John to come at once. His illness had taken his strength, he said, and the mill stood idle for lack of help. 'If you don't come and give me a hand, to tide me over till I'm well, I shall be a ruined man.'

'What d'you think?' John asked, as Will handed back the note.

'Seems pretty genuine, I would say. I'd heard he was getting the asthma bad. One or two folk've told me that.'

'Then you think I should go and do as he asks?'

'I dunno what to say to that. If you want to go, that's up to you.'

'I don't want to go. It's the last thing I want. But maybe I ought to. I wish you'd say.'

Unhappily, he stared at Will, but Will was reluctant to give advice.

'You know how things are between me and your dad. I reckon you've got to decide for yourself.'

'Yes. You're right. I reckon I have.'

'I'll tell you what,' Will said. 'Seems to me you should ask your mother.'

So Ellen, during their midday meal, had to give judgment on the matter, and John saw by her clouded face that she was as unhappy about it as he.

'I don't like the thought of your going there, after the threats Richard has made, but he is your father and I suppose he's got some right to ask for your help. But you're a grown man and as Will says, it's up to you decide for yourself.'

'I think I should go,' John said. 'It's only for a week or two, and he's got no one else to turn to for help. I'd better go up and pack a few things.'

He rose, having eaten little food, and pushed his chair in under the table. The thought of the mill, like a dark prison, and the thought of his father, sick as he was in mind and body, filled him with a kind of dread, and he would have given anything to be rid of the burdensome sense of duty.

'I wish to Heaven he hadn't asked me!' he said, and the words burst out against his will. 'I wish to heaven he'd leave me alone!'

'Strikes me you're daft,' Peter said, 'going where you don't want to go.'

'No, he's not daft,' Ellen said. 'John is doing what he thinks is right.'

'Oh, he's a great one for doing what's right, our John! But what about us others in the smithy, having to do his work for him, while he plays the miller down at Pex Mill?'

'Peter, be quiet!' Will said. 'What're you talking such rubbish for?'

'I'll go and pack,' John said. 'I may as well get down there at once.'

A little while later he left the cottage and set off across the green. Peter stepped out from behind the oak.

'You're going the wrong way,' he said. 'That's not the way to Pex Mill.'

'I've got a call to make first.'

'Going to say a fond farewell?'

'What're you on about?' John asked.

'I'll tell you what!' Peter said. 'I'll go up to Neyes myself if you like and do what I can to comfort Hannah. I can take over where you've left off. After all, if I've got to do your work in the smithy, I might as well do it elsewhere as well. She's maybe a bit on the old side for me but I daresay we'll get along all right – '

'Look here!' John said. 'I don't much like the way you talk. I ent going to listen to nothing more. If you can't talk about Hannah with some respect, you can d— well keep your mouth shut! Otherwise I'll shut it for you!'

'You *are* in a temper and no mistake.'

'I ent too well pleased, I must admit.'

'You shouldn't take it out on me, just cos you've got to go to the mill. I was only joking. I meant no harm.'

Peter, amused at John's bad temper, was suddenly smiling. He was showing his teeth, as Jim would say. Those beautiful teeth, very white and strong, square and even and all of a size.

'We ent going to part bad friends, I hope?'

'You talk as though I was going for good.'

'You never know!' Peter said. 'You might take a shine to the miller's trade and stop there for good.'

'Oh, no, not me! I shall be back in a week or two, or maybe even sooner than that. You don't get rid of me so easy as that, my lad!'

And John swung off across the green, a few belongings in a bag, slung by its handles over his shoulder.

* * *

The day was a dull one, much overcast, but the weather was still unusually mild, and under the trees in Berry Lane, as John and Hannah walked there, the midges were thick on the windless air.

'I don't want to go to the mill, but I couldn't hardly say no, could I?'

'Of course you couldn't,' Hannah said.

'I doubt if I shall see you much, for a week or two at any rate.'

'Surely you won't be working every minute of the day?'

'I dunno. Maybe not. But I'd just as soon stick it out, down there at the blasted mill, and get it all over as you might say.'

'All right. It's up to you.'

Hannah felt his unhappiness. She put a hand in the crook of his arm.

'The time will soon go – what's a couple of weeks out of a whole lifetime?' she said.

'I'd give anything in the world to have it over and done with, though, and be back in the smithy where I belong. I'm no miller! I'm a smith. Always will be, come what may!'

'Very well,' Hannah said, teasing him for his vehemence. 'No one's trying to persuade you any different.'

'It was just something Peter said. Oh, I dunno! I'm feeling

sore. I don't like my life getting upset like this.'

'You're getting too set in your ways,' she said.

John stopped and turned towards her. They looked at each other for a time. There was a smile in her light brown eyes and it soon awoke a smile in his.

'You've nothing against marrying a blacksmith, I hope?' he said.

'If a blacksmith should ask me,' Hannah said, 'I might perhaps consider it.'

'You mean to say I've never asked?'

'Not in so many words. No.'

'I suppose I was taking it for granted.'

'How like a man.'

'Well, I'm asking you now, right enough.'

'Then I'd better say yes, straight away, just in case you change your mind.'

'That's settled, then. We know how we stand.'

'Yes,' she said. 'But you ought to be getting on to the mill.'

'Ah. You're right. I better had.' The thought of it weighed on him heavily. 'No sense in putting it off.'

A few minutes later they parted company at the stile, and John took the footpath down to the river, where the midges were biting worse than ever.

The mill and the millhouse, to any stranger coming there, would have seemed derelict, dead as the grave, for the buildings were in disrepair and bits of planking were nailed across two broken windows. The place was quiet; both river and stream were running deep; but when he opened the gate on the bridge, there was a loud clanging noise, because of the sheepbells and old tin cans tied along the lower rail. Promptly, in response to the noise, his father's face appeared at one of the broken windows. Then came the noise of rusty bolts being drawn, and the door, scraping the stone-flagged floor, was opened just wide enough to let John in.

'I knew you'd come, boy! I knew you'd come! Blood is thicker than water yet and you're the only kin I've got. Here, light that candle on the table there, so's we can see enough to talk.'

The millhouse kitchen, close shut, smelt of sickness and old sweat. When John lit the candle and held it up, the place was everywhere thick with dirt, and his father's narrow makeshift bed was a tumble of blankets green with mould. Sacks were nailed across the windows, the fireplace was full of soot, and in the space beneath the dresser, a heap of empty brandy bottles glinted darkly through their dust.

'I'm a sick man,' Richard said. 'You can see that, can't you? It ent a lie. I need looking after and that's a fact. If you hadn't come, I'd have likely died. Nobody else would care at all.

The truth of his illness was plain indeed, for he breathed with immense difficulty and pressed his hand to his chest in pain, and as he struggled across the room, sweat trickled slowly down from his brow, into the beard that covered his cheeks. His skin was pinched and bruised-looking. He sat down heavily on the bed and stared before him with filmy eyes.

'I ent got the strength I was born with, let alone to do my work. That's why I need you running the mill, otherwise I'm a ruined man.'

'Have you had the doctor?' John asked.

'What use is he? You tell me that! The doctor would come and look at me and he'd say to me, "Lancy, you are a sick man!", and then he'd go home and write out his bill. Why should I pay to be told I'm sick? I know I'm sick. I'm just about done.'

'Have you eaten today?'

'My stomach's against the sight of food.'

'You ought to eat. It'd give you strength. And you ought to have more air in here – '

'Ah, I can see you're looking round. It's a lot different from the old days when your mother was here and kept it so trim. Remember when you was a little lad? You could eat off that floor in them days, and see yourself in them pots and pans, so bright and shining they used to be. We was happy in them days. Do you remember, when you was small?'

'Yes, I remember,' John said. But he also remembered how, in this room, his father had tried to make him eat slugs, and he felt the horror of it even now. 'I remember everything,' he said, and, taking a rag, began cleaning the dust from the table.

'She had no call to go off like that, leaving me to struggle alone. You can see what I've come to, without her.'

'Let's not talk about that,' John said, 'or we shall end by quarrelling.'

'Ah, that's right,' Richard said. 'Let's talk about the mill instead. You'll get it going, first thing, and put me back in business again?'

'Yes, if you tell me what to do.'

'I'll tell you all right. I can at least talk! Except when the coughing gets my guts. I'll get you to put this bed in the mill and then I can watch how you go on. Tomorrow morning, first thing. I'll soon make a miller out of you, boy, and we shall be well away, working together. Lancy and Son! That's the style. Working together the way we ought.'

'Now look here!' John said. 'I'm willing to stop a week or two and give you all the help I can, but as soon as you're on your feet again, I shall be going back to the forge.'

'Supposing I never get on my feet again?'

'Then it's up to you to employ a helper. But you'll get well. I'm sure of that. It's just that you need looking after a bit.'

'You going to nurse me and molly for me?'

'I'm going to do the best I can. And the first thing is to get you to eat.'

'I feel better already, having you here. I do, that's a fact, it's a real tonic. I've been so long alone, you see, and it does me good to see you here.'

'Just so long as it's understood that I shan't be stopping once you're fit.'

'We'll see about that when the time comes. Maybe by then you'll have changed your mind.'

'No,' John said, 'I shan't change my mind.'

'All right, all right, just as you say! Seems like I've got to be in your hands.'

For a while Richard sat in silence, watching as John, unpacking his bag, brought out bread, cheese, tea and sugar, a jar of meat jelly and a cold roast fowl, a boiled ham and an onion pie.

'Your mother send them things to me?'

'Yes.'

'Paid for by that swine Will Gale!'

'You don't have to eat them, if that's how you feel.'

'I'll eat them all right. You see if I don't! He owes me something, the rotten swine, seeing he stole my wife from me!'

John made no answer. He laid out the food on the bare table, and went to fetch water from the pump.

* * *

It was a strange experience for him, to be back in the old mill again after nineteen years, and during the first morning's work, when the sluice-gates were opened and the waterwheel began to turn, the sound of it brought his childhood back in a rush that threatened to overwhelm him. Inside the mill, as the runner stones turned and the whole building rumbled and shook, he knew a moment of childish panic, for he was in charge of all this cumbrous machinery that drew such strength from the river flood, and he felt its power like a living presence, as though it had a will of its own and would surely never submit to him.

The fear attacked him again and again as he ran to obey his father's instructions, and often his heart was in his mouth. When the warning-bell tinkled up above, he felt he would never get up the ladder quickly enough to feed the grain into the hopper, and when the water needed adjusting, his hands shook so badly that he could hardly grasp the control lever. He felt sick in his stomach. He was sure he would do the wrong thing. And in his mind's eye he saw the most dreadful catastrophes: the stones heating up and starting a fire, or the millstream flooding through the mill.

His father's instructions, shouted hoarsely from the bed against the wall, were often difficult to understand.

'God almighty! Are you daft? Don't you know what I mean by clewers, boy? Don't you remember nothing at all from the days when you was a little lad?'

Sometimes, enraged by his own helplessness, Richard shouted such abuse that his voice broke altogether and he would be seized with a fit of coughing. Once he struggled up from his bed, took a hammer from the wall, and hurled it straight at John's head, missing only because John was quick to duck. Then he fell back, gasping and coughing, blue in the face, pressing his hand against his chest.

'You want to go easy,' John said. 'You'll kill yourself if you go on like that.' He picked up the hammer and hung it back in its place on the wall. 'You'll very likely kill me too if you don't mind your temper better than that. I don't take kindly to having hammers throwed at me. Nor shall I work any better for being bawled at all day long, so just you tell me in simple words, which is what I'm used to at the forge.'

Richard, recovering, sat propped against a few bags of bran, chewing the ends of his long moustache. He watched John narrowly by the hour, and sometimes swore under his breath, but he made some effort to keep his temper under control, and often sat with his fists stuck muff-like into his sleeves, to keep them out of temptation's way.

'I shan't hurt you,' he said once. 'My own son? Oh, dear me, no! I shan't hurt you, I give you my word.'

By the third day, John no longer feared the mill, but became calm and confident, attuned to each small telltale sound, heard under the rumble and clack, and sensing the need of every straining shaft and cogwheel. He even came to enjoy the work and when, in the millroom, the fine flecked flour ran from the shute into the bag, he felt some pleasure touched with pride. But it was his father, hobbling across now and then to rub the flour between finger and thumb, who pronounced on its quality, good or bad; who knew by its texture and dryness and warmth whether the stones were grinding too close or, perhaps, not close enough.

'I dunno how you do it,' John said. 'It all seems much of a muchness to me. I dunno what you can *feel*.'

'That takes time,' Richard said. 'But you'll come to it in the end, my son, and I'll make a miller out of you if it takes me from now to my dying day.'

'I shan't be stopping as long as that. As soon as you're well enough, I shall be off. That was our bargain, don't forget.'

'Don't you like the work here?'

'I'm a blacksmith,' John said. 'I ent much good, away from the smithy.'

'You got no business being a blacksmith. Gale had no business making you one. Your place is here with me.'

'Why go on about it all the time? You ent going to make me change my mind.'

Sometimes, at the end of the day, when the waterwheel came to a halt and the mill was hushed, John would walk a little way along the towpath, listening to the quiet sounds of the river, coming to him through the thickening dusk. The voice of the water in its shallows and the voices of the feeding waterfowl were a part of his earliest memories, and when he pulled the dead dry seeds from the tall hemlock and crushed them in his hands to get the scent, he was a little boy again, out in the dark, all alone, marvelling at the evening star. The river-world was a world apart and had a feeling all its own. The quietness of it went down deep into the soul. The stillness of the waters soothed the mind.

Inside the mill, there was no such quiet feeling, for Richard, growing gradually stronger, followed John from place to place; questioned every move he made; ran him about without pause. In the house, too, it was the same, and when they sat down to their meals together, he grudged every mouthful of food John took. He himself ate very little. It hurt him to see John eat so well. And he would sit grumbling, clicking his tongue, till a moment came when, unable to control himself any longer, he would rise and gather the food together, all anyhow, within his arms, and put it away in the corner cupboard.

'Strikes me you've had enough. Food ent got without money, you know. You can't go on eating for evermore.'

'I brought that food,' John said.

'What about when it's all gone? I can't afford to feed you, boy, if that's the way you always eat. I'd be in the poorhouse in no time at all.'

'Then I shall have to buy it for myself.'

'That ent good for any man, eating as much as you do, boy. Just look at *me*. I never eat as much as that.'

'It must be the brandy that keeps you alive.'

'Tales! All tales!' Richard exclaimed. 'When've you seen me drinking, boy?'

'Never once,' John said, 'but I can smell it all the same, and I've seen enough bottles lying about.'

'It's Will Gale that's set you against me like this. Him and your mother, telling you tales. They've brung you up on a pack of lies.'

'I'm not against you,' John said.

'Then why don't you treat me with proper respect? I'm your father. You seem to forget.'

'I came when you asked me, didn't I? I'm here helping to work the mill.'

'You know which side your bread is buttered, that's why. You've got your eye on the future, my lad, when I'm dead and gone and the mill is yours.'

'That's nothing to me cos I don't mean to stop. I made that clear from the very start.'

'*I* mean you to stop, though!' Richard muttered. '*I* mean you to stop, and stop you shall!'

'What's that you said?' John asked sharply.

But his father, instead of repeating his remark, cleared the last of the supper things and firmly closed the cupboard door.

'You've had enough for tonight,' he said. 'You've had enough to sink a barge!'

* * *

The millhouse, so often surrounded by mist, was chilly and damp, but Richard rarely lit a fire. 'Work is the best thing for keeping warm,' he said, 'and you may be sure there's plenty of that.' John, every morning at five o'clock, rose from the mildewed mattress where he slept in a single worsted blanket, washed and shaved in cold water, and ate a cold breakfast in the cold kitchen, lit by a single tallow candle.

His day's work, eighteen hours long, was no harder or heavier than many a day's work in the smithy. He and Will, at busy times, had often been known to work all night. But in the smithy, there was always cheerful companionship, and at the end of the day's work, there was the comfort of the cottage kitchen, the reward of good hot food and drink, the ease of a chair drawn up to the hearth. There was friendly talk and a few jokes, perhaps, about the happenings of the day. The place was home. The people lived in friendliness. The warmth of it was shared by all.

At the millhouse, however, the only time Richard allowed a fire was when he caught a fish or two on the lines which, fixed all day from one of the mill windows, trailed in the water down below. Then he would light a fire in the rusty broken stove, on top of the heap of ash and soot, and would sit crouched in front of it, with the black smoke blowing out in his face, cooking a couple of tiny perch, stuck on the prongs of the toasting-fork and held among the meagre flames. John, receiving his share of the fish, found it more than half raw and pushed it from him in disgust. But his father finished every scrap.

'You've been spoilt by your mother's cooking. It's made you particular and I ent surprised. There's nobody cooks so well as her. I was particular myself once when she was here and cooked for me. But now I've had too many years alone. I can't afford to be fussy now. I must do the best I can.'

In the mill and the millhouse, shut up as they were, the windows covered with old sacks, day and night were almost the same, and the darkness often got on John's nerves.

'I wonder you choose to live like this, shut up in the dark, after what you went through that time, getting shut in that there cellar.'

'D'you think I choose to live like this?' Richard asked, shouting at him. 'If I didn't keep the place shut up I'd have the villagers snooping around, spying on me at every turn, poking their noses everywhere – '

'Nobody spies on you,' John said.

But Richard was convinced that they did: the bargemen plying up and down the river; the river-keepers; the wandering boys: he was determined they must be shut out. And if John removed a corner of sacking, to let in a tiny ray of light, Richard would rush to put it back and would hammer two or three nails into it.

The weather was still quite mild and sunny, although it was early January, and sometimes when John went out to see to the sluices he would linger a while on the river bank, watching the ducks swimming about and the dabchicks diving among the reeds. Often their antics made him laugh and one day he lingered there so long that his father came out to call him in.

'What're you up to, mooning about, when you ought to be getting down to work?'

'I was watching them dabchicks, that's all. Seems they're all wound up today, the way they're playing about out there. It's this mild weather. They think it's spring.'

'H'mph! Is that so? Seems there's some truth in what they say, that little things please little minds!'

Richard turned and went into the house. John went back into the mill and was soon busy working the hoist. A few minutes later he heard a shot. When he ran outside again, his father was standing on the bank with his gun in his hands, and smoke was squirming from one barrel. Down below, on the river, feathers floated among the reeds and the two dead dabchicks, stained with blood, were being swept away downstream.

'What did you have to do that for?' John cried, hating the

look on his father's face.

'They eat the fish, that's why!'

'Ent there enough blasted fish without your killing harmless birds?'

'You get back to your work!' Richard said. 'It's none of your business what I do.'

John said no more. He knew he was only wasting his breath. But every day after that, if any waterfowl came near the mill, he frightened them off by clapping his hands.

Sometimes, when milling was finished for the day, John had to take the horse and waggon and deliver meal at distant farms or flour to the bakehouse at Sutton Crabtree. Richard had quarrelled with every farmer in Dingham itself, and all his trade was further afield, so that John had to travel a great many miles.

Once, after dark on a cold wet night, he was returning from Upper Mayse, and when he reached the green at Dingham, he stopped the waggon on the round road and sat for a moment, hunched in his jacket, looking across at the old smithy. The upper half of the door was open and a wedge of light shone out on the rain, while another light, ruddier, duller, glowed at the opening in the roof. The sound of iron ringing on iron came, chink-chink, to John's ears, and the smell of the forge, burning coal, caught in his nostrils, acrid and rough.

He felt he had been away for a lifetime, although it was only ten days, and such a longing came over him that he half rose from the box of the waggon, thinking to run across the green and put his head in over the hatch, just for a word or two of gossip. But he sat down again, still holding the reins, for he felt that if he once set foot inside the smithy, it would be all the harder for him to return again to Pex Mill.

'Stick it out,' he said to himself. 'Another week should see the end. Then I'll be back for good and all.'

* * *

Sometimes, during the night, John would awake on his

comfortless bed and hear his father moving about in the room below. One night the shuffling, unsteady feet came very slowly up the stairs, and John's bedroom door creaked open a little way. But when he spoke there was no reply and after a while he heard the footsteps shuffle away again down the stairs.

Once he awoke to a smashing of glass and in the morning, when he entered the kitchen, the floor was covered with the fragments of five or six brandy bottles. He never once saw his father in the act of drinking, but always in the morning the smell of it was hot on his breath, and a sullen redness burnt darkly in his face.

'What sort of time d'you call this?'

'I reckon it's just about after six.'

'Is that the earliest you can rise?'

'It's early enough,' John said, 'seeing I had a disturbed night.'

'It's a funny thing,' Richard said, 'that although I'm only a sick old man, I should always be up before you.'

'Not so funny,' John said, 'seeing you never go to bed.'

'You'd better go and find a broom and make yourself useful sweeping this rubbish out of the way.'

'I think I'd better open a window, too, and let some fresh air in here. The place is stinking like a drain.'

'Don't you touch them windows, boy! They're all nailed up to keep out the thieves.'

Even when the sun shone, the sacking must never be pulled aside. Richard disliked the light of day, shortlived as it was in wintertime, and his one idea was to keep it out. The mill, too, was kept close and dark.

'No wonder your asthma's bad,' John said, 'cooped up so close with all this dust.'

'Who owns this mill, you or me?'

'Please yourself,' John said, and although he felt stifled, imprisoned there, he comforted himself that he would soon be returning home.

After the rain, there came a spell of cold weather, sunny

and dry. Richard's health was improving apace. He was growing stronger; coughing less; and no longer came out in a sweat at the slightest exertion.

'Seems to me you're a lot better,' John said at supper one evening. 'You'll soon be able to manage alone.'

'I ent a hundred per cent yet. Look at my hands, the way they shake.'

'It's not your asthma that causes that. It's the medicine you take for it.'

'I doubt if I shall ever be fit enough to run this mill by myself again. I'm an old man now. I've lost my strength. I need you here like I need to breathe. What'll I do if you go off?'

'You'll have to do what every other miller does – get another man to help.'

'Not while I've got a son of my own. Why the h— should I, in G— name? It's little enough to ask of you, seeing the mill will be yours when I'm gone.'

'I'll stay to the end of the week,' John said. 'Then I'm going and that's final.'

'You're a good son to me,' Richard said. 'You won't let me down. I'm sure of that. You know how I depend on you. You're all I've got in the whole world.'

Chapter Fourteen

One bright afternoon when John was out on the wooden footbridge, looking down into the leats, a voice spoke to him from behind and there was Hannah on the towpath, wearing a brown cloak with a hood and carrying a basket. The hood was pushed back and her hair in the sunlight was golden brown. Her look and her smile gave him a little jolt inside, and he was struck dumb, in a strange shyness. He had kept away from Neyes Farm, denying himself a sight of her as a test of his own strength and endurance. His task at the mill must be got through alone. But now that she had come to him, seeking him out so openly, without any silly girlish pride, his self-denial seemed absurd. A childishness. A waste of time.

'Your mother sent you a basket of food. She thought you might be going short.'

'She's about right. I ent getting half what I get at home.'

'There's one or two things from the farm as well. A piece of bacon and two score eggs. I made you a mutton pasty too.'

'Your arm must be breaking, carrying all that food like that. What am I thinking of? Give it here.'

He opened the rickety wooden gate and there was a clangour from the bells. He took the basket and exclaimed at its weight.

'Glory be! We shall feast like kings!'

'You seem surprised to see me,' she said. 'You're looking at me as though I'm not real.'

'Yes, well,' he said, still shy, 'I hadn't thought of your coming here.'

'It's strange to see you dressed like that, all dusty and white, instead of black.'

'I suppose you're laughing at my apron, like that time when I was a lad, wearing one of Will's old leathers.'

'How've you been getting on?'

'Muddling along, like, just about keeping the wheels turning. But my father's better, I'm glad to say, and I shall be home in a few days more.'

'Where is he?'

'Oh, he's around. He'll have heard the racket of them bells and he's probably watching from a crack somewhere. D'you want to come in?'

'I'd better not,' Hannah said. 'I've got to call at Uncle Bob's. I'm already later than I said.'

'Hang on a jiff, then, and I'll empty this basket,' John said.

At that moment, his father appeared at the open hatch, eyes narrowed against the sunlight, looking Hannah up and down.

'What's all this? Visitors?'

'Hannah's brought us a basket of food.'

'Hannah? Hannah? Hannah who?'

'Hannah Draycott from Neyes Farm.'

'You two getting married, then? Seems you're pretty thick together.'

'Yes, in due course,' John said.

'Then let me warn you, young woman! – You'll have your work cut out to keep him fed!'

'I'm used to that,' Hannah said. 'My menfolk at the farm are just the same.'

'When's the wedding going to be?'

'We haven't decided yet,' John said. 'We've got to find a place to live.'

'Stop here with me,' Richard said, 'and you've got a home all ready made.'

'No, no, I've told you before. At the end of this week I'm going home.'

'What about Hannah? What's she think?'

'John will do what he wants to do,' Hannah said, in her clear voice, 'and that is to go on working in the forge.'

'Then it's up to you to try and talk some sense into him. This mill could be a flourishing business and that'll be his when I'm dead and gone. He's my one and only son and the milling trade is in his blood.'

'Oh no it ent!' John said with a laugh.

'Then it d— well ought to be!' Richard snapped. 'Lord almighty! Can't you *see?*' Then, with a sudden agreeable smile, he addressed himself to Hannah again. 'You're a sensible-looking girl. You don't want to marry a d—— blacksmith when he could be a miller and own his own mill. Oh, I know the house has been neglected! I see what you're thinking right enough! But you and John could put it to rights. Take a pride in it. Make it nice. And John and me, us two men, we could set the mill on its feet, doing good trade and flourishing, just like it was in days gone by.'

'No, Mr Lancy,' Hannah said. 'John's heart is in the smithy. You'll never get him to give it up.'

For a moment Richard stared at her, his smile dying on his lips, giving way to a tremulous anger. Then he pushed himself away from the hatch and slammed the upper half of it shut, and a moment later, listening, they heard him flinging about the millroom, rattling the chain of the sack-hoist and sending it smashing against the wall. Hannah's eyes opened wide. She looked at John in anxiety.

'Now I've put him in a temper. I hope he won't take it out on you.'

'There's nothing for you to worry about. He threw a hammer at me once and he likes to smash things now and then. But I don't think he'd do me any harm. Not while I'm useful in the mill!'

'It's nothing to laugh at!' Hannah said. 'I've heard strange stories about your father. I'll be glad when you're safe back home again.'

'Ah, well, it won't be long now.'

Her look of anxiety made him feel warm, and the warmth went spreading slowly out inside him, so that he stood and smiled at her, moved by the fearfulness in her eyes. He was filled with a knowledge of his own strength. His youth and manhood. His lack of fear. No harm could come to him, for his life was set on a definite course, and Hannah was part of it, his to keep. He saw it so clearly in his mind that he *knew* no harm could come to him. But her fearfulness moved him all the same.

'I can take care of myself,' he said.

'Then see that you do,' Hannah said.

'Hang on a jiff. I'll take in this food. No doubt you'll want the basket back.'

When he returned with the empty basket, his father was calling from the mill. John made a face and gave a shrug. He parted from Hannah cheerfully, breezily, with a smile and a wave, but when he went inside the mill, its darkness and closeness pressed on him, and the days ahead seemed very long.

Over at the workbench, his father, with a lantern in his hand, was searching for a lost chisel. John found it and gave it to him. They both had work to do on the cog-wheels.

'She's a fine-looking girl, that Hannah of yours.'

'Yes, she is.'

'A bit of a madam if I'm any judge. You'll have your hands full, managing her. But she's the sort that gets things done. She'll soon have the house all shipshape again, when you've married her and brung her home. She'll make things hum for us, no doubt, but I shan't mind too much about that, so long as she's a good wife to you and does her duty, caring for us.'

John, who was turning the pitwheel and knocking out the damaged cogs, stopped and stared at his father's face.

'Didn't you hear what Hannah said? We shan't be coming to live here with you. We're getting a cottage of our own.'

'I heard what she said, right enough, but she'll come round to it, given time.' Richard, working with hammer and chisel, was intent on shaping a new cog. His mind was closed to everything but what it suited him to believe. 'She'll come round to it. You mark my words. It's up to you to see that she does.'

* * *

Saturday came, and it was the day for John's departure. He had been at the mill for nearly three weeks. His father was fully recovered now, or as nearly as he could hope for, anyway. His breathing was easier; he no longer coughed; and his stamina was astonishing. He could work without tiring from dawn to dusk, though his strength, when it came to lifting weights, was now a thing of the distant past.

'It pleases me to see you so strong. It's like myself all over again. You've done pretty well by me, my son, seeing me through while I've been bad, and if you stop on you shall have your reward.'

'No, father,' John said. 'I must go and today is the day. We'll get this last lot of barley done for Mr Treeve and then I'm off home.'

Richard looked at him with a sidelong glance.

'That's the first time you've called me father,' he said, 'in all the time you've been here with me.'

'Is it?' John said. But he knew it was. 'It don't come all that easy to me, after nineteen years apart.'

'It means a lot to me, my son, to hear you give me my proper name. I *am* your father. You can't escape that. And blood must count for something, I'm sure, especially between a man and his son. I'm only sorry it don't count for more.'

John had no answer to make to this. He went and busied himself at the shute, putting the wooden stop-board in, while he took away the full sack and put an empty one in its place. There was some change in his father today. A quietness.

A softness of speech. His eyes were not so dulled by drink, nor was the smell of it on his breath. His fretful temper was under control. John was puzzled. The change, instead of comforting him, filled him with a vague unease.

By two o'clock, the whole day's milling was done. Mr Treeve's barley was ground, and the twelve sacks of meal stood tied and labelled near the door, awaiting collection. John went out and closed the sluice-gates. He removed a dead branch of wood from the stream. A strong wind was blowing from the cold northwest and there was a hint of drizzle in it. He stood for a while on the river bank and watched it roughening the dark water. Then he went into the mill again, hung up the sluice-key, and removed his borrowed miller's apron. His father was cleaning the weighing-machine.

'Seems you're just about ready for off.'

'Just about,' John said.

'Won't you stop for a bite of food?'

'No, I shall eat when I get home. I'm just going up to get my things.'

'In such a hurry?' Richard said. 'In such a hurry to be gone?'

John stood, hesitant, at the door.

'If you need me again, I'll always come. So long as I'm able to, that is, and it don't hinder my work at the forge. I'd be quite willing to spare a day or two helping you out.'

'A day or two! What use is that?'

'I reckon that's up to you,' John said.

He went through the mealroom into the house and up the stairs to his bedroom. He threw his belongings into his bag. Outside, the drizzle had turned to rain, and was skittering hard against the window. The sky was heavily overcast.

When he went down to the mill again, the millroom was even darker than usual, for both halves of the door were now closed and the curtain of sacking covered the cracks. When he went to the door he found that the bar had been put across and the padlock inserted into the hasp. He tugged at the padlock and found it secure. Anger got him by the throat and he swung quickly round to where his father, stooping low, was lighting the lantern on the kist. The bearded face was watchful, intent, purposeful. The hand, holding the lighted match, shook and was clumsy with curbed excitement. And as the light of the lantern grew, he turned to John with a little smile.

'You ent leaving here, my son. Oh, dear me, no. You're stopping on. You're going to help me run this here mill. I'm going to set it on its feet and you got a duty to help me out. You ent leaving. I'll see to that.'

'D'you think you can keep me against my will?'

'There'd be no need if only you could see some sense.'

'If you think a locked door can keep me here – '

'It's only until we've had time to talk.'

'We've talked and talked these past three weeks! We've thrashed it out a hundred times! I'm not going through it all again!'

John turned and strode through the mealroom into the house. His father followed, holding the lantern high in his hand, and by its dingy, flickering light, John saw that the house-door too was barred and locked.

'You can't get out of here, my son. The door is padlocked, as you see, and the windows is all nailed up to the frames. You got no choice but to stop with me.'

'I've just about had enough of this! If you don't open up I shall do some damage breaking out!'

'You're my son,' Richard said. 'I've got first claim on you, my boy, and I aim to keep you where you belong.'

'I'm warning you! I mean what I say!'

'And I'm warning *you*!' Richard said. 'I know my rights.'

John looked at his father's face and knew it was useless to reason with him. The old man's eyes, though watchful, intent, were blind to the light of the daylight world. His mind, like his mill, was full of dark places, shuttered and barred, and in the thickening shadows there, his thoughts gnawed like imprisoned rats. Shut up in himself, inward-coiled, he was a man who needed help. A man whose reason had gone astray because of an accident in his youth. A man to be pitied, not reviled. And John did indeed feel pity for him. This man was his father, his own flesh and blood, alone in the world, cut off by his madness. It was John's duty to reason with him.

'Father, give me the key and let me go, and I promise I'll come and give you a hand whenever I can spare the time. One day a week, say. I'll do my best.'

'One little day is no use to me.'

'Then let me find you a man full-time.'

'I don't want strangers in my mill.'

'Then there's nothing I can do to help you.'

'You've got a duty to stop here with me and help me to put this mill to rights.'

'I've got a duty to myself!' John said. 'If you won't open up for me, I must get out as best I can!'

He went to the window and wrenched the sacking from its nails. He picked up the nearest kitchen chair and smashed it with all his strength against the casements, which splintered apart and swung outwards, hanging askew from their broken hinges. Richard gave a cry of rage and lunged forward, swinging the lantern. It struck John on the side of his head and cut his scalp above the ear, and a few drops of paraffin, spilt from the drum, splashed over his face and neck. As the lantern swung again, he yanked it out of his father's hand and hurled it into the fireplace, where its glass broke and its flame was extinguished in ash and soot. He snatched up his bag and dropped it out of the open window. Patience and pity had left him now. His one idea was to get away. He wrenched himself free from his father's grasp and vaulted over the window-sill.

'You'll be sorry for this!' Richard cried. 'You'll be sorry for leaving me all alone! I gave you your chance! I was always willing to do well by you! And this is how you turn me down!'

Sobbing and crying in his rage, he suddenly snatched off his ragged cap, and, leaning out after John, struck him two or three blows with it and eventually hurled it at his head.

'You'll be sorry for this, my son, and so will some others I could name! You and your mother and Will Gale and all, you think I'm nothing, you laugh at me! You think you can trample me underfoot! But I'll make you sorry, the pack of you, and you won't laugh at me for long!'

John shouldered his bag and walked away. He felt rather sick and there was a sourness on his tongue that he longed to be able to wash away. The smell of the mill was in his clothes; the mustiness was in his hair; and the stale bad smell of his father's breath seemed to lodge forever in his nostrils. But he was free of the place now, out in the Godsent wind and rain, and as he walked towards the village he took deep breaths of cold clean air.

* * *

Richard, left alone in the millhouse kitchen, pulled the broken casements shut and tied them together with a piece of string. He fetched a hammer and a handful of nails and nailed the sacking back in place. The kitchen was now dark again, so he took the lantern from the hearth, shook off the ash and broken glass, and set it on the table. He struck a match and touched the wick and reluctantly, because of the dirt, there came a circle of dim blue flame. His hands were trembling. He breathed heavily, making a noise in his nose and throat. Now and then he licked his lips.

He went to the cupboard in the corner where, in the leg of an old boot, he kept a bottle and a glass. He brought them to the table and sat down to drink, and the brandy went noiselessly down his throat in a single draught that emptied the glass. For a moment more he sat unmoved; it might have been water flowing down; but the sudden spasm, when it came, shook him as a terrier shakes a rat, and afterwards he sat bent and cowed, the moisture running from his eyes, the sweat standing out on his brow and forehead. But his hands were a lot steadier now. He tilted the bottle and refilled the glass.

After a while he got up and took his shotgun out of the clock-case. He laid it on the table with powder-flask, wads, the bag of shot, and the clay pipe-bowl broken off at the stem which he used as a funnel for the powder charge. He sat down again, placed the gun upright between his knees, and set to work, loading both barrels carefully. His face was clenched in concentration. His lips were tight-pressed and he breathed very heavily through his nose. He was always careful when loading his gun. His wads were cut exactly to size, powder and shot were measured just so, and the charge was always rammed well home. The gun had been his for forty years.

The brandy bottle was empty now. It went on the heap under the dresser. Richard turned down the lantern-flame, wrapped his gun in a piece of sacking, and let himself out of the side door, carefully pocketing the key. The afternoon was already dark, and gusts of rain came down now and then, blowing on the changeable wind. Richard turned up his coat-collar, pulled his hat over his eyes, and set out towards the village. He held the gun very close to his side.

Behind him, the mill stood dark and quiet, doors locked and windows sealed, safe from entry except by marauding rats and mice. But the lantern, although he had turned it down, had not been extinguished. A speck of flame remained on the wick and was drawing oil from a crack in the holder. The oil-drum, too, had been damaged in its fall, and where the joint had opened a fraction, oil was seeping onto the table. Soon the speck of flame would grow, fed by the fumes rising around it. The bits of burning wick would fall and ignite the paraffin on the table. And the trail would lead to the dusting of gunpowder Richard had spilt when filling the pipe-bowl from the flask. The flask itself still lay nearby.

* * *

When John arrived at the smithy, work was almost done for the day, and the fire in the forge was burning low. Jim Pacey had gone home and Peter was sweeping the workshop floor.

Only Will was still working, in his absent-looking way, cutting shoe-lengths on the anvil, and when he looked up to see who it was who had walked in, his face came alive in a smile that warmed John through to the very marrow of his bones. Stooping over the anvil again, he beat out a tune with his long-handled hammer and cold chisel, lightly, cleverly, drawing a different note from each part and making a joyous message of welcome. Ting-tinker-*tink*-tink! – Ting-*tink*!

'Peter! Peter! Look who's here! Your mother's son as ever was!'

'Lord almighty!' Peter said, sweeping the dust to John's feet. 'You back for good or just for tea?'

'We'd given you up for lost,' Will said. 'We thought you'd done with the smithing trade and turned a miller after all.'

'No lections of that!' John said, and because of the warmth of Will's welcome and his own joy at being back, he was stricken with shyness and awkwardness, looking around at the old place and trying to think of something to say. 'Everything looks pretty much the same, don't it?'

'We done our best,' Peter said, 'to keep it tidy while you was away.'

'I should hope so indeed.'

'We heard your old man was up and about at the mill again. We heard he was running you around.'

'How did he take it, John,' asked Will, 'when you upped sticks and came away?'

'Well might you ask!' John exclaimed. 'He tried to stop me. He locked me in.'

'Is that how you got that cut on your head?'

'Yes, he catched me a clout with a storm-lantern.'

'The man is mad,' Peter said. 'It's high time he was put away. There's proper places for folk like him.'

'Yes, well,' John said.

'You'd better get indoors,' Will said. 'Your mother'll be nearly over the moon. She's been looking out for you enough!'

'Yes, I'll go in,' John said. 'I could do with a clean-up and that's a fact.'

'Anything troubling you, John?' Will asked.

'My dad, that's all. You know how he is. He was saying what he'd do to us and how he was going to pay us out.'

'Don't lose no sleep over that!' Will said. 'He's been singing that song for nineteen years and it's never come to nothing yet. You get indoors and see your mother. Peter and me will be in pretty soon. We're having an easy day today so tell her to get an early tea and we'll celebrate your coming home.'

'Ah!' Peter said. 'Tell her to kill the fatted calf!'

'Take no notice of Peter,' said Will. 'His nose is out of joint a bit but he'll soon get over that.'

'I'll go on in, then,' John said. 'I'll be glad of the chance of a good wash and shave. The way I smell right at this moment, my mother will put me to eat with the pig.'

As he went to the door leading into the cottage, he was smiling to himself in expectation, picturing the brightness of the kitchen and himself going in, very quietly, to take his mother by surprise. He had his hand on the sneck of the door when he heard someone come into the smithy. He glanced back, over his shoulder, and saw his father among the shadows, outside the central circle of light cast by the fire in the forge and the lantern hanging overhead. Will and Peter also saw him and both became still, peering questioningly into the shadows. Will, who still had his hammer and chisel in his hands, straightened himself to his full height.

'You got business with us, Mr Lancy?'

'Certainly I have,' Richard said. 'You're a blacksmith, supposed to be! Maybe you can fix this here.'

'What is it?' Will asked.

'It's this!' Richard said, and stepped forward into the light, allowing the sacking to fall from the gun. 'What you should've had long years ago!'

Will, at a range of only three or four yards, received the murderous charge of shot in the abdomen, yet such was his enormous strength that when they reached him he was still on his feet, supporting himself against the anvil. The front of his shirt was a glistening mess, and as they lowered him to the ground, he reached out and pulled at his leather apron, drawing it up to cover himself, to spare them the sight of his terrible wound.

Peter, seeing his father's plight, turned away, his face contorted, and seized the shotgun from Richard's hands. He gave a terrible strangled howl.

'D'you see what you've done to him?' he cried.

'Yes, I see it!' Richard said. 'I always said I'd pay him out!'

'Well, it's *your* turn now!' Peter said. 'And *I* shan't wait for nineteen years! If both these barrels is loaded up, you're getting the other in the guts!'

The gun was pointing at Richard's stomach, but as Peter began squeezing the trigger, John sprang forward and struck at the muzzle and the shot went up into the rafters. Peter, beside himself with rage, struck at John's face with the gunstock, and John, wresting the weapon from his hands, hurled it into the water-trough.

In that instant, Richard quickly left the smithy, vanishing into the winter darkness, and when the brothers turned to Will, their mother was on her knees beside him, cradling him within her arms and weeping, weeping, hopelessly, knowing that he was slipping away. His blood had soaked her pinafore, and her hands were stained with it, so was her face. With such a wound, he could never live.

As her lips kissed his forehead and her fingertips gently touched his cheek, he moved a little, against her arm, trying to look at her, trying to speak.

'All my own fault – ' he said weakly, and turned his face towards her breast.

Ellen continued to hold him close and would not be moved for a long time. Her sons could do nothing. The dead man was hers. She would not leave his side so long as some warmth remained in him; so long as his spirit still seemed near; so long as she still had strength enough to hold his body in her arms. All her sons could do for her was to close and bolt the smithy door against the villagers gathered outside. Only when Dr Nathan came would she consent to leave the body and by that time she was perfectly calm. She watched as the doctor closed Will's eyes and covered him with a clean white sheet.

'Where is the murderer, Richard Lancy?'

'Ask my brother!' Peter said. 'If I'd had my way he'd be lying there dead the same as my father and I should be wiping my feet on him! I got the gun out of his hands. I'd have shot him without a second thought. But my brother had to interfere and the murdering swine just walked away.'

'Better to leave it to the law,' Dr Nathan said to him. 'The police will be here in due course. They'll probably find him at the mill.'

'If I get to him first,' Peter said, 'I shall save the law a lot of trouble.'

* * *

But soon it was known throughout the village that Pex Mill was on fire. The glow of it could be seen in the sky and the smell of it was on the wind. The first men to have raised the alarm were the two river keepers patrolling the bank. They had seen the bright glare in the mill windows and had done what they could with water-buckets. But the fire had already got a hold. The heat of it had driven them back. And one of them swore that the Mad Miller had been inside, trying to rescue his sacks of meal, at the moment when the roof collapsed, bringing with it a part of one wall.

Even when extra help arrived, and a stream of water was piped from the leats, there was no hope of saving the mill. By the time the fire was out, the place was gutted, a black shell, and when at last the ruins were cool enough for men to enter, Richard Lancy's dead body, charred, blackened, unrecognizable, was dug out of the smoking rubble and taken to the mortuary in Runston. Outside the mill, where he had thrown it for safety, lay an iron-bound box with a padlock on it. Somebody took it to the smithy cottage and handed it over to Ellen Lancy. She in turn gave it to John. It contained a few coins and a small roll of banknotes, a total of seven pounds three shillings and sixpence.

* * *

All through Sunday, in the smithy cottage, Peter was almost completely silent, even at mealtimes, and whenever John spoke to him, he turned away with a savage gesture. Ellen, who had moved Will's chair from the head of the table because its emptiness gave such pain, looked at these two sons of hers and knew that she must speak her mind. But she knew, too, that although she could often influence the one, she could very rarely influence the other.

'How long is this silence to last between you?'

'Peter must answer that,' said John. 'He's the one that's dumb.'

'Let them that feel like talking, talk by all means,' Peter said. 'For my part, there's little to say.'

'Where's the good in adding hurt to hurt?' she said. 'Isn't it enough that your father is dead?'

'It's more than enough for me,' Peter said.

'Do you think it's any different for John?'

'Oh, John's lost a father, too, I know! The Mad Miller of Pex Mill! Does anybody care for that?'

For the first time that day, Peter looked directly at John, and the effort brought the tears to his eyes. He was only seventeen. His rage and bitterness knew no bounds.

'Well, brother?' he said harshly. 'Your father is dead! Do you grieve for him?'

'No,' John said, 'but I grieve for Will.'

'Do you? Do you? Oh, I daresay!'

'He was as good a father to me as he was to you.'

'And was murdered for it at the end!'

'You don't hold me to blame for that?'

'It was *your* father that murdered him!'

'I'm not to blame for what he did.'

'You're to blame for striking up the gun! I'd have shot the

miller, sure as fate, if you hadn't stopped me and let him go. I'd have watched him die in agony, as I had to watch my father die, and sent his stinking soul to Hades!'

'Then you'd have been a murderer too.'

'D'you call that murder? I don't!'

'My father was mad. He didn't rightly know what he was doing.'

'Why should a madman be spared, pray, more than a man in his right mind? A man that's mad is better dead.'

'Yes, well, he is dead now,' John said, 'and had a worse death than he would've done if you'd shot him.'

'Yes!' Peter said. 'And I wish I'd been there to see him burn!'

'Don't!' Ellen said, and there was horror in her eyes. 'You don't know what you're saying, my son. Such a thing is too wicked for words. Richard was a man. A human being, like any other. Besides which he was also – '

'Also what?' Peter asked.

'Never mind,' Ellen said.

'He was still your husband, wasn't he? – That's what you was going to say. I suppose it still counts for something with you, does it, even after living with my father all these years and bringing his b——d into the world? Does it, mother? Does it count? Then no doubt we shall be seeing you going into mourning for two husbands at the same time?'

'By G—!' John exclaimed, and half rose from his chair. But his mother touched him on the arm and after a moment he sat down again, his clenched fists on the edge of the table. 'Do you think you're the only one with feelings?' he said.

Peter, upright in his chair, sat like an image, hard-faced. But he was ashamed, under his mother's steady gaze, and his glance shifted once or twice, while he made the effort to speak.

'I'm sorry, mother!' he said in a burst. 'I shouldn't have said that. I take it back.'

'You shouldn't be saying these things to John, either.'

'What've I said that ent true?'

'Your father would have hated this. To hear you talk as you have today. To know there was badness between you and John.'

'How long d'you aim to keep it up?' John asked. 'Are you going to be at odds with me even working in the smithy? That's a darn silly thing if you like!'

'There'll be no work done in the smithy tomorrow. I'm keeping it closed as a mark of respect.'

'*You're* keeping it closed?'

'That's what I said. I've got business in Runston in the morning. I shan't be home till about twelve o'clock.'

'Then I'll see the vicar,' John said, 'and make arrangements for Will's funeral.'

'No,' Peter said. 'I shall do that when I get home. He was *my* father, not yours. It's my duty to see the vicar.'

John and his mother exchanged a glance. Neither spoke, but their thought was the same. Peter watched them without expression and then, leaning forward over the table, began cutting the loaf of bread. He dropped a slice onto John's plate.

'*You've* got the Mad Miller's funeral to see to. I hope you hadn't forgotten that.'

'No. I hadn't forgotten.'

'That'll come pretty hard on you, but at least he left a few pounds in that box. It'll pay for his burial, I suppose.'

'I shall manage,' John said. 'I've got a bit of money saved. But there's no need for you to worry about it. He was *my* father, not yours.'

Peter glanced at him and smiled.

* * *

The next day, in the early morning, John and Hannah walked on the hill in sunshine so warm that steam rose from the wet grass and larks sang in the sky above. The hem of Hannah's skirt was drenched, but she made nothing of the matter, and they continued up the hill till they came to the log beside the pond. They sat together and talked about Will.

'My grandfather cried when he heard the news. He said Will had helped him a thousand times. He said the world would not be the same without Will Gale to send it round.'

'It certainly won't be the same for me. Things is already changing a bit. They'll change a lot more in the days to come.'

'What do you mean?'

'Peter's taking it badly,' he said. 'There's going to be trouble between him and me.'

'Are you worried?' Hannah asked.

'I'm preparing myself, that's all. I shan't cross my bridges till I come to them, but I'm getting things sorted out in my mind, and there's one or two things I must talk out with you, about our future, yours and mine.'

'Talk away,' Hannah said.

Later that morning, John went into Runston to see about his father's funeral. He thought it best that the burial should be a quiet affair, and he made arrangements accordingly. He and his mother would be the only mourners.

When he returned home at midday, Peter was there, standing on the hearth in his best suit, his hands behind him. Ellen, pale-faced, sat very still and erect in her chair, and her eyes, seeking John's, gave him some warning of what was to come.

'I've been to town to see the lawyer,' Peter said. 'Not that I had any doubts at all, but I thought I'd like to get things straight, especially seeing I'm illegitimate. The lawyer says, there being no will, the smithy and cottage belong to me.'

'Yes,' John said, 'I daresay they do.'

'I'm his only living kin, so it's all pretty simple, the way things fall out, and you've got no claim on the smithy at all. Nor the cottage nor nothing else. Everything here belongs to me.'

'I reckon I'm following so far, but what happens next, might I ask? D'you want me to touch my cap to you before starting work in the smithy every morning?'

'You won't be working in the smithy no more. Nor living under this roof neither. I've decided it's better if you move on.'

'Ah! I see. So it's come to that!'

'You don't seem all that much surprised.'

'I thought there was something in the wind. I smelt it like you smell bad fish.'

'You've got no claim on my father's property.'

'I don't care tuppence who owns what, but I would've thought we could at least have gone on working together, the same way we have done in the past.'

'Yes,' said Ellen, looking at Peter. 'You know well enough what Will intended. He spoke about it oftentimes. He always said, when the time came for him to retire, you and John would stop on in the smithy and work together on equal terms.'

'He didn't know, when he said that, that John's father would shoot him down!'

'He looked on John as his own son. He'd want him treated more fairly than this.'

'John won't want for nothing much. He's got the old mill if nothing else.'

'The mill?' she said. 'What use is that?'

'It's better than having nothing at all. He might be able to salvage something and get the mill working again. He says he's got some money saved.'

'I'm a blacksmith,' John said. 'What do I want with running a mill?'

Peter gave a little shrug.

'Beggars can't be choosers,' he said. 'But if you don't want to be a miller, you can go as journeyman to some other smith. It should be easy enough to get a job, so long as you don't mind going further afield. You've got your indentures, after all.'

'Which is more than you have!' John exclaimed. 'You've got another couple of years yet before you've properly served your time.'

'Seeing I own my own smithy, I can call myself a master smith.'

'You can call yourself whatever you please! It's what you *are* that really counts!'

Peter was silent. He looked away. His lips were set in a hard line.

'What about me?' Ellen asked. 'I've got no lawful claim on Will, either. Am I to be turned out along with John?'

'Don't be silly,' Peter said. 'This is your home.'

'Then my word should count for something here!'

'It's no use, mother,' John said. 'I shan't stop where I ent wanted. We could never work as a team, him and me, not with him feeling as he does. The best thing is to do as he says.'

'I am still mistress in this house, whether I have a lawful claim or not, and it's me that says who comes and goes.'

'I'd have to find somewhere to live in the end, when Hannah and me get married,' he said. 'I may as well go soon as late.' And to Peter he said bitterly: 'I know you've always been jealous of me on account of my being a better smith, but I never thought it'd come to this. I'd have been willing to work with you. I'd have helped you every way I could, for Will's sake if nothing else. But seeing you've chosen to sling me out I shall ask you to remember this – the moment I step outside that door, I owe you no duty nor favour nor nothing, and the same goes for you, too.'

'Amen to that,' Peter said.

'I'll go upstairs and pack my things.'

'So soon? So soon?' Ellen said. She was reaching out to take his hands. 'No, I can't bear it to be like this!'

'It's better this way,' John said. 'Too much has been said between him and me. It'll only get worse now, the longer I stay. I'll go along to Grannie Naylor's. She'll give me a lodging, I daresay.'

'Will would have been so distressed by this!'

'I shan't say goodbye to you, mother, cos I shall see you oftentimes. I'll be at Will's funeral for a start. At least Peter can't grudge me that! And if you ever have need of me, be sure to send word without delay.'

'She won't want for nothing with me,' Peter said.

'As to that, I ent so sure!'

'Are you going, did you say?'

'Yes, I'm going,' John said.

Half an hour later he left the house, his belongings packed into two canvas bags. He went to Mrs Naylor's cottage and she agreed to take him in. He paid her ten shillings in advance. He sat on the bed in the room she gave him and counted his savings carefully. It came to nearly fifty pounds.

* * *

The day was still fine, and as he stood in the burnt-out mill, he could feel the sunshine warm on his head, for the upper floors and roof had gone and the place was open to the sky. Bits of charred rafters stuck out, pointed, from their wall-sockets, and the central beams, although still in place, were burnt to half their original thickness. By a strange chance, the hoist-chain still hung from the main roof-beam, and when he touched its twisted links, he found that they had been welded together by the heat.

The mill machinery lay in ruins, the wooden shafts and cogwheels burnt, the metal twisted, shrunken, deformed, and among the heap, which smoked even now, the broken mill-stones lay about, their grooves filled with a fine soft black dust that had once been flour.

The smell of the place was foul and loathsome, for such a fire, far from purifying, left behind it blackness and filth, and the evil smeech of it, catching in the throat and nostrils, could turn a man's stomach and make him retch. John had known that smell before, as a small boy, four years old, in the ruined mill at Cutlowell Park, when his father had taken him to the sale. And he thought how very strange it was that his father's misfortunes should have begun and ended with a burnt-out mill.

He had put on his working-clothes to come to Pex Mill this afternoon. Now he took his sweat-rag from his neck and pressed it against his nose and mouth. And as he went from place to place: to the mealroom where his father had died; to the stockroom and sheds and the house itself; he wondered if the smell could ever really be cleansed away. With the smoking refuse gone; the stonework and brickwork scraped clean; with all the timberwork replaced and a roof of new tiles overhead: could the place be made decent and wholesome again, brought to life out of the past, inhabited by a new spirit?

'Well, now, I wonder!' he said to himself.

He stooped and picked up a piece of stone and went around with it, using it as a hammer, testing the condition of the walls. Crunching across the bed of ash, he trod carefully, picking his way, for he felt the heat of it underfoot and saw how, when the wind breathed, the bits of charcoal glowed bright red.

Just after two, Hannah came to the mill door, and he went to meet her.

'Don't come in. You'll dirty your clothes. You might get burnt. It's hot enough.'

'It's all over Dingham that you and your brother have fallen out.'

'It would be,' he said. 'I've taken lodgings with Grannie Naylor.'

'Is it true you've left the smithy for good?'

'Yes, it's true. He's turned me out.'

'Well, for goodness' sake!' Hannah exclaimed. 'Aren't you going to tell me about it?'

'First I want to tell you my plans. Let's go outside, where the air is clean, and I'll tell you what I've got in mind.'

So they went and sat on the lock-gate, and he talked to her in a quiet voice, pointing now and then to the mill. He would lower the mill walls by half and use the spare bricks to build a new chimney and a blacksmith's hearth. A few sheets of corrugated iron would serve as a roof for the time being and then it was just a question of gear and tackle.

'I've wrote a list of things I'll need, and the anvil's about the biggest item, specially if I get it new. Then there's bellows and tools and iron and maybe a couple of tons of breeze but once I've really made a start – '

'So you'd set up as smith against your brother?'

'That's right. Why not? It's my proper trade. He hoped to drive me right away. He thought I'd have to go pretty far afield and give myself to another smith. Well, he's made a mistake, and I'm stopping here. I'm setting up shop in this old mill and if he don't like it that's just too bad.'

'Is there work enough for two smiths?'

'I dunno. We shall have to see. There was four of us working in the smithy. Now there's Peter and Jim Pacey. It's his own fault if he loses trade.'

'He may take on new helpers.'

'He'll never take on a first-rate smith cos he can't bear to be with any man whose work is better than his own. That's half the reason he's pushed me out. He knows I'm a better smith than him, and that's not bragging, it's just plain fact. He's only a lad of seventeen. I've had a start of seven years. I've got the experience. It's in my bones. And there's plenty of people round about who'll come where they know they get good work.'

'So you mean to take half Peter's trade?'

'I shall take it all – if it comes!' John said. 'I owe him nothing. I told him that.'

'It's quiet out this end of Dingham.'

'It won't be, however, when the new bridge is built and the new road links up with the main turnpike.'

'Seems you've got it all worked out.'

'I shall start clearing tomorrow morning, so's I've got somewhere to lay my head, to save paying out for lodgings and that. I'll get a mason to give me a hand, and the moment I've got a fire going in my forge, I shall start smithing straight away. The house'll have to wait a bit. I shall work on that in my spare time.'

'So!' Hannah said, with a faint smile. 'We'll be living next to the smithy, then, with the smoke your mother grumbles about?'

'We may have to wait a bit, before getting married,' John

said. 'And I may make a botch of things, when I start, if folk don't come to me with their trade. You don't want to change your mind, do you, now that you know what risks there are?'

'Supposing I was to say yes?'

'Ah, just supposing!' he agreed. 'Women are known for it, so they say.'

Hannah was joking. He knew that. And he answered in kind, with a teasing smile. Yet a certain fear took hold of him now and Hannah, seeing it in his eyes, leant towards him and kissed his mouth. Her arms went round him. She held him close.

'You mustn't look at me like that.'

'I dunno so much. Seems like it pays.'

After a moment she drew away. She became cool and composed again, matter-of-fact and rather grave, though the little flickering smile of warmth was still alive in her hazel eyes.

'Tell me more about your plans '

Chapter Fifteen

On a boisterous day in March, 1899, when the southwest wind, blowing up the river, hurled spray at the mill walls and thumped around in the new-built chimney, John lit a fire for the first time in his own blacksmith's hearth, and, working the bellows with his foot, watched as the coals began to glow. In front was the cooling-trough, ready filled, and from the rail hung his shovel and slice, bought second-hand at a sale near Gloucester. Nearby stood his anvil, brand-new, on a great block of elm bedded deep in the floor, and beside it stood a strong sturdy table, where his precious tools lay ready to hand.

The first task he had set himself was to stock up with horseshoes, different sizes, for, as old Mr Draycott had said to him, any blacksmith working alone would need to keep an extra good stock to save time when impatient customers stood at the door. And for a start, to encourage him, the old man had promised that all the horses at Neyes Farm should come to John to be shod by the year.

First he cut up the shoe-lengths, until there were scores of them, on the floor. He then took a bundle in his hands, set them on end upon the anvil, and selected four of them, all of a size. He placed them among the hot coals.

Overhead, as he tended his fire, the wind made music of a whining kind in the roof of galvanised iron sheeting, and outside, on the river, he could hear the calls of the waterfowl nesting among the reeds and rushes. Soon his hammer would ring on the anvil yet again and he would hear nothing else, but all these sounds, worked in a pattern, would be part of his life from now on and he would hear them even in dreams.

Throughout the morning, as he worked, people, mostly in ones and twos, would wander along the river bank or stroll straight down from the village itself to see what was happening at the mill turned forge. Some passed without a word. Others, like Tommy Breton, stopped and looked in at the open door.

'Morning, John! How're you doing? Making the sparks fly already, I see!'

'Morning, Tommy. It's a fine day. Anything I can do for you?'

'I thought I could maybe light my pipe.'

'Help yourself. The tongs is there.'

'You've done a good job, making the place neat and tidy. When're you starting on the house?'

'All in good time,' John said. 'I've got to earn a living first.'

'It's a great thing for Dingham, having a smithy at either end. There ent many places can boast of that, especially places as small as Dingham.'

'No,' John said, 'I reckon that's right.'

'Think you'll get trade, do you, right down here, where nobody comes much nor even knows there's a blacksmith here?'

'Half Dingham's been past this morning. By the time they've had their say, I shan't need to advertise in the papers.'

'What does your brother think of it, your setting up as a smith like this?'

'I dunno. I've never asked him.'

'Well, good luck to you, John. You'll need it for sure. Thanks for the light-up. That saved me a match.'

Later that morning, about eleven, an elderly knife-grinder came to the door, having heard the sound of John's hammer. His name was Bert Toms and he travelled the roads with a treadle grindstone set on a ramshackle pair of wheels.

'Didn't know there was a smith this end. That'll save me a lot of swither. My old axle's packed up on me. Think you can fix it for me, eh?'

'Bring it in and I'll have a look.'

John replaced the broken axle, put new cotter-pins in at the wheels, and put in a rivet to strengthen the brake. Bert was well pleased. He took out a little leather purse.

'How much do I owe you for doing that?'

'I reckon we'll call it sixpence,' John said.

'Then I'll pay cash,' Bert said. 'I reckon you've done a good job. Not everyone would've took such pains. I can just about run to a sixpenny piece. Trade ent good for me these days. Not many folk've got knives and scissors for me to grind, or so they tell me, anyway.' Bert, in disgust, pretended to spit. 'They better prefer to go to the town and get it done dearer!' he exclaimed. 'I hope you do better in *your* chosen trade.'

When the knife-grinder had gone, trundling away towards the village, John went back to his work at the anvil. By noon that day, when he paused to eat his bread and cheese, one beam overhead was hung with foreshoes, six on a nail, ranged along according to size. By the time he had finished that day he was resolved that the second beam would be hung with an equal number of hindshoes.

At about three in the afternoon Hannah arrived, bringing his washing tied up in a cloth. She carried it through into what had once been the old mealroom, where John now slept on a bunk-bed, and gathered up his dirty clothes. She came back into the smithy and stood watching as he worked.

'You've started, then?'

'*And* had a customer, if you please!'

'Whoever was it?' she asked, surprised.

'Bert Toms, the knife-grinder. His trolley-axle had packed up.'

'However much did you earn doing that?'

'I earnt sixpence,' John said.

'Sixpence!' she said, laughing at him. 'I suppose you'll be taking that straight to the bank!'

'It's all very well for you to laugh. Sixpence is sixpence, say what you like.'

He took a shoe-length out of the fire, hammered it round on the anvil-beak, and then, with a movement of his tongs, laid it upon the flat 'table' and proceeded to hammer out the crimp. His movements were easy, unhurried, unfussed. The work seemed to cost him no thought at all. But because the knowledge of it was in his bones, every blow of the hammer told. And Hannah, seeing how it was, took pride in the man because of his craft.

'You're very quick.'

'It was Will who learnt me that quickness,' he said. 'Everything I do I get from him. You could say, and it'd be true, that Will Gale is still working in me, at least so long as I'm at the anvil and got a hammer in my hand.'

'What would he say if he knew you'd set up against his son?'

'The skill he gave me, I've got to use. I couldn't do that

half so well if I had to work for some other smith. Will would agree with that, I'm sure. I've got to stand on my own two feet. It's up to Peter to do the same. He's got his name and all his customers ready made. I've got my skill and not much else. Seems to me it's a fair fight.' He glanced briefly at her face. 'Do you think I'm in the wrong?'

'No,' she said, 'but I doubt if it'd make any difference if I did.'

Walking about the new workshop, she looked at the tools hanging up on the walls, the hopper full of pale sand, the shoeing-stalls and halter-rings, the farrier's toolbox, as yet unused.

'The place is as clean as a new pin.'

'It won't be, however, by the time I've worked here a day or two and had a few horses in and out.'

'Not to mention the smoke and smuts.'

'You'll have to get used to that,' he said, 'seeing you're marrying into the trade.'

Hannah came from the shoeing-stall and stood again close by the anvil.

'You're very high and mighty today. You seem to think you're on top of the world.'

'Ah. Well. And why not?'

'Just cos you've had a customer? Seems to me it's gone to your head.'

'There'll be others. You'll see. The sound of my hammer will bring them in, just the same as it done with Bert Toms. There's no sound like it in the world.'

'You're very pert and sure of yourself.'

'I've got to be. It's the only way. And I ent done too badly, first day off.'

'A knife-grinder!' Hannah said, and her eyes mocked him, cool and amused. They were still learning about each other, he and she. Their discoveries often brought them close. And there was always a current of humour, running between them, provoking, alive. 'A knife-grinder!' she said again. 'And he paid you sixpence? Oh my stars!'

'Yes, well, it's a start,' John said, and paused long enough in his work to smile at her across the anvil. Then his hammer rang out again, and the iron, answering to the blows, submitted itself to his design.

CHRISTIAN HERALD ASSOCIATION AND ITS MINISTRIES

CHRISTIAN HERALD ASSOCIATION, founded in 1878, publishes The Christian Herald Magazine, one of the leading interdenominational religious monthlies in America. Through its wide circulation, it brings inspiring articles and the latest news of religious developments to many families. From the magazine's pages came the initiative for CHRISTIAN HERALD CHILDREN'S HOME and THE BOWERY MISSION, two individually supported not-for-profit corporations.

CHRISTIAN HERALD CHILDREN'S HOME, established in 1894, is the name for a unique and dynamic ministry to disadvantaged children, offering hope and opportunities which would not otherwise be available for reasons of poverty and neglect. The goal is to develop each child's potential and to demonstrate Christian compassion and understanding to children in need.

Mont Lawn is a permanent camp located in Bushkill, Pennsylvania. It is the focal point of a ministry which provides a healthful "vacation with a purpose" to children who without it would be confined to the streets of the city. Up to 1000 children between the ages of 7 and 11 come to Mont Lawn each year.

Christian Herald Children's Home maintains year-round contact with children by means of an *In-City Youth Ministry.* Central to its philosophy is the belief that only through sustained relationships and demonstrated concern can individual lives be truly enriched. Special emphasis is on individual guidance, spiritual and family counseling and tutoring. This follow-up ministry to inner-city children culminates for many in financial assistance toward higher education and career counseling.

THE BOWERY MISSION, located at 227 Bowery, New York City, has since 1879 been reaching out to the lost men on the Bowery, offering them what could be their last chance to rebuild their lives. Every man is fed, clothed and ministered to. Countless numbers have entered the 90-day residential rehabilitation program at the Bowery Mission. A concentrated ministry of counseling, medical care, nutrition therapy, Bible study and Gospel services awakens a man to spiritual renewal within himself.

These ministries are supported solely by the voluntary contributions of individuals and by legacies and bequests. Contributions are tax deductible. Checks should be made out either to CHRISTIAN HERALD CHILDREN'S HOME or to THE BOWERY MISSION.

Administrative Office: 40 Overlook Drive, Chappaqua, New York 10514
Telephone: (914) 769-9000